Lake City

A NOVEL

THOMAS KOHNSTAMM

ADVANCE PRAISE FOR *LAKE CITY*

"Kohnstamm delivers a blistering, clear-eyed, and sure-footed debut novel about the perils and pitfalls of misdirected ambition. More than that, *Lake City* is a hilarious and sneakily incisive examination of the cultural tensions and widening class divides in an increasingly homogenized and gentrified urban America." —JONATHAN EVISON, author of *Lawn Boy*

"*Lake City* is a darkly funny and extremely relevant debut novel about American inequality and moral authority, featuring a sad-sack antihero who takes way too long to grow up. When he finally does, the results are beautiful, and the book ultimately becomes an elegy for a now-gone Seattle, and a lesson in how the place we're from never fully lets us go."

—ANTHONY DOERR, author of
All the Light We Cannot See

"Kohnstamm has written a novel of Pale Male Fail above and below the poverty line, a Dickensian tale of a fledgling philosopher who's taken flight from trailer parks to Gramercy Park and then . . . had his wings clipped. This is the American Dream cut thin on a grocery store meat slicer, laced with oxy, stolen booze, and an unfinished dissertation. It's a rotgut to Dom Pérignon rainbow, which is to say: *Lake City* is a crucial black comedy about the myths of money and happiness, and whether nature, nurture, or AmEx rears a better man."

—MARIA DAHVANA HEADLEY,
New York Times–bestselling author of *The Mere Wife*

"There are so many reasons to admire Thomas Kohnstamm's astonishing debut novel: his astute and cutting depiction of urban gentrification, his pitch-perfect evocation of a young man's endless ricochet between self-aggrandizement and self-hatred, his vision of Seattle's grungy underside that is so richly related one can almost smell the cedar and cannabis wafting off the pages. And yet, it is Kohnstamm's innate storytelling verve—his taut, noirish knack for plotting and his ability to make the reader laugh, cringe, worry, and feel for his characters all at once—that makes *Lake City* truly unputdownable."

—STEFAN MERRILL BLOCK,
author of *Oliver Loving: A Novel*

"Kohnstamm knowingly illuminates the underbelly of Seattle—a place of beater cars, strip clubs, and a subpar hypermarket—far from the hipsters and gentrifiers. Hilarious as it is cutting, *Lake City* offers an all-too-insightful critique of clashing classes and misguided ideas of success."

—SHARI GOLDHAGEN, author of
In Some Other World, Maybe

Lake City

Lake City

A Novel

THOMAS KOHNSTAMM

COUNTERPOINT
Berkeley, California

Lake City

First Counterpoint paperback edition: 2019

Library of Congress Cataloging-in-Publication Data
Names: Kohnstamm, Thomas B., author.
Title: Lake City : a novel / Thomas Kohnstamm.
Description: First Counterpoint paperback edition. | Berkeley, California : Counterpoint, 2019.
Identifiers: LCCN 2018018899 | ISBN 9781640091429
Classification: LCC PS3611.O3695 L35 2019 | DDC 813/.6—dc23
LC record available at https://lccn.loc.gov/2018018899

Jacket design by Nicole Caputo
Book design by Jordan Koluch

COUNTERPOINT
2560 Ninth Street, Suite 318
Berkeley, CA 94710
www.counterpointpress.com

Printed in the United States of America
Distributed by Publishers Group West

10 9 8 7 6 5 4 3 2 1

To my parents, Ed and Linda Kohnstamm,
who always encouraged me to be whatever I wanted to be

Mine the miners, not the mines.

—DOC MAYNARD, founder of Seattle

Lake City

ONE

LANE STARTS THE MONTH WITH two bottles of decent pinot noir from the Washington State Liquor Store up on Lake City Way. He determines these wines to be decent, based on their price and minimalist label design. Plus, Mia always drinks pinot noir or pinot something. In the winter, anyway.

"Just enjoying a long Christmas break." Lane nods to the liquor store clerk as she checks his face against his recently issued New York ID.

She keys Lane's birthdate into the register and swipes his credit card. He tries her again. "Needed a little time off from my PhD . . . after what happened in September and all." Lane waits for the clerk to bite on his story. To be inspired by a visitor with such big things afoot.

To be fair, this is not the Seattle of Microsoft, Starbucks and Amazon. It's nowhere, deep Seattle: Lake City. Moss. Lawns matted with decomposing pine needles. Mud-licked streets without sidewalks. The Seattle that fueled the melancholy of what came to be known as grunge; not the one that sells Sub Pop coffee mugs and tote bags at its international airport.

But the clerk knows better than to engage wild-eyed liquor store customers in anything resembling a personal conversation.

Lane makes a final attempt, doing his best impression of a functional human being. "I'm looking forward to trying these Washington varietals."

"Card's declined." She cleans her glasses on her dark orange work vest, clicking the plastic lenses against the edge of her name tag: SHIRLEY.

"Gotta be the magnetic strip," he says, realizing that Mia's father must have bucked him off the last of her credit cards. He pulls the other card from his wallet, a relic of his premarriage finances that's survived in the back of his underwear drawer. "Try this."

He doesn't breathe while she runs the card.

"This one's no good either, Professor."

Lane stands in silence, unpacking the effects of market and state-run forces on the store's décor: a 1970s Bulgarian post office pastiche pocked with Jägermeister neons and a Captain Morgan mirror. He fails to reconcile the culture-specific neo-Marxist development theory he's proposed for his interdisciplinary dissertation in social policy with the fact that the smell, lighting, and vinyl flooring of state-owned buildings make him feel as if he were being strangled. Not a painful strangulation. More of a soft choke by someone with bad taste and sweaty palms.

He goes to return the bottles to the shelf.

The clerk waves him back. "Leave 'em up here."

"Don't worry . . . Shirley." Lane laughs but then second-guesses whether the words even rhyme. He returns one bottle to the display and slides the other neck-first under his armpit and down the sleeve of his jacket. "It's all a big mix-up. I'm not even supposed to be— Let me run to the ATM real quick."

Lane pushes through the door, arms flush at his sides, and jogs into the light rain. The sun is on its way over the horizon at 3:08 p.m.

LANE DEDICATES THE NEXT WEEKS to crying, drinking and sleeping as many hours as possible in his mom's TV room. The same room where she hoards newspaper coupon inserts and the NFL mugs she won playing bingo at the Tulalip. The same room where he lived as a kid. The room where he washed up on and off throughout college. But this time, things aren't as cool. Which is Lane's Seattle way of saying completely fucking terrible.

He surprises himself by how fast he can put back twenty-dollar bottles of shoplifted pinot noir from a sixteen-ounce ceramic Seahawks mug. As sobriety is not an option, he soon descends into his mom's stash of Carlo Rossi jugs she keeps inside the long-broken dishwasher and her boyfriend's mother lode of Rainier tallboys in a yellowed foam cooler out in the garage. *That loser's boning my mom,* Lane justifies to himself. And Lane's right; the boyfriend never says a word about the beers. Dude even goes out and buys more when the supply runs low.

Some days or weeks into this, Lane gives in and starts trying to call her, the her who matters, back in New York. Mia should have called him first. That's the least she could do. But she hasn't. Nobody's called. Except for Lonnie, the top weed dealer in Lane's high school from about '92 to '93. And everybody knows that call doesn't count.

The problem with contacting Mia is that the house phone can't make outgoing calls beyond 206 and the unspeakable 425, 253 and 360 area codes. Lane needs 212s and 917s and 646s. Even a 347 or a 718 might do. He coaxes, complains and breaks down to his mom, but she won't upgrade her service. She wants to help but keeps repeating some story about one of her various deadbeat ex-boyfriends, his penchant for 976 chat lines and the resulting issues with the phone company.

Lane resolves to do what any self-respecting twenty-seven-year-old man who's spent weeks using alcoholic blunt force trauma to play Whac-A-Mole with his every emotion while watching an endless stream of Christmas TV specials and post-9/11 coverage would do: he masturbates. A few times. To clear his head. And then he starts calling Mia—collect. Every four hours. That's the schedule he sets for himself, and he has his eye on the VCR digital clock right up until that last minute clicks over and the receiver is in his hand and he's asking the operator to put through the call.

He can't be sure if it's the second or third day of calling that Mia accepts the charges.

"Don't you think we need some time?" she asks. Lane recognizes her father's coaching in this assertive stance.

"Time?" Lane's voice bends.

"Time without talking. Time to think."

"I do nothing but think: think about us, think about how to not think about us."

He wants to scream that time's easy when she's the one in their apartment in Gramercy Park leading the life that he was meant to lead. That they were meant to lead together. How would she feel about time if she were sipping off his mom's eight-dollar jugs of room-temperature Chablis right down the road from Rick's strip club, Discount Gun Sales and a sixty-block corridor of used car dealerships?

Instead, he kicks over the stack of books he brought home to read during the break. Wallerstein on dependency theory. Sen on human capabilities. Benedict Anderson on the origin and spread of nationalism. He hasn't opened a single one, but it doesn't matter because he can feign participation in any lower-level grad seminar by name-dropping the author and the philosophy with which they are most often associated. "Well, because Comte and positivism . . ." can be followed by a quick retreat to a general argument about why social malaise is bad or injustice is unjust. If nothing else, the books provided a serviceable end table for his Seahawks mug.

"We have a lot to figure out." Mia sounds distant, scripted.

"You're not figuring out anything," he fires back as he assumes the fetal position on his side on the floor.

Whether she thinks she needs time or not and whether her father has convinced her that Lane is a parasite or not, Lane knows he is going to find a way to get back to New York, get back on his feet and prove that they are meant to be together.

"You're holding a pillow over the face of our marriage," he cries.

"I'm not. I'm—"

"You're right. You're not. It's your dad." He leaves the dagger in for a moment and then twists. "I believed you . . . that you weren't like him."

AFTER THE LAMP (MIA'S) AND cell phone (his on her family plan) smashing incident back at their apartment (technically also hers) on Twenty-First Street, he also made a studied effort to not mention the management-consultant motherfucker she spent the night with. The guy Lane was certain Mia's father foisted upon her as part of his ploy to sabotage their marriage. The same guy Lane then called at work and tried to shame into feeling as bad as he was feeling. The one who not only didn't feel bad but countered, "Why don't you go cry about it like Mia tells me you always do, Bueche . . . douche . . . whatever your name is?"

"It's Bue-*shay*. Lane Bue-*shay*." Lane crumbled. "Like *touché*, you piece of sh-sh-sh . . ."

In order to overcome his childhood stutter, Lane spent years practicing his diction by reading his Dungeons & Dragons *Monster Manual* and the *Deities & Demigods* cyclopedia out loud in front of a mirror, wrestling with *psionics, alignment, lycanthropy, dexterity* and the like. Those years of repeating the names of the hand-drawn enemies in the books could even be utilized to feign a deeper classical education. For example, he could recall that Isis is the Egyptian goddess of magic and fertility, Ushas is the Hindu goddess of the dawn and Tlazolteotl is the Aztec goddess of vice. But only because they were the ones with exposed nipples in the book.

Yet, even with all of this practice, many types of mocking still took him right back to being called "Slow Lane" and "Douche-Gay" by Matty Ericksen on the tetherball court in third grade. He could envision the single syllable he needed to conjure now to this consultant prick, but it wouldn't arrive on his tongue.

Lane wondered about creative ways to let the dude know that after all that self-imposed language practice, he earned straight As in high school English. That he scored a perfect 800 on the verbal section of the SAT. It was actually a 720, but he deserved to round up. Maybe he could forge an email to this guy from Mia's account and slide those details in there, although she'd changed her password a lot in recent weeks.

Lane reloaded. "You piece of sh-sh-sh ..."

Even the homewrecker on the other end of the line couldn't bear it any longer and offered, "Listen, man, perhaps I shouldn'ta said—"

Lane disconnected the call, took two deep breaths, said "Shit" as loud as he could and hurled his cell against the wall.

The lamp, which he later learned was a late nineteenth-century family heirloom that was given to Mia by her mother before she passed away, happened to be located between his phone and said wall. And, just like that, everything about her cheating and poisoning their nascent marriage became secondary to his "unpredictable violent outbursts and disregard for

other people's property." As Mia's fuckface father would char-
acterize Lane's behavior thereafter.

LANE KEEPS IT TOGETHER FOR most of his phone call
with Mia. He no longer expects her to finish with the once-
customary "I love you." He's not waiting for her to confirm that
he's still The One. At this point, he's more realistic than that.
But she doesn't say, "Sorry, I've got to go," or, "We'll talk soon.
Take care of yourself." That would be too decent.

She says, "I'm late. I've got a birthday party in Chelsea."

A fucking party. In Chelsea. He feels as if half of his per-
sonality, half of his emotional being has been cleaved away.
While he lies in tatters, bleeding to death on the fetid floor, the
other half is coordinating shoes with handbags and heading to
a birthday party.

He looks around the room at the stacks of long-expired
coupons for discounted margarine at Albertsons and two-
for-one Capri Sun value packs at Safeway. He is wrapped in
a patchwork quilt with the comforting yet repulsive smells of
his long-ago deceased Wally the Collie and the Winston Super
Kings his mom smoked until the early '90s.

"Whose birthday?" he asks.

BEFORE HE LEFT NEW YORK, Lane formulated a plan. A
plan with an eye on the long game. A plan that accounted for
the asymmetrical warfare in which he was engaged. He figured
that if he kept his mouth shut, laid low in Seattle for an ex-

tended holiday and played the conciliator, his earlier conduct, in fact, the whole situation, would blow over. He was confident about this due to the fact that it all went down on Friday, September 7. That September 7. 2001. The day that shit really hit the fan, at least in Lane's estimation.

The conversation changed in the days that followed, which made it easier for him to defer the rest of the semester toward his PhD in social policy at Columbia.

"I know this is a lot to ask in my first year, but all this, what happened downtown, I'm taking it hard," he groveled to his PhD advisor in her narrow, windowless office. He didn't think she was convinced. He hadn't lost any friends or relatives and was nowhere near the Financial District, but the advisor seemed to have bigger issues on her mind.

"I'll be back and catch up on everything right after the holidays," he promised.

And he still stands behind that pledge. After all, he isn't another lost rich kid biding his time in a doctoral program for lack of better things to do. He's the Bill Clinton of Lake City Way. Sure, Lane knows that not everyone can rise out of Hope, Arkansas, or whatever shithole nowhere to become president of the United States. But if Clinton could do it, Lane can at least expect to head up an NGO of some sort. An international NGO was not unreasonable. Or he'd even settle for one with a national footprint, but not some local charity run like an afterschool activity. He wants one of those jobs advertised in between the articles in the *Economist*: directors of rarified international institutions with acronym names like WHO, ILO, UNHRC that mesmerize Europeans and are over the heads of most Americans, noble titles that require dark suits and gravitas and meetings in Davos to decide the fate of people like his mom's boyfriends. The jobs—the callings—that impress Mia and professors and the other well-intentioned, affluent liberals who've opened doors for Lane at challenging points in his journey toward realizing his intellectual destiny.

He is a courageous figure, clawing his way up from the mud and blackberry thickets to become a great humanitarian. Fighting to give back. To create social change. There's no way he's about to let it slip through his fingers. He'll be the first person in his family to go to college, let alone earn an MA and a PhD. Academic success has allowed him to transcend class, and soon he'll be free to live a sophisticated life governed by ideas and unburdened by the petty quotidian concerns of life in Lake City.

As for the conversation with his academic advisor, Lane avoided mentioning that he was, in reality, spending all of his waking hours battling the image of his wife getting penetrated by some dude named Bray. First name. A guy who'd played squash since he was a kid and not as a way to get ahead at work. The asshole had all he could ever need, so why did he have to take everything from Lane too?

Lane also failed to note to his advisor that he lost the rent-free status of living with his wife in the three-bedroom apartment she inherited from her mom. The advisor wouldn't understand how it felt to go from having a guest room and a home office and a key to Gramercy Park to unsuccessfully scouring Craigslist for apartment shares in Ditmas Park. Or how an Ivy League PhD candidate couldn't even get a call back from a temp agency, let alone for busing tables during that autumn of uncertainty, those shaky months when New York City was an armadillo jabbed with a sharp stick. Furthermore, he didn't want to admit that Mia was the primary investor in his doctoral degree. Or another way to say that would be: Mia was paying his tuition with her trust fund. All of his tuition.

"WHAT DO YOU MEAN, WHOSE birthday?" Mia fires back, emotion returning to her voice.

There is a stretch of dying and then dead air.

"*Yours.* No, I totally knew that." How to explain? "I thought, under these circumstances, that . . . either way . . . I totally got you a present. I was waiting to—to give it to you in person."

Lane knows that his birthday lapse is the kind of thing Mia's dad latches on to. But her dad looks for anything he can use as a proof point to bolster his predetermined narrative of Lane and Mia's relationship.

It's not as obvious on the surface level, but Lane has been helping Mia become her best self as much as she's been helping him to do the same. That, to the best of Lane's knowledge, is the foundation of a sustainable and fulfilling marriage. How he's helping her isn't as tangible as the quantifiable financial support that she gave to him. But money is just money and he, by being who he is, is uniquely suited to complete her on an emotional, intellectual and spiritual level.

She too wants, or at least wanted, to fight for social justice, to make a difference, but lacked follow-through, her resolve blunted by the thickness of her own financial cushion. That

and an ever-shifting set of goals and influences. Monday was
Naomi Klein. Tuesday was Marc Jacobs. Wednesday, Deepak
Chopra. Her greatest act of both rebellion and ambition was
eloping with Lane. A former welfare recipient. A student of
mushy social sciences. A Democrat.

Her father views their union as further confirmation
of Mia's long track record of impulsivity and pathological
free-spiritedness. Once her father reentered their lives, it was a
straight path to Mia and Lane finding themselves on the opposite ends of this collect call.

MIA TELLS LANE TO NOT worry about forgetting her birthday. She hadn't been planning to celebrate. It just came up.
She's had a tough time too, whether he believes it or not. Some
friends wanted to make sure she got out of the house. Enjoyed
her special day and all.

He wants to know who "some friends" are but holds his
tongue. There are clicking noises in the background. Lane assumes she is applying makeup.

Then Mia thanks Lane. For what, he isn't sure. Maybe she
isn't either. There's a short pause when they both struggle to
come up with the next thing to say. She hangs up the phone.

He refuses to associate any sense of finality with her thank-
you. But he is forced to consider that his plan might not be
working. Unless drastic measures are taken, he might not
have everything resolved by January. By the start of the new
semester.

He contemplates how he can find out which restaurant or

bar her birthday party is at in Chelsea so he can phone in a bomb threat. To cancel it. She can't be having fun while he's suffering. Nothing more sinister than that. Really. But he realizes that most restaurants won't accept a bomb threat by collect call. Even if they do, the White House is getting all serious about this stuff and might trace the call back to his mom. Or worse, to him.

He decides to walk up to the pay phone at the liquor store on Lake City Way. That said, people in New York don't have much of a sense of humor about fake bomb threats these days, even ones that are justified. And it's a twenty-minute walk to the liquor store. Each way.

He opts instead for another Rainier.

A few hours later, it's time for his next scheduled collect call to Mia. Lane is drunk and wearing nothing more than a pair of boxers he picked out of his dirty laundry strewn across the floor. He's watching *The Road Warrior* on TV and crying because he loves the touching bond between Mel Gibson and that little feral boy who lives in the hole by the fence. Even though they never share an intelligible word.

If only Lane and his own father had even had that much of a relationship. His pops dropped dead of a heart attack in his late thirties after a double shift on the lot at Bill Pierre Ford. It happened right before Christmas; they were coming up on the anniversary though neither he nor his mom ever mentioned Perry Bueche. Poor bastard went facedown in the December slush next to a used '84 Tempo he was hawking to a Vietnamese family.

Lane can't remember a single specific conversation he'd had

with his father, and the man never connected with Lane's interest in reading and wanting to know about the world beyond Lake City, but—right up until the point that Perry's diet of Gordon's Gin, Dick's Deluxe cheeseburgers and filterless Pall Malls exploded his heart in his chest—he sure as hell never played the victim.

Lane makes up his mind. Instead of collect calling Mia, he too is going to go to a birthday party.

Tonight. Right now, as a matter of fact.

TWO

LONNIE THE WEED DEALER LEAVES another message, and Lane decides to call him back. That's his single option. It's not like he still keeps in touch with other people in Seattle or even has any other phone numbers.

Sure, he has some good friends from the neighborhood. Childhood friends, friends who have and still would jump into a fight on Lane's behalf with no questions asked. But he'd had to distance himself from all of his Lake City boys by the time he met Mia, or in the following months.

What would he even talk about with them? Which high school classmates have now impregnated which? How Vin Baker seems like a nice guy but will never fill the hole left by Shawn Kemp? How Gary Payton can't return the Sonics to being NBA championship contenders all on his own? Lane had read a bunch of Foucault (and understood some of it, maybe even half) and made a twenty-minute PowerPoint presentation on political ecology this last semester. He could drop words like *discourse, dialectics* and *semiotics* into any conversation. If he called his old friends, they'd give him crap about how he is a fake, how he thinks he's too good for them. But that's not his concern.

"Why don't you call J.C. or Robbie?" Lane's mom asks him over and over again. "They'd love to know you're back."

"I told you, Ma, I'm not back," he answers.

As for lasting friends from undergrad: he had zero. Lane had always been a commuter student with a full-time job. He did his first two years at North Seattle Community College, living with his mom and knocking out the cold cut preslice shift at Lake City's Fred Meyer superstore deli department. Lane had believed all of his dreams would be achieved when he got enough credits to transfer to the University of Washington, but once there he still found himself as a commuter student but now with a longer bus ride, larger classes and needing to work ever more hours to pay basic tuition and bills. During his limited hours on campus, he turned his attention to professors, TAs and program coordinators: people who could help him get ahead to whatever *ahead* meant.

Of course, he'd yearned to be part of the student community, to have UW friends. After months of searching, he found a rare opportunity: a small shared apartment on the edge of the U District that he could (almost) swing and that was close enough to the bus line that he'd be able to reverse his commute and continue his shifts at Fred Meyer. On the day he was to close on the apartment, the super informed him that, without a suitable cosigner or better credit, he'd need both first and last . . . and a deposit. He had enough cash saved up for his first month and his last. It was the deposit that put independence beyond of his reach. The super gave Lane forty-eight hours to come up with the rest.

Lane attempted to amass the deposit by selling two ounces of Super Silver Haze to the white-hat Wrangler-driving frat daddy from Bellevue who was always pestering him about weed hookups in their Sociology 213 study group. Turned out that dude was working down his own Rohypnol and ketamine possession conviction. The worst charges didn't stick and Lane used up every faculty connection he had to make sure he didn't get kicked out of school, but he ended up buying himself a three-year suspended sentence, a felony conviction and, therefore, a lifetime disqualification from federal student aid. Not to mention he didn't get the apartment and, after fronting all his savings on the doomed weed deal, was flat broke.

The last thing Lane needs right now is to be calling up a known drug dealer, but at least Lonnie will know about a birthday party. He knows everyone and everything going on in North Seattle. They used to call him the Lando Calrissian of Lake City Way. Except he's white, unattractive and awkward around women.

Lane's unsure how Lonnie knows he's in town, but he doesn't have to guess what he wants. He'll have to play Lonnie's game and say he'd like to purchase an intent-to-distribute amount of weed. He'll make the plan to meet up the next day and then cancel a few hours prior. The excuse will have to sound dramatic, perhaps something involving law enforcement.

Lane winds Lonnie up with the prospect of making a few hundred bucks and then asks about birthday parties. He asks about friends and friends of friends.

"Birthday party?" Lonnie puzzles at Lane's request.

"I'm showing a colleague around. A foreign— European colleague. He's doing an ethnography on American microcommunities and endogenous influences such as ... well, you know, social construct, cultural identity stuff. Sorry if that sounds kinda out there."

"Yeah, but, nah, that's cool. I've been calling you 'cause there's this rich lady. She asked to meet some of my friends," Lonnie says. "She's at this Hawaiian bar tonight. Like a luau place."

"You know I'm married, right?"

"You should talk to her."

"She's at a birthday party?"

"Maybe somebody there's having a birthday, right?" Lonnie continues on about some other details, but Lane more or less stopped listening after he heard there was a birthday-like party.

Lane's mom demurs at letting him borrow her Chevy Celebrity station wagon because she knows how much of her wine and how many of her boyfriend's tallboys he's massacred. Of course, she has some excuse about an ex-boyfriend and a drunken hit-and-run while he was driving her car.

She offers to drive Lane to the party instead. It's the least she can do considering she hasn't washed any of his clothes and he's forced to go out with no underwear. He's made sure she's aware of her malfeasance.

He accepts her offer with the stipulation that she drop him off a block away from the bar so nobody'll see. And the poor lady would do it too. She'd do anything in her power for her only child, always has. But after watching the triumphant final scene of *The Road Warrior*, Lane decides to take the bus instead.

He prides himself on the decision not to lean on his mother. Not exactly drastic measures, but it's an initial victory. Another bit of proof that tonight is about building his own momentum.

On the way out the door, he convinces his mom and her boyfriend to loan him ten bucks each so he can have something to spend. "Super short-term," he guarantees them as he pockets the boyfriend's last beer to nurse on the bus.

LANE RIDES FOR THIRTY-THREE MINUTES in the back of the sixty-one-foot articulated Metro bus and then walks another eighteen minutes in the misting December rain to get to the luau bar. The walk doesn't need to be that long, but Lane yanks the cord on the wrong block and is too prideful to stay seated when the empty bus pulls to the curb. As a true Seattleite, he wants to save face and not inconvenience the driver.

Although he can't see as he walks in the dark, Lane's mom told him that Green Lake is no longer besieged with its eponymous avocado-colored algae. He notices that the car mechanics and Vitamilk factory that ringed the east side of the lake are shuttering and giving way to new condo developments.

It seems that people are realizing that a neighborhood with a huge lake in the middle of the city is a desirable place to live and not just a puddle of green sludge with a minefield of Canada goose shit on the shores. SOLD signs punctuate the parking strips like billboards along a freeway. Most are adorned with a headshot of the same blond TV-weathercaster look-alike.

Once at the bar, Lane finds that the party looks more like a group of intoxicated coworkers than a birthday. Two men have their ties flipped over their shoulders and are arguing about the trajectory of mortgage rates. Lane squeezes in at the corner of the long, rectangular table without saying a word to any of the dozen or so people. After these weeks holed up in his mom's TV room, after the blowup in New York, after all of the drinking and crying, he needs some time to get out of his own head.

He focuses on all of the fun that Mia must be having right now, flirting and drinking Bellinis with her friends. Friends who work at Condé Nast and Publicis to supplement their clothing allowances and gain access to better parties. Maybe Bray is there too.

He has a sudden impulse to run into traffic. Not to kill himself; he is too talented and too destined for eventual greatness to do that. But he needs something tragic enough to happen so she will have to stop everything she is doing and occupy all of her thoughts with him. She will have to medevac him to New York, where she can tend to his bandaged body in a well-appointed, if not outright stylish, suite room in an Upper East Side hospital. Maybe he can even get a view of the East River.

He busies himself playing with his new cell phone: the one he upgraded to on Mia's family plan during that short window between destroying his earlier phone and her father taking over her finances. This is the phone he imagines pulling out to take a call from the head of an international think tank or NGO, or perhaps Secretary-General Annan himself. The phone is some cutting-edge shit that he figures people still didn't have out here in provincial Seattle. His Nokia 8310 has an internal antenna, FM radio, a calendar and predictive T9 text messaging that speeds the process of hitting the keys three times to get to the letters C, F, I, L, O and V or four times to get to S and Z.

Getting brunch in Nolita after the holidays is the subject of the numerous texts he taps out. Even if he had service on the phone, he has no one to send the texts to, except Mia.

The woman next to him watches with a mix of interest and bemusement as she finishes a cocktail that reeks of grenadine. She is a good ten years older than him and more than a touch bigger than he usually likes, but she has an attractive face: arching smile and dimples, even if her expression conveys an aggressive intensity. Her hair is bleached blond, a bit fried from the chemicals and cut into an executive-looking bob.

He nods to her. "Having trouble getting a signal out here."

She gives him a West Coast Courtesy Smile™.

"Roaming . . ." He flashes the phone to her, holding it between his thumb and index finger to showcase its size. "East Coast cell plan."

"Smoke?" she asks, opening her crinkled black lambskin handbag to fish out a pack of Camel Lights.

He waves off the cigarette. But his eyes are drawn to the wadded bills, at least one of which is a hundred, mixed in with a mess of makeup compacts, receipts, notebooks and glasses cases in the purse. Some white boxy thing with a tangle of white headphones also catches his attention. He's never seen anything like it.

She catches him staring. "It's an iPod."

He mouths the syllables: *eye-pahd*. He sucks in his cheeks in the way he knows make his cheekbones more pronounced, juts his jaw forward and clenches his eyes into his determined, if not a little bit dangerous, look. Since the tail end of puberty, a not insignificant number of women have told him that he is charming, if not good-looking. He doesn't believe it but often counts on it being true.

"MP3 player," she rasps between drags. "Like a Walkman, but this is like 'a thousand songs in your pocket.'"

Lane is smitten with this piece of technology and intrigued by, if not jealous of, this woman who possesses it.

"Just came out. Five gigs of storage. Crazy, huh?" she continues, weighing the John Varvatos black leather slip-ons that Mia bought for him, his dark jeans and long-sleeved black T-shirt. "You're not from the East Coast."

"Not originally. But I live in Manhattan." He dusts off his stump speech. "Needed a little time off from my PhD . . . after what happened in September and all." This time he leaves his mouth ajar, the word *all* dangling. He maintains eye contact and then lowers his gaze. Lane's pleased that he's getting a sense of how to optimize the pacing and accompanying physical expressions.

The tension leaves her face. He has her on the hook. It is Lane's coup de grâce. This is the first time he's witnessed the full power of his trump card story outside of New York.

Of course, he had so much vodka and Vicodin on 9/10 trying to forget about Mia and the consultant's transgressing penis that he was in the hospital having his stomach pumped when *all* went down. He assured the doctors that the overdose was an unfortunate accident. That he had a legitimate prescription for the Vicodin for an old skiing injury (back strain from loading five-gallon drums of premixed coleslaw at the Fred Meyer deli) and needed another day or two to recuperate. They still kicked him out of his hospital bed to make room for triage. That was Lane's most direct experience with the attacks. His story was pathetic in New York, but he recognizes its clout here and runs with it.

"It makes you think about how fragile it all is. What's really important. Family and the people you love. That's it. The rest is distraction." He tries to clench his eyes even more but wonders if he's overdoing it. He'll need more practice on this section.

"What did you—"

He throws a roadblock into her line of questioning. "It was horrible. Truly terrible."

She rests her hand on his knee. "I love New York."

"Me too. So much better than this place. Nothing happens here." He extends his hand. "Lane."

"Nina." She gives him a salesman's grip. They lock on each other's eyes, their hands still clasped. "So, you're Lonnie's friend, huh?"

"Lonnie? Oh, hey. Yeah. You're . . . ?"

"Nina. I just said that."

He nods, trying to recollect what all Lonnie told him.

"You're heading back in a few more days?" she asks.

"A bit longer than that." He coughs from her cigarette. "But still, in and out."

"In and out." She pauses again to look him over, perhaps guessing at his height. "Shot? . . . Reposado? Añejo?"

He makes an empty promise to buy the next round as she stubs out her Camel Light in an ashtray made from a lacquered half of a coconut shell.

THREE

"YOU'RE A DECENT-LOOKING GUY." NINA licks the remaining cocaine off her index finger, rolling it around on her tongue. "Charming even, if you don't talk too much." She inches toward him but stops at the perimeter of his personal space, daring him to take the next step.

They stand in silence between the condo's staging furniture and an oversized Le Chat Noir poster. He considers his angles: the value of a rebound hookup or even an ongoing affair. Although he shouldn't sleep with Nina, his ego still needs her to want to sleep with him. "I'm flattered." He shows his ring. "But I'm also—"

"You told me that before." Her tongue searches under her fingernail for more white residue.

He should have run when he had the chance. When she was doing key bumps and listening to Matchbox Twenty in her gunmetal gray Mercedes E320 with California plates. When she was fumbling with the lockbox on the front door of the townhouse and Lane stared at her face on its FOR SALE sign.

Nina Radcliffe. On all of the FOR SALE signs up and down the street. When she was stabbing her same ignition key into the cork of the Syrah she'd yanked from the seasonal cornucopia display between the open-concept kitchen and great room.

She offers him the glass vial of cocaine, but the one thing he promised himself after his Ketel One and codeine incident was no drugs, prescription or otherwise. Quitting drinking would have been a prudent idea too but wasn't realistic under these trying emotional circumstances. A person has only so much discipline to go around.

Lane is close enough to catch her aroma of conditioners and moisturizers not sold at drug stores. He smells top notes of monogramed towels and large-denomination bills. Scents that transport him back to his beloved in Gramercy Park. His mind and his body veer in different directions as his pulse quickens in his chest, flooding blood into his penis like an unruly mob down a dead-end alley.

He feels guilty for his unintentional erection and fights the notion that he's attracted to someone other than Mia. He's heard about fear giving men a hard-on, some sort of fight-or-flight survival mechanism. He wonders in terms of evolutionary biology how that would have come in handy when faced with a saber-toothed tiger or a wooly mammoth.

He turns his thoughts to Mia and the first time he slept with her, which was the first time he met Mia, at a house party near the University of Washington. Lane was there backing up a Fred Meyer coworker who moonlighted as a DJ and bartender, if you call playing Top 40 CDs between mixing rum-and-Cokes in red plastic party cups to be DJing and bartending.

It was great timing, as Mia had come to Seattle to participate in the WTO protests and stuck around, houseboat-sitting
for an old college friend who was on an extended assignment
for Amazon in Beijing. She filled her days with sleeping late,
snowboarding at Snoqualmie Pass and auditing psych, religion
and anthro classes at the UW. She'd taken a hit and a half of
ecstasy earlier that evening and was going through a phase that
Lane now saw as less about her and more about not being her
parents.

She reveled in a kind of East Coast rich kid fantasy of lib-
ertine West Coast life where shoes are optional and everyone
pretends to be super outdoorsy (even if they hate camping) and
weed is good for you. She told him about how she lived in Jackson Hole for the year prior to coming to Seattle with some
boyfriend she met at Dartmouth. She'd dropped out when he
graduated, bought a new Range Rover with a full-grain leather
interior, Bose speakers and six-disc changer, and drove west.

Meanwhile, Lane was still spending most of his time wearing a vinyl apron, polyester tie and latex gloves while machine-
slicing honey turkey and provolone at the Lake City Fred
Meyer, flailing through his last semesters of college without
financial aid. Three years in total. That's what it took him to
finish his senior year, a handful of credits and fifty-hour work-
weeks at a time.

As they lay on the king-sized waterbed in Mia's friend's
houseboat, Lane lost himself in the wraparound view of Lake
Union. He'd never seen such a vista in an entire lifetime in
Seattle. He fell in love with Mia's strawberry blond hair. The
light freckles sprayed across her nose. Her passion for those

less fortunate matched with a laugh that could be heard a block away. He knew at that moment. She was both his muse and his rope out of the pit.

But now that rope is running through his hands, flaying his skin on the way down.

Nina snaps her fingers an inch from his nose. "You still with us, dude?"

"Me? Yeah, for sure."

"Well, you gonna be the man here or what?"

He notices that without underwear or a belt to restrain him, his erection has crested the waistline of his pants. He feels something like the panicked realization that he's left an open *Penthouse* in his mom's bathroom—exposed, vulnerable, betrayed by all of his baser intentions. He steps—almost hops—to her, trying to get close enough to narrow her field of vision. Lane overshoots his mark and ends up pressing himself against her.

The pressure from their bodies pushing together forces the throbbing from his crotch back into his chest, where it overflows, rebounding up to his neck to his temples.

She swivels her neck so her lips line up with his, her breath—an antiseptic wintergreen stacked atop the dimly sweet cocaine, alcohol and tobacco—entering his mouth.

"You're not much of a closer." She turns and starts walking away. "But you'll do the trick."

"Wait. Where're you going? What trick?" He feels his face flush and tries to force air to the bottom of his lungs.

"Don't go anywhere." She points at the phone in her hand and keeps walking. "We have more to discuss."

"Wait. Seriously. What trick?" His eyes follow Nina until she disappears into one of the back bedrooms.

He stands in the middle of the kitchen, overcome with guilt and shaking out his feet to try to redistribute his blood supply.

LANE DIDN'T NOTICE THE FAKE plasma TV above the fireplace or the plastic Christmas tree in the corner until now. He rushes through the index of his brain, thumbing for a topic of conversation for when she gets back, something to segue into explaining why he has to leave.

He cranes his neck to hear. She's pacing and only audible when closer to him. "Yeah, whatever, fuck that little bitch," she repeats in tones that are at once frustrated and soothing. "She's not gonna do shit."

Never taking his eyes off the hallway, Lane kneels to slip one finger into the top of her purse and pulls it open. He starts to feel through the bag, searching for the loose bills. It is like rummaging through a recycling bin. He pulls out a few wadded receipts before extracting a twenty. He sticks it into the pocket of his jeans.

"Yes, I'm listening," Nina says in the other room. "Yes, attachment parenting, I understand." She is pacing faster now. "Yes, I know what fucking attachment parenting is. I read the book, remember?"

He rubs the papers in the purse between his thumb and index finger to try to locate the grainy stock of currency. Instead, he finds the smooth stickiness and sharp right angles of a photograph.

"I promised you I'm gonna take care of it, right?" she proclaims. "You know me."

Lane brings the photo to the mouth of the purse and tilts it so he can see. It is Nina posing with an Asian woman and a darker-skinned boy, not a baby but not yet in kindergarten, Lane guesses. Maybe what people who know about these things call a toddler.

He returns his gaze to the hallway and is met with a waist-level view of Nina and her smooth leather and black python belt.

"Find what you're looking for?" she asks.

"I, uh, I wanted to check out your ePod."

She eyes the photo in the top of the purse, "And? What do you think?"

"Of what? That?" He shrugs. "Like a Benetton ad."

"My son." She smiles. "And my wife."

Lane joins in on the joke. "Yeah, your wife."

"Yeah, my wife." She lowers her tone. "You got a problem with that?"

"Problem? No. No problem. Not at all."

"Actually, she's not my wife."

"Shit." He holds his hands over his face and exhales. "Got me again."

"No same-sex marriage in Washington State. But we've been a couple for a decade."

"Oh, OK, no. That's cool. I love lesbians." He swallows. "I mean, not as like a fetish thing, but like I respect and appreciate all people, but I believe it's, I— So, you're selling this place?"

She rolls her eyes, pauses and decides to let it slide. "Pretty much the whole neighborhood. I'm bringing some of the best practices I learned in the Silicon Valley e-commerce space to bear on the Pacific Northwest residential real estate market."

This exchange strikes the deathblow, putting his erection out of its misery.

"Listen." She coughs. "I need you to do something for me."

"OK?" He worries that a cameraman and a production assistant with a release form on a clipboard are about to emerge from the closet.

She searches through her handbag, pulls out a Motorola pager, and tosses it onto his lap. "It's alphanumeric."

"It's alphanumeric." He nods and repeats the word. He thinks he understands what it means but is unsure how exactly that applies to a pager.

"When I send you a message, you need to call me back. Right away."

"What for?" He doesn't trust that he has the right words to ask if she is planning some sort of illicit heterosexual affair. Better to let her say it.

"I need you to talk to somebody for me. Somebody from your neck of the woods."

"Gramercy?"

"Not exactly."

"I got my own cell," he says as he picks up the beeper.

"It doesn't work. We both know that."

FOUR

"LANE. LANE." HIS MOM POUNDS on the door to the TV room.

He's dreaming about the forty-foot Norway spruce in Gramercy Park, the one at eye level out the window of his home office. He thinks of long afternoons drinking double Americanos near the Columbia campus, how he feels twirling the stem of a nineteen-dollar martini at the Gramercy Park Hotel's Rose Bar, and, for the first time in a while, he ponders his dissertation. Soon, he'll be a doctor of philosophy. A few more years and the degree will be something that nobody, not even Mia's father, can take away from him.

He battles the voice drawing him back to consciousness. He wants to stay where it all makes sense, where his efforts deliver the life he deserves. But he's mouth-breathing with his lips on the pleather couch and his feet are cramped with cold from sticking out below the quilt. The space heater crapped out again. Either that or his mom came in before and turned it off. She was always a Nazi about the electric bill.

"That cross-eyed kid's here," his mom announces.

"Who?"

"The ugly one."

"Lonnie's not technically cross-eyed. He's—" Lane notices the clock on the VCR. It reads 1:26, a few minutes short of two hours after he was to meet Lonnie. "Goddamn it."

He yanks a semi-buttoned dress shirt over his head and staggers barefoot and hungover toward the front of the house. Lane opens the door to see walleyed Lonnie standing on his front porch in a full denim outfit and a Mariners hat, eating a red plastic bag of corn nuts.

"Hey, man. How you been, Lonnie?" Lane smiles and extends a hand. "What's up with the Canadian tux?"

Lonnie wipes bits of corn nuts from his beard and folds his arms across his chest. "Dude, I called you like six times, dude."

"Can we talk outside?" Lane nods his head toward his mom in the kitchen.

They walk out to the front lawn toward Lonnie's white Toyota Tundra, its two front wheels rutted into the foot-long wet grass. Lane's feet cramp more from the cold lawn.

"Tell me why I shouldn't be hella pissed." Lonnie was always a big guy. Fat and big. He's at least three inches taller than Lane but has never shown too much of a temper. Then again, business is business.

"You see, my colleague, he had to go home—"

"To Europe?"

"He is . . . He was . . . No, you know . . . It's, you see, the cops—"

Lonnie hits Lane in the stomach with a short right hook. He

has good form, building from his right foot and up through the rotation of his hips. Lane doubles over and drops to the ground.

"I can't . . . can't believe, you did that." Lane struggles to breathe, feeling as if his liver has burst and shot hot bile throughout his body cavity.

"Fuck, dude." Lonnie shakes his head. "I don't even sell trees no more. You know what I had to go through to get that much weed for you on short notice?"

"Everything OK out there?" Lane's mom shouts from the front door.

"Hey, Mrs. Bueche." Lonnie waves to her. She disappears back inside.

Lane tries to pick himself up. "It's Bue-*shay*, like—"

"Shut up. I've known your ass since middle school, motherfucker."

"We pronounced it wrong then 'cause it was easier for—"

"I know you're all *Boo-shay* and New York 'n' shit and think you're all hella filty now."

"Filthy. *Th*. *Th*. There's an 'h.'"

"Filty. Yeah, that's what I said. Either way, this weed—I didn't get it from Nordstrom's. There ain't no return policy, dude."

Lane spits and rolls to his knees, still unsure if he'll vomit or not, and starts to cry. He isn't sobbing, per se, but he can't fight back the tears that streak down his cheeks.

"Seriously, Lane?" Lonnie kneels down to clean bits of wet grass off of his Jordan 6s, while swearing under his breath.

"I was with— I was at that party." Lane fights to get it out. "With the lady."

After a few deep breaths, Lonnie heads toward his pickup, dialing on his Ericsson T68 with a color screen as he walks. He leaps into his driver's seat, talking in a hushed voice and nodding his head.

Lane eyes the woods at the far end of his mom's street. He doesn't think Lonnie will hurt him. Not too bad, but who knows? He'd rather Lonnie beat the crap out of him than force him to pay for the weed, as he can spare a bruise or two. But, as for money, well, that's what he is crying about. He decides to run, but as he tries to stand, his feet are stone and his abdomen won't unfurl.

Lonnie walks back over, removing his Mariners hat and running his hand over his shaved head. With the bald scalp leading to mid-mounted eyes and then the beard, it appears that Lonnie's head is on upside down. "We're cool, player," he mumbles. "Don't never fuck with me like that again, though."

"Why didn't you tell me you don't sell anymore?" Lane pants.

"I was trying to help you out." Lonnie pulls Lane to his feet. "I heard you're going through a hella hard time."

"What? I'm great. Who'd you hear that from?"

"People."

"People?"

"People. And Toby."

"Who the fuck's Toby?"

"Uh, your mom's boyfriend, dude." Lonnie motions his head toward Toby, who is now looking out the kitchen window along with Lane's mom.

"That's his name?"

"Dude works at my cousin's fireworks stand. Sometimes. Up on Lake City and 145th there, past the city limit, you know? Nice guy."

"I wouldn't exactly call him her boyfriend." Lane doesn't remember the end of his conversation with Lonnie. Something about how Lonnie was trying to get his GED, but the teacher got sent to jail for some sort of mail or welfare fraud. Otherwise, it was a series of Lane's excuses and counting the moments until he could get back in the house to yell at his mom for not waking him up earlier and to tell Toby to stop spreading rumors and focus on minding his own goddamn business.

After his mom and Toby have been reprimanded, Lane grabs his shoes and storms out of the house, slamming the front door behind him. "Don't expect your ten bucks back either, Toby." He marches down the walkway.

He makes it to the pay phone by the liquor store, and before he knows it, he's placing another collect call to Mia. He knows better than to use his name at this point, so he tells the operator he is Tad, Mia's autistic cousin who lives in a group home in Connecticut. He's been saving this one for a special occasion.

She answers the call. "Tad? Everything OK, sweetie? Where are you?"

Lane is silent. He hasn't thought about the next step. How to manage the pivot.

"Taddy? Are you there?"

He imagines her in their apartment, shouldering a nice Nokia to her ear and scanning the floor-to-ceiling cherrywood bookcases in the living room. Shelves he was busy filling out with novels he'd been buying from the Strand that he hadn't had the chance to read yet.

"Lane? Is that you?"

He doesn't answer. He's trying not to cry or, worse, stutter.

"I'm— I can't talk to you." She tries to maintain control of her voice. "My dad, he knows about all the collect calls. He wants me to meet with a lawyer."

Lane feels a trembling sensation in his ribs. Shit. Here comes the coronary. He's always known it would get him. It was a matter of when. He's almost in visual range of the used car lot where his pops met the same fate. His chest pulses and rattles. Then the feeling stops. All feeling stops. His vision starts to dim.

He falls forward against the pay phone.

Am I dead? he wonders, grasping at his own torso, searching for something tangible, some proof of life. His hand finds its way to the hard edges of Nina's pager in the left chest pocket of his faux fur–collared Armani Exchange jacket.

Of course, he knew it was the pager all along. It's the hangover making him jittery, that's all.

"You there, Lane? I told my dad I'm not ready for that," Mia continues. "But I promised I wouldn't answer any more calls. To calm my nerves, you know? Before any decisions . . . I'm sorry," she says. He is sure he hears just enough intentional sensitivity to let him know that she still has feelings for him.

"Buy me a ticket. I'll pay you back. I'll come to the apartment and we can talk about this. I know this'd be different if you talk to me in person. Don't talk to a lawyer until we can speak face-to-face. Please. Please, Mia."

There's no answer.

"Mia?"

The line clicks over to a dial tone. She disconnected the call after saying she was sorry.

He punches the pay phone as hard as he can. He imagines the number pad on the phone as Mia's dad's stupid, angular WASPy face, and he hits it again and again until blood streams down the back of his fist.

Lane goes through the coins at the bottom of his pocket. He scrounges a dime and three nickels, and calls the number on the pager.

FIVE

A PASTEL-COLORED WOLF LEAPS ATOP a brick house and enters the chimney.

Lane gets back to murdering the pronunciation of the children's book in Spanish: "*Des-cen— Des-cen-dee-o por el* . . . No, *damn*, it's *la—la chi— chi-mee-nuh.*"

He glances at Jordan, Nina's two-year-old, in the back seat of the parked Mercedes. The kid doesn't seem to be listening. He's hypnotized by the passing traffic on Lake City Way, his eyelids at half-mast. Lane's not even sure if the little guy talks.

"Don't you have anything in English?" Lane asks Nina as she returns to the car with fingernail clippers and a sugar-free Red Bull she procured from the Shell station.

"My wife, she won't let me. It's about Jordan's cultural whatever." She sets about clipping any visible white parts off her nails.

"*Chimenea*," Jordan says without a hint of an accent.

"Good job, honey. Mommy and Momma are so proud of

you." Nina grins and then turns to Lane. "My wife read me this thing about how bilingual children are high achievers."

The wolf drops down the chimney into a cauldron of boiling water. The Three Little Pigs slam closed the lid and climb atop, as the wolf struggles to escape.

On the next page, a bit of limp, furry tail sticks out from under the lid. The pigs celebrate.

"Jesus." Lane slams shut the book, shielding Jordan from the grizzly denouement. "I remember the English version as a bit more, I dunno, kid-friendly."

"Babar's got a murder and an incestuous marriage. All in the first chapter. But I bet they've sanitized that now too 'cause everything's so vanilla these days that—" Nina sits up straight. "Wait. There she is." She grabs a small pair of binoculars from under the seat and puts them to her eyes. "Yep, that's her. For sure." She hands the binoculars to Lane.

He watches through the windshield of the Mercedes as a woman, a few years younger than him, emerges from a dirt trail and climbs—careful not to rip her pants or lose the cigarette between her lips—over the guardrail onto the far side of Lake City Way. Lane can't make out where the path leads down through the maple trees and thicket, but he knows the encampment of busted mobile homes, blue tarpaulin roofs and makeshift plywood walls known as the University Trailer Park infests much of the ravine below.

"That's the chick?"

"Inez," she whispers. "The little crack baby herself."

From what he can see, the woman's skin is darker, like Jordan's, and her hair is jet-black, stretched so tight into a pony-tail that it seems to peel back her eyelids. And it is all secured in place with a shellacking of hairspray. Her clothes look to be black polyester and fake patent leather trimmed with white stitching: a desperate attempt at work casual by someone who gets her sense of sophistication through primetime network dramas. She doesn't strike Lane as the vicious street junkie Nina made her out to be. In another world, another dimension, he might even say that she's attractive. Or, at least, his type, if no one else knew about it.

He imagines the pungency of her discount-aisle perfume. The opacity of her overapplied foundation makeup. As she starts to walk down the sidewalk, Lane watches how her ass curves into her upper thigh. She is slender through the torso, a bit thicker though the legs. Impressive for someone he assumes to be surviving off of boiled hot dogs, Newports and Safeway Select. Maybe it's due to her youth. Maybe it's the meth. But seeing where she lives, he knows all he really needs to know.

Nina fires up the engine and noses the car out of the Shell station parking lot. As Inez chucks her cigarette on the sidewalk and breaks into a sprint, Nina whips the Mercedes across four lanes of Lake City Way traffic. Lane drops the binoculars to the floor and braces both palms on the dash.

Inez is wearing low heels, and her patent-leather handbag swings with each stride, hitting her in the back. She doesn't run like someone who has ever run for fitness or because she wants to run. She runs out of pure, panicked necessity.

The 72 Metro rounds the bend, decelerating for the stop

ahead. Nina falls into place behind the bus. Inez catches the 72 as it starts to pull away again.

"Keep your eyes on her." Nina finishes a smoke, flicking it out the open window. "Use the binoculars. That's what they're made for. Come on, man."

Lane digs around on the floor, searching for the binoculars. They must have slid back under the seat once the car accelerated. "I can see her fine. No worries. Really."

"And to think: we were this close to signing the paperwork." Nina grinds together her thumb and index finger. "This close to being done with her trashy Mexican ass."

Nina tails the bus, winding north along Lake City Way. They drive past the Seven Seas, the Shanty Tavern, the Italian Spaghetti House, Bill Pierre Ford, the Frigate, the Rimrock, Bakers candy store, the Value Village: the places that mark the borders of the only world Lane knew for so long. The one he now wants to forget.

"I mean, look at this." Nina motions at Jordan's elaborate car seat, one that would be at home in a NASA cockpit. "You think she can even afford bus fare for him? How about health insurance? Or college?"

"Here we go," Lane warns as Inez pulls the stop cord and gets up from her seat. Nina veers to the side of the road with half a block to spare.

"I think it's better if you talk to her yourself," he offers. "I can still help. You know, keep an eye on your kid and all. Like you said: babysitter no-showed; wife's at a meditation retreat."

"No direct interaction. That'd blow our whole case."

Inez jumps off the bus and resumes running, her bag still whacking her in the back.

"Talk to her. Get to know her a bit. Become part of her life." Nina double-checks that Jordan is asleep and continues, "All she wants is money. Money from us. Money from welfare. Money either way. And I'm gonna give her what she wants. But you have to make sure it's her idea. It's gotta be her asking, not me offering. You follow me?"

"I've got some legal complications that—"

"Do it for my little Jordan. Make sure he isn't a pawn in some scheme by the druggie loser who never did anything more for him than get barebacked in a mobile home."

"Listen, I've already dedicated my career to helping those who—"

"So, do it for Jordan. And three thousand. Cash."

A terse, exaggerated laugh bursts from somewhere inside of him, forcing out white flecks of spittle that hit the dashboard before he can tamp it down and redirect his attention to his split knuckles. He turns his hand over and over, following the contours of the ragged flesh. "Dollars?"

Nina and Lane watch as Inez affixes a name badge to her shirt while jogging through the front doors of the Fred Meyer superstore.

"C'mon. I'll throw in the iPod. That's my last offer before I go with Lonnie's other friend. The one with the forehead acne," she says.

Lane looks at the red Fred Meyer billboard and drops his head into his hands.

Nina lights a smoke and opens her Red Bull in a single

motion. "Let me tell you something: when people're trying to fuck you over, sometimes you've gotta be like those piggies. You gotta make wolf soup."

She exhales smoke into the car. "Honestly, Lane . . . today is not the day to be a pussy."

SIX

"YOU LOOKING FOR SOMETHING?" INEZ says as he passes the end of the aisle.

Lane opens his eyes wide, scavenging for some sense of surprise. He taps his chest with two fingers and mouths, *"Me?"* But he doesn't stop walking.

"Yeah, you. C'mere." She fluffs a purple poly-cotton and rayon-blend pillow, the kind with attached bolster arms, and shoves it back on the middle shelf in the Home Essentials section. The air is sticky with clearance-priced Green Apple, Warm Breeze and Chocolate Fusion scented house candles fatter than soup cans.

The moment he starts sweating, Lane can smell his own body odor. He's sure that Toby's Old Spice is the culprit. It must be infected with some sort of noxious white trash bacterium. Lane makes a mental note to tell Toby to get a new deodorant as soon as he gets home. That said, he's not sure he likes the fact that Toby feels comfortable enough to keep toiletries at his mom's house.

He takes as few steps as possible toward Inez and nods to the purple pillow and its orange-corduroy brethren. "Yeah, I was wondering, uh, what do you call those things?"

"These? I dunno. A TV-watching pillow?" She smooths back the sides of her hair into the ponytail.

"That's funny. I always thought they were called reading pillows."

Due to her lack of reaction, Lane deduces that she must not have heard him.

"My mom, she used to call them a lazy husband," he tries while surveying her chewed nails, torn cuticles and a couple of hot-Bic smiley scars between her index finger and thumb. "But I bet the real name is like a bed rest pillow."

Lane realizes he's still wearing his wedding ring and slides his hands into his back pockets.

"Wow. Really?" She leans toward him. "Can I ask you something?"

"Yeah?" he inches closer, arms still behind his back.

"The fuck are you up to, dude?"

LANE NEVER TOLD MIA THAT he worked at the Fred Meyer deli, even though he was still there full-time when they met. "I dedicate my time to working with disadvantaged youth" is what he explained to her. And it was true, except the disadvantaged youth were he and his coworkers.

Mia never set foot in Lake City. During daylight, anyway. Lane made sure of that. It was one thing to tell her stories about where he was from. To describe his youth as "Algeresque" or "hardscrabble" and swaddle his bootstrapping tales in a layer of authenticity and grit. It was quite another thing for her to witness him in his indigenous habitat, especially as he'd always felt himself a non-native species marooned there from more cosmopolitan climes.

Lane knows what she would have thought. Lake City looks like nothing more than a strip of downtrodden and often sleazy businesses adrift in a sea of cracked parking lots and brambles. And although he didn't want the responsibility of explaining it to her—of defending a place he'd hoped never to see again—he knew Lake City was Lake City for a reason.

He knew that the day the Volstead Act was passed in 1919, there was but a single commercial business, a family-owned general store, on the whole length of the road. By 1922, it had been rechristened as "Victory Way." And this first cement highway in the United States was teeming with road-houses named the Plantation, the Jungle Temple, the French Inn and Joe's Hot Lunches, where they offered no lunch, only booze, cards and female companionship. Tusco's was housed in a barn and owned by a doctor who served up both drinks and abortions.

Seattle absorbed Lake City in the mid '50s. Like proto-mammals feasting on fallen dinosaurs, smaller taverns over-took the roadhouses. The last of the old guard, the Jolly Roger, was torched Lane's freshman year of high school and became a Shell station. Frank Colacurcio Sr., or Frank Sr. as they called him, built a strip club empire up and down Lake City Way from Rick's to the group houses where his strippers lived to Talents West where their books were kept. But not much else changed.

Lane does remember the construction of a large blue castle across the street from Fred Meyer when he was about eight years old. As they tacked on the prefab crenellations, he dreamt that it would be the Lake City outpost of Enchanted Village or maybe an indoor waterslide park like they had up on Aurora. In the end, it became a windowless self-storage block. One of dozens to follow. That was progress for Lake City: as a receptacle for the crap that Seattle didn't want but couldn't quite bring itself to throw away. That's the last time Lane would ever get his hopes up about the neighborhood.

By the end of the dot-com boom, the rest of Seattle had cut its hair and gotten a job. But Lake City was the mistress that grown-up Seattle kept around from its younger, untamed years. The one with electric-blue eyeliner and a missing incisor. The one Seattle would never introduce to its friends, but also the one who is always there when it needs to drink a forty and get a hand job in a parked car and not have to discuss what it all means.

"WHAT AM I UP TO?" Lane fires back at Inez. "I'm shopping for Home Essentials. Jesus, lady."

Inez crosses herself in what Lane figures is the direction of the *Virgen de Guadalupe* votives. "I seen you pass by here three times. Looking all weird 'n' shit. You got something in your jacket?"

"In my jacket?"

"Yeah, you gaffle something?"

"You accusing me of shoplifting?"

She shrugs, "Go over to the 99 Cent Store or Value Village. But here, it's gonna be my ass and I'm already—"

"I'm a— Do I look like a shoplifter to you?"

"Kinda. Yeah."

"Listen, what's your name?" He makes a point of searching for her name tag. "Listen, Inez, I can't believe you'd—"

The clap of a hand across Lane's shoulders forces him to pause and regain his breath before turning around.

"What up, Lame-o?"

Once Lane turns, his tongue clutches in his throat.

"It's me. Tom. Tommy Tucker the Mommyfucker." The man fingers his name tag and takes a long swill from a can of orange Crush. "C'mon, brainiac. You don't recognize me outside the deli?"

Tom was, in fact, unmistakable with his faithful preservation of an '80s hustler motif: a feathered butt-cut parted down the middle, caressing the tops of his ears. Throw in a bulletproof black mustache and a copious chest pelt surmounting his open collar and he added up to a kind of a third-tier gentile Harry Reems. Or, more precisely, the former home run king of the grocery union softball league. A total "plab," as they used to call the look in high school.

"Tom. Hey." Lane struggles to get the words out. "I was planning to come over to the deli."

"So, how's it hangin', guy?"

"Not really sure. How's it, uh, hanging with you?"

"Long and loose and fulla juice." Tom laughs as if he didn't say this whenever given the opportunity. "Man, how long were you gone? A week? Who woulda thought? I can't wait to tell everybody you're back."

"No, I'm not. I'm—"

"You know this dude?" Inez asks Tom.

"The new chick sweating you, Lame-o?" Tom tracks Inez from her chest down, craning his neck to try to evaluate her rear.

Lane catches himself checking out her body too and then redirects his eyes. "We're cool. We're just talking."

"Just talking . . ." Inez trails off.

"Carefula this guy, Maria," Tom says. "He don't look like much, but he gets chicks' heads spinning with all his big words."

"My name's not Maria," she says as she retreats to the pillows.

Tom puts his hand back on Lane's shoulder and leans in close, the burnt coffee acidity of his breath curdling the contents of Lane's stomach. "I might be able to pull some strings. Get you some holiday shifts." Tom flicks his name tag again and smiles.

"Assistant store manager . . . nice. Moving on up." Lane grabs the purple pillow off the shelf, puts it under his arm. "This is what I was looking for. Uh, perfect."

Tom steps to Lane again and delivers his main point before he can slip away. "Us guys gotta stick together. This place is getting overrun with homos and beaners."

"Don't worry, Tom. Lake City's not catching up with the modern world anytime soon."

"You'd be surprised," Tom says, ditching any veneer of humor. "If it were up to me, I'd check 'em all for drugs and green cards. Send 'em back to wherever they came from."

Lane waits until Inez slips up and makes eye contact. "Thanks again for your help. See you soon?"

Inez turns her back and fluffs another pillow.

SEVEN

"I TOLD YOU TO KEEP your head down." Nina pushes on the back of his neck, trying to fold him in half. The seat belt fights back harder than he does. Lane unbuckles and slides into the passenger-side footwell, the pillow still clutched to his chest.

As they pull to a stop at the edge of her driveway, she drapes her jacket over his head and secures it with a tuck between his shoulder and the car door.

"We'll finish this conversation in five." She removes a sleeping Jordan from his car seat and carries him over her shoulder, up the steps and into the corner-lot new construction. "Don't go anywhere."

While tempted to rifle through the glove compartment and find out if there's anything under the seats, Lane stays put. He counts his age. He counts from his age back down to zero. The smell of the leather interior reminds him of Mia and their cross-country move to New York in her Range Rover. Every mile they traveled east, every mile closer to their new life together, Lane felt one step closer to his destiny.

At least five minutes pass. Probably ten. Or fifteen. He raises his head and peeks out from under the jacket to admire the house: a three-story box built of cement, metal, composite paneling, dark-stained tropical hardwood accents and numerous balconies with frameless frosted-glass balustrades. He isn't sure, but it looks like the place has a decent roof deck or two with million-dollar views of Green Lake.

Nina passes inside the house's front window. He drops back down into the footwell, only to rise up again. Now he sees a second woman, the Asian woman from Nina's photograph, carrying the sleeping child—his head leaning against her neck.

The two women pace their front room. Nina wrings her hair with her hand, as if squeezing the water from a dish sponge. Her wife grips Jordan to her chest with her one arm and slices at the air in front of Nina's face with the other.

They use some sort of remote to lower the automatic blinds. Nina spots Lane and mouths *"Get down"* as the blinds drop past her face. As her wife steps to the last open window, Lane plummets below the edge of the door and holds his breath.

Before he can count to his age and back again, Nina opens the driver's-side door and gets in. She doesn't say a word. She starts playing with her phone and PalmPilot, resting them on the dashboard.

"Don't worry. She didn't see me," he whispers from under the coat.

No answer.

"It's really none of my business, but doesn't your wife think it's weird that you're back out here?" he tries again.

Nina dials a number on her phone but never hits *call*. She puts the phone to her ear and keeps facing out the windshield. "In my wife's world, even drinking from plastic water bottles'll give you cancer. And she's even more *allahu akbar* about smoking 'cause it's corrupting Jordan. I'm out here like every fifteen minutes."

"*Allahu akbar* means 'God is great,'" Lane says.

"Yeah, thanks. I get it." She clears her throat. "What's up with the pillow-thing anyway?"

He considers it for a moment. "Strategy. Like a prop. Maybe if you'd let me get a word in edgewise before I coulda explained what—"

"I take it you bought that pillow instead of my smokes?"

He slips three dollars and some change next to the stick shift.

"Not inspiring a lot of trust here, Lane." She uses her free hand to search the car for a loose cigarette.

"Well, I— I talked to her, which is already more than I said I'd do today. OK?" He squeezes the pillow tighter.

"And?" She produces the nail clipper from her pocket and searches in vain for more white in her nails to trim.

"And what?"

She motions toward Jordan's empty car seat. "In a work situation, you see, you report back to your employer."

"Not much to say. Like you told me, she's pretty scratchy."

"Listen, Lane: You ever felt like the most important thing in your world might slip between your fingers? Disappear forever?"

"I'm assuming Lonnie filled you in about all of that too."

She gives up on the nail clipper, picks a butt out of the ashtray and struggles to straighten it out enough to light it.

"For some reason, I have trouble picturing you as an I-was-born-to-be-a-mom type," he pries.

"I can make my company happen. I can achieve all these successes." She waves the cigarette stub at her house. "But don't I also deserve to have a regular life with a family, like everyone else out there? People who are otherwise totally unremarkable get to take that shit for granted. I've had to fight for every bit of it. And if we lose Jordan, I don't see how my wife can recover. How we can recov— Shit, here comes Tracey."

"Who?"

Nina pulls the pillow out of Lane's arms and punches it down on top of him, forcing him further into the footwell.

She opens the window some three inches, signaling to the cigarette smoke and her phone call as the obstacles to normal communication.

"Jordan's down," Tracey says, straining to see inside the car. "I'm sorry I made you rush back like that, but I just feel so freaked out. So overwhelmed. Like we have no control."

Nina holds her palm over the phone's mic and presses her lips toward the open gap at the top of the window. "Don't worry, we have more control than you think."

"Come back inside, sweetie," Tracey says.

Nina arches her eyebrows and nods to the phone with her head. "The lawyer. Gimme a minute."

"This late?"

"High priority . . . Gimme a minute."

"Tell him I want— Tell him we need results. Right now,"

Tracey says as the window rolls up. She continues to talk at Nina through the glass, "I swear to God my head will explode if he says 'my hands are tied' one more time."

Neither Nina nor Lane speaks a word until the house door closes behind Tracey.

"I canned that lawyer the other week. Got a new one the next day and already dumped her too. I don't tolerate inefficiency. And I don't lose. Ever." She continues to fake-talk into the phone. "In forty-eight hours, you're gonna show me some progress or I'm going to have to move on. Got it?"

"That's maybe, I dunno, a little fast."

"I'm sure—if you really want to—you can find a way to convince someone with a marginal IQ to do something in their own best interest. And in the best interest of a young child." She gives him twenty bucks. "Get a cab. Not here." She uses her index and middle fingers to simulate a person running.

Dramatic measures, Lane thinks as he exits the car.

"Take this thing with you." Nina tosses the pillow out on the pavement before she closes the door.

EIGHT

GETTING HIS JOB BACK AT Fred Meyer should be easy. In terms of paperwork and such. But emotionally, it would be one of the hardest things Lane has ever undertaken.

He waits for Tom at the edge of the parking lot and tries to intercept him on the way to his bus stop. After blowing the first night and a few hours the next day standing out in the cold, he resolves to go inside and pretend to shop until he locates his target.

"I knew it," Tom shouts down the aisle as Lane browses the candy section. "Lame-o wants his old job back."

Lane laughs at the ridiculous comment. No way. He's on winter break. Shopping for candy. For his nephew.

"I hope that kid doesn't grow up to be a liberal bookworm gay-ass too." Tom pretends to knee Lane in the thigh. The ol' charley horse. A Tommy Tucker classic.

Lane conjures a final stilted laugh and, after a few moments of quiet, mentions that the store does seem a bit understaffed. He knows how things get around Christmas. If Tom twists his arm, he'd be willing to pick up a couple of holiday shifts. But as a favor to Tom. If he needs him. And only through New Year's.

"AA folks call that 'backsliding.'" Tom sucks something out from between his teeth.

Lane has tried to prepare himself for this. He's repeated it over and over in his head. This whole thing is another step toward becoming the Bill Clinton of Lake City Way. The "Comeback Kid" Clinton in the "Hope" TV ad from '92, not the ex-president who nutted all over his own narrative.

When Lane first saw that ad in high school, he found what he'd been missing: the role model, the father figure that he'd so long desired—a kindred spirit, born at the bottom, but who was also intelligent, hardworking and, of course, preternaturally charismatic.

Lane too could dream to make something of himself. And now, a decade later, he digs up a few lines from the Clinton ad: "I worked my way through law school with part-time jobs, anything I could find. And after I graduated, I really didn't care about making a lot of money. I just wanted to go home and see if I could make a difference." There. That was Lane. And this is the "anything I could find" moment.

The moment, with conditions. Lane explains to Tom he can't work the deli counter—under any circumstances. That's his proviso for picking up these shifts. He figures that, best-case scenario, he'll do a couple of days in the back, get the line on Inez and have the whole thing sorted before anyone notices that he's there. Worst-case scenario, Inez'll require a few more days and he'll end up making a few extra bucks at the store in the process. Like some political economist, probably Keynes, said, money is the link between the present and the future.

Tom listens to Lane's pitch. "C'mon up to the break room. I'll do your interview."

"Really?"

"Next time, think about shaving. Men have standards in the real world."

On the way upstairs, Lane thinks about running for the door, punching Tom in the back of his head or at least blackmailing the piece of shit to get out of jumping through all of these embarrassing and unnecessary hoops. After all, on Lane's last day before quitting the deli to get married to Mia and move to New York, Tom took Lane out for drinks and started running his mouth. "Out for drinks" was a single can of Carling Black Label for each of them out on the loading dock. And Lane was pretty sure Tom had lifted the beers from the refrigerated aisle.

Thinking that it was their last time together, Tom unloaded on Lane about how he had lived with his mom since being released from jail for pandering. Lane assumed at first that pandering was another way to say panhandling. It seemed out of character for Tom, and he soon found out it was a bit more complicated.

Tom used to do the books and work the front desk at night at a North Lake City motel frequented by hookers. Tom said he'd been smoking a lot of base in those days and needed to generate some additional cash. He agreed to give the hookers free rooms by keeping the rentals off the books in exchange for a steady cut. It worked well for a couple of months until some

other individual with more experience in the pandering industry tipped the cops to arrest him, but not until after he slapped
the shit out of Tom and threatened his life. Since getting out,
Tom's been working his way through rehab, living at home,
paying down fines and legal fees and working at Fred Meyer all
the way up to his big comeback as assistant manager.

Even as Tom grills Lane about what makes a quality Fred
Meyer employee, three ways to improve a customer's day, how
Jews are infiltrating the grocery union and a long digression-
cum-debate about which part of a turkey deli slices come from,
Lane doesn't have the nerve to bring up any of the dirt he has
on Tom. If he's going to be the Bill Clinton of Lake City Way,
he'll have to know when to keep his head down and when to
go for the kill.

THE NEXT DAY, HE FINDS her timecard in the metal rack in
the hallway. First name. No last name. Printed in pencil. She's
here. Punched in late. But she's here, for sure.

The clipboard hangs a few feet to the left on a nail between
the hooks holding vinyl aprons and a mix of Burlington Coat
Factory, Carhartt and Seahawks Starter jackets. Lane thumbs
through the pages of printed spreadsheets, searching for her
schedule. He found it when last in the store and remembers
that it is about two-thirds of the way through.

He double-checks her breaks against the hour on the wall-
mounted timecard machine and then spots her garish patent
leather handbag.

He reaches inside the bag. Bills and tissues and a Chapstick. Lots of bills. Overdue bills. Electric. Phone company. Trailer park fees. Collection notices. Welfare statements. An overdraft charge from Washington Mutual. Lottery tickets. Food stamps. More lottery tickets. A pay stub from Fred Meyer: $6.72 per hour. Not a single photo of Jordan.

The jacket pockets yield a bus transfer and a box of Parliaments with four cigarettes left. He steals her smokes and buries them at the bottom of the wastepaper basket.

He was hoping to find a wallet or cell phone, although nobody in their right mind would keep their valuables here. The handful of lockers are monopolized by the store managers and union journeymen from the meat and fish departments.

But Inez is her real name. It's on the pay stub and welfare statements. Inez Roberts. He snakes the pay stub so that he'll have her address and phone number, just in case.

"Hey. Lame-o," Tom shouts from down the hallway. "Don't be late for your shift. No tardy slips here—just pink ones."

IN THE GROCERY STORE KINGDOM, lunch meat is the lowest species of the esteemed meat phyla. Some would argue it's closer to the grab-and-go snack foods than to an elite filet. It's the meat with a sketchy, if not unknown, provenance. Meat product propped up with preservatives. We're not talking about Katz's or 2nd Ave Deli here. These are the wares of a regional superstore that sells as many or more bath mats and jumper cables. But it is still meat. Sort of. It's lunch meat.

Lane works out his frustrations on the meat slicer. On the poor little pigs and turkeys and steer that have been mechanically separated, tumbled, pressed and colored into cold cuts that deliver a consistent look and uniform sandwich-eating experience.

He rams them into the spinning blade. Some unknown part of them. The carriage returning and returning in a hypnotic rhythm. He moves his hands in a practiced pattern around the knife's edge. He is part of the machine. The machine is an extension of him.

He's done this for years. Knows it better than riding a bike. Better than typing on a keyboard. Way better than driving a car. By late high school, he graduated from spraying down the meat department and carrying the bin of offcuts to the loading dock to be taken away and rendered. He started donning an apron and gathering a roller cart full of the different meats and cheeses for the preslice shift. There were roast beefs, honey smoked turkeys, oven-browned turkeys, York hams, Black Forest hams, turkey pastramis and a variety of deli cheeses running from Jarlsberg Lite to fluorescent yellow American.

Today, as he always does, he lays down the black rubber floor mats, sprays the deli slicer with bleach water, adjusts its gauge plate for ideal thickness for a given type of meat or cheese and sets the blade whirring at a vicious 530 rpm. He holds the meat with his left hand and reaches across with his right to operate the push arm.

He sings "Miss Mary Mack" to himself while executing the complex hand routine around the revolving vorpal blade and inserting the paper sheet between each slice of the softer cheeses. When he finishes the shift, he reloads the roller cart and starts all over again. He was—he is again, at least, for the

next few days—North Seattle's Sisyphus of sliced sandwich
meats.

"DILL, SON," THE CUSTOMER SAYS, not taking his eye off
the game of *Snake II* on his blue-and-silver Nokia 3310 brick.
"And hurry up, I got business."

"Lemme check," the deli clerk answers, snapping on a pow-
derless latex glove. He does an about-face, spinning on his all-
black discount sneakers and calls to Lane in the back, "Biz?"

Lane already told dude not to call him that. Twice. This
time he was going to straight-up pretend he didn't hear him.
When Tom introduced them at the beginning of the shift, he
mentioned that they look like Bizarro Superman versions of
each other. The guy started calling Lane "Bizarro" and then
truncated it to "Biz" within five minutes. Lane assured him
that they have nothing in common. Nothing. Even if they both
have brown hair, blue eyes and a similar height.

"You got that Havarti back there? With the dill?"

And what's wrong with "No, sorry, we're out of that?" Lane
thinks as he finishes cleaning the slicer, running the bleach rag
around the edge of the blade on low rpm. Fuck this guy. He's
supposed to have Lane's back, not make things more difficult.

On top of it, he already invited Lane to go to a Mars Hill
megachurch service after work. Lane figures he's the kind
of kid, fresh off the bus from Idaho, Eastern Washington or
Alaska, who refers to Seattle as "The City" and says shit like
"Shut the front door" and "Cheese and rice."

Little bothered Lane so much as a narrow-minded, earnest

person with a poor sense of humor. Go ahead and be provincial
or a philistine, but at least be funny. Most of Lane's childhood
friends were, in fact, hilarious idiots. And, on the other side, if
you decide to shackle yourself with earnestness, at least come
up with something interesting to show for it.

Lane gives a cursory—if not altogether fake—glance in the
freezer. "Nope. Not here."

"I saw one back there. Bottom of the roller cart," the clerk
shouts from the front.

Lane finds the loaf on the cart, but it's room temperature.
Doesn't the kid know Havarti needs to be frozen in order to
cut on a slicer? That's Superstore Deli 101. When Lane picks
it up, his thumb leaves an indentation in the side. The blade
would chew up the ends and require at least a half-dozen passes
before he could consider getting a slice of appropriate sandwich
thickness. By then, the gauge plate would be so gummed up
that nothing would get through. Even if he could cut a clean
slice, he'd have to delay his break in order to get the slicer ready
again for the coming lunch rush.

"Can you come up on counter and I'll look?" the kid tries
again.

Lane refuses to answer.

"Biz?"

Lane grabs the bleach rag and wipes the brown roast beef
blood juice off his apron as he walks out from the back room.
Best to handle this directly with the customer: tell him there's
none left, time to settle for some regular, standard, old-fashioned
Havarti and—with some luck—the bus'll get you back to your
recliner in time for the second half of *The Price Is Right*. It took a

lot of maneuvering for Lane to get his break from 10:45 to 11:00, right when he needs it. Whether or not there's a culinary herb in some loser's cheese is not going to screw that up.

"Listen." He approaches the counter. "We don't—" *Shit.* He stares right at Robbie. Robbie who he's known since the third grade. One of the more hilarious of the hilarious idiots. Blazed as usual, Robbie battles to add one more square onto the zigzagging, pixelated snake on his phone screen before looking up.

Lane's already thrown himself to the floor, rolling behind the lowboy as if he'd just seen a man in a trench coat stroll into the store and rack the pump action on a shotgun.

"You OK?" the clerk calls out.

Lane military-crawls into the back room.

"Yo, you OK? . . . You slip?"

Lane crouches against the wall, waiting for Robbie to shout his name, to clown the hell out of him for being back in Lake City, back in the deli. No further than when they were kids: but in today's depressing version, Lane is supplying the cheese for Robbie's sandwich. Aside from the odd insurance scam, intermittent landscaping gigs and overcharging friends for gas money, Robbie doesn't even work. He used to brag to Lane that he didn't read a single book or do a night of homework in high school.

"Fucking why, Mia?" Lane asks the dropdown ceiling panels. "Why couldn't we work through this together?" Lane braces for Robbie's fusillade. But it doesn't come.

"I need two or three slices of shaved ham," a lady's voice calls from the counter.

"Can I get some help up front then? I'll come back and look for the cheese," the clerk insists. "Biz?"

"Wait a minute." Lane knocks his voice down an octave, like he used to do when calling into high school as his (already departed) father to get a waiver from gym classes. He races to the wall phone and hits 3 for the customer service desk.

Moments later, a voice crackles over the store paging system. "Hello, Fred Meyer customers. Would the owner of the red 1988 Chevrolet Z24 please come to the parking lot? Immediately. Your parking brake is off and the car is rolling. Again, that's a red 1988 Chevy Z24."

Lane watches fifteen seconds tick off the clock and then peeks his head around the corner. Robbie is gone, his sandwich open and cheeseless on the bar. The wall clock reads 10:51.

On his way out of the deli, Lane heaves the whole loaf of dill Havarti on the cutting board next to the sandwich.

He bags and tosses a handful of ham to the woman. She watches him grab it from the presliced stack in the front case. "Is that shaved?" she asks, spinning around as he jogs from behind the counter to the aisle. "I like it rather thin."

"Yeah. Sure, lady. Of course."

"Hey, I need you here," the deli clerk shouts after him.

Lane heads toward the upstairs break room. "UFCW Local 367 mandate. Nothing I can do, man."

NINE

LANE GIVES HIMSELF A FEW quick slaps on the cheeks,
straightens into a power pose he learned from Sage, Mia's
Reiki and Pilates instructor cum nutrition and life coach, and
stares at the door into the break room.

He tries to visualize how he will approach Inez but ends
up thinking of sitting on Central Park's Great Lawn on the
first day of September. His head rests in Mia's lap. The worst
of the humidity has passed, but it is still seventy-three degrees
and he's in short sleeves and flip-flops. She passes her hands
through his hair. Runs a finger around his brow and ears. They
smoke a joint of Sour Diesel from her delivery guy and debate
whether they should go walk around the Museum of Natural
History or take a cab out to Jackson Heights to hit up their
favorite Tamil restaurant for a long lunch.

They're already discussing summer break and where they'll
travel. Mia prepaid his whole year's tuition on the Amex card,
which means a shit-ton of frequent-flier miles. Lisbon and Ber-
lin have been discussed. Amsterdam is always up there. Maybe

a service project in someplace like Bolivia or Mozambique. They speak about "flexibility" and "realistic impact" to be sure it's understood that neither wants the service part to be too time-consuming or, God forbid, too depressing.

He focuses on the optimism, the fulfillment he felt that day.

Lane takes a final deep breath from his abdomen, like Sage showed him. He slouches out of his power pose and pushes through the break room door to find Inez sitting by herself at a far table by the microwave. Considering how many employees here have Washington State Food Handler Permits, Lane wonders how the microwave area could be so defiled with the encrusted remnants of Marie Callender's chicken potpies and Lynn Wilson's frozen burritos.

Inez holds her head up with one hand and reads the comics in the *Seattle Post-Intelligencer. Marmaduke. The Family Circus*. All that. She picks through a box of turkey-and-cheddar Lunchables with the other hand.

He walks up to her, an unopened pack of Parliaments conspicuous in his hand. He'd considered trying to pass off her own pack of smokes back on her but decided that the risk outweighed the cost of new ones, no matter how little cash he had. "Can I join you?"

She surveys the room. Three other employees are eating in silence at their own tables. "Why?"

"I think you got the wrong impression of me the other day."

She shakes her head: no recognition.

"Remember? The TV pillow?"

"Oh yeah, you're boyfriends with Tommy the Motherfucker." The other employees in the room shrink at her blasphemy.

"*Mommy*fucker," Lane manages to keep a straight face. "He's very specific about that."

She stands up and tosses the Lunchables box into a garbage can.

"Want to join me for a cigarette?" he asks. "You still got like six minutes."

She cocks her head to the side.

". . . I'm guessing. The break times, they're pretty much standardized."

"Got my own," she says as she walks out the door and into the hallway with the jackets.

He unwraps the Parliaments, waits until he hears her start cursing, and then follows after her. "C'mon. I know the best outdoor spot to stay outta the rain."

THE FRED MEYER IS THE lone large commercial establishment Lane ever visited (or remembers visiting) until he was a teenager. Sure, it used to be located in a smaller building across the parking lot back in the day. And they didn't sell much in the way of groceries or deli meats then. The store was on its trajectory from starting out as a horse-drawn coffee cart for Oregon lumber camps in 1909 to pioneering the concept of one-stop shopping in 1933 through becoming an independent Pacific Northwest regional superstore to the point it was bought out by Kroger while Lane was working there in 1998. These days, the Lake City store has the honor of having the highest shoplifting rate of any company's locations in Washington, Oregon, Idaho and Alaska. That and a nonpareil selection of Mad Dog 20/20. They even stock the elusive Lightning Creek flavor.

Although Lane doesn't smoke, he's known about the secret spot for years. It's little more than a few feet of extra roof hanging over the back edge of the second-floor, open-air parking lot. The fact that you have to squeeze behind rows of stacked shopping carts and a massive HVAC output to get there is what makes it worth visiting. There's no chance a customer or a non-smoking manager would wander back by accident.

There's a view north up the length of Lake City Way toward the city limit. Lane and Inez are shielded from the rain but not from a biting wind that drops down the same corridor from British Columbia and, he imagines, Alaska before it.

The cement floor is spotted with black remnants of chewing gum, red cellophane pull strings and a few dozen butts in a Folgers can. An overturned milk crate serves as a coffee table for tattered back issues of *People* and *Stuff*. The best part is the wall, which always features new Sharpie murals including what looks to be a man getting head from a cat—Garfield?—with the title UPPER-CLASS LAKE CITY.

Inez admires the artwork. "This place should be called Shit City. Or Used Car Dealership and Strip Club City."

Lane traces a finger along the horizon and riffs to her about how the land was carved out by the Vashon glacier some fifteen thousand years ago. How the primeval forest, once dominated by Douglas fir, bison and mastodon, is now the wet pavement that melds in the distance with the graphite sky. How the factory that shipped bricks the length of Lake Washington to rebuild much of downtown after the Great Seattle Fire of 1889 was the first non-logging or farming business in the area. How railroad workers hung a sign that read LAKE at the train platform near the brickyard and the region earned its name.

He looks at her from the side of his eye.

Inez focuses on smoking. She does it with a certain rough grace, as if she knows he's paying attention.

Perhaps he's made too cerebral a gambit. Yes, he should have known better. Inez is no Mia. He yanks his Nokia out of his pocket and spins it around in his hand a few times. He checks for incoming texts. To show her the kind of world to which he has access.

His chest gets tight. It's hard for Lane to tell if he is nervous or cold. He jams his phone and hands into his pockets and bounces on the balls of his feet.

"You all right, dude?" she asks.

"Me, yeah. Of course."

She pulls her hair back with one hand. He focuses on the faint whorl of dark peach fuzz on the side of her neck. He thinks of the indigenous influences in Mexico and the effects of racial miscegenation, how conversion-driven Spanish colonization differed from the British sense of order, bloodlines and racial purity. He read *Open Veins of Latin America* in a postcolonialism course earlier in the semester. He's tempted to bring up the book but is certain she's never heard of Galeano.

"Ain't you gonna smoke?" she asks.

"Nah, I'm OK." He's never smoked a full cigarette in his life. This was to his advantage because Mia hated everything about cigarettes, including the fact that discount tobacco brands were the source of much of her family's fortune. Not smoking was one of the primary articles in the Constitution of the United State of Mia and Lane.

"Why'd you bring me here then?" Inez lets go of her hair and it sweeps back like a stage curtain, shielding her neck and ears. "You some kinda nerd rapist?"

"Never raped a nerd, no." He gets it out without a stutter.

"Rapist nerd, then?"

"First a shoplifter, now a rapist. OK." He pulls a Parliament from the pack. "I was— I bought the pack, but my asthma, you know." He doesn't have to tell Mia about this cigarette. She doesn't have to find out. It'll be one of a few random things that happened while they were going through this hard time, things best never mentioned again. "And, you know, it's not cool to make rape jokes."

Inez laughs as he hacks up a lung and mixes excuses about asthma and the cold weather between coughing bouts.

They then stand in renewed silence as she finishes her smoke and he tries to get a handle on his head rush and churning bowels. They watch the rain falling on the boarded-up Mandarin Grille and used car lots down the street. Lane feigns another drag by pulling the smoke into his mouth. He coughs anyway.

"So what's your story?" he asks, looking at her through blurred eyes. "Where're you from?"

"What's *your* story, man?"

"I'm back for the holidays. From New York." He dusts it off. "Needed a little time off from my PhD . . . after what happened in September and all."

"The fuck're you doing here then?"

His delivery was solid. He's thrown by its apparent lack of impact. "Doing a little extra work to, you know, keep busy. Idle hands, right? Helping out my mom and all."

"I know all about that." Inez checks her watch. "The family stuff, I mean. Never met nobody from New York." She takes one more drag off her cigarette, chucks it on the ground right next to the Folgers can and walks off. "Thanks for the square."

"See you next break?" He waves with the pack of smokes in his hand.

"Maybe."

The pager buzzes. He knows it's not a heart attack this time, but it's still enough to make him jump. The gray display screen reads: PROGRESS???

TEN

MIA ADMITTED TO LANE THAT she first became interested in moving to Seattle after watching *Say Anything . . .* , *Singles* and *Sleepless in Seattle* back in high school.

She, along with much of Lane's generation, bought into the idea of an earnest alt-utopia of overeducated, progressive do-gooders and amiable slacker artists. An organized metropolis with efficient public institutions, a low crime rate (beyond the few elusive serial killers) and quirky, if a bit depressed, type-A culture. Norway on Puget Sound. It's a place where Tom Hanks's heartbroken Sam Baldwin would move to start his life over in a tidy, multimillion-dollar houseboat with an elaborate tropical fish tank in his kid's bedroom.

The town that Lane grew up in was less Sam Baldwin and more the realm of James Caan's John Baggs Jr., a sailor who shacks up with a hooker while on shore leave in Seattle in 1973's *Cinderella Liberty*.

Lane doesn't deny the dominance of the Sam Baldwin narrative. Arthur Denny—the guy who's credited as the founder of the city, at least in the mainstream history books—was such a teetotaler that he refused to sell liquor in the main store or let others drink in his presence. He was ambitious to the point of naming the settlement "New York Alki"—*alki* being Chinook Jargon for "eventually."

But he had an unwelcome neighbor in the form of David "Doc" Maynard, a divorced, hard-drinking and likely bipolar physician who'd been chased out of the regional political and cultural center of Tumwater (current population around twenty thousand) for fornicating with the Widow Broshears.

Maynard and Denny came to despise each other. That much was inevitable. But they did agree to cede a strip of land between their territories to the city's first industry, a new steam power mill, so it could roll its logs down a greased road to the waterfront. This original "Skid Row" became the official dividing line between Denny's striver side of town and Maynard's south side of brothels, taverns and live music.

THE DENNYS AND THEIR ILK squeezed Maynard and the native Duwamish out of Seattle and tried to wipe them from the history. But the Maynard/Denny dichotomy, the Baldwins versus the Baggs Jrs., remains encoded in its cultural DNA the way *Homo sapiens* has stray Neanderthal genes. And the dark side still peeks through in a few mutant spots, primarily in Lake City.

The Rimrock is one of those places.

"You couldn't pay my ass to go to New York these days," says Lonnie. Lane thinks that one of his wonky eyes is on the

TV behind the bar, but it's hard to tell which way Lonnie's looking. The cable news anchors scream about some guy on a plane who tried to set his shoe on fire. A bomb, they report. Lonnie turns to Lane. "I swear, if I knew what Nina really wanted . . . and about your parole—"

"I told you it's not parole." Lane finishes his pint of Rainier and slams the glass down on the bar with a little too much emphasis. A few people turn their heads his way, not that anyone at the Rimrock cares about one man's personal problems. "It's a suspended sentence." In fact, it's a conditional suspended sentence, but Lane doesn't want to confuse Lonnie.

Lane admires the padded red Naugahyde and the big western mural full of mesas and cattle on the wall of the Rimrock's Stirrup Lounge. A bedraggled band seems to be over two decades into playing the same Van Halen and CCR covers. As the low stage isn't large enough to accommodate the whole band, the singing drummer is set up off to the side. A trio of drunks sway and stagger on the pitted dance floor that's divided by a load-bearing square post smack in front of the stage. One woman attempts some sort of pole dancing move on the post. Lane's not sure what she's hoping to accomplish, but it's unlikely that she planned for her result.

Lane picked this place because of the low probability of running into any old friends. Lonnie likes it because it's one of the last places in town where anything still goes. It is comfortable, you might say. A man can smoke and drink doubles while eating a four-dollar steak-and-egg breakfast anytime from open to close. There is never a question that everything is cooked in butter and there's full cream in the coffee. You can say whatever you want, as loud as you want. You can ash your cigarette on your plate. The owner, Connie, is always behind the bar, and it's rumored that she's never cut off a single paying customer. The Rimrock's days are numbered.

A scabby old guy in a wheelchair with a patch on his eye sips a well whiskey and rants about how subliminal messages hidden in CNN broadcasts of old Bin Laden speeches are giving commands to terrorist sleeper cells throughout suburban America. "We're next. Mark my words, people. Seattle's next," he shouts over the music.

"You blow it, you go to jail for three years then?" Lonnie asks.

"Nah. The conditional sentence lasts three years." Lane is annoyed to have to hold Lonnie's hand through the whole explanation. "The jail time's a different thing."

"How long in jail then?"

Lane holds the thought as if summoning the courage to put the horrendous specifics into words. When he's good and ready, he exhales. "Three months." He nods his head to convey the gravity of the consequences. "Straight to Walla Walla. No appeal. No questions asked."

"*Three months?*" Lonnie laughs. "I thought you had a suspended sentence. That's a long weekend. I'm looking at twenty-four and consider that lucky." Lonnie straightens up in his chair, thinks a second and says, "I mentioned my sentence to Nina. I bet that's why she didn't ask me."

Nina told Lane it was because Lonnie is "about as seductive as toenail clippings." But Lane doesn't think it worth challenging him on the point.

Lane feels his cheeks burning hot. Lonnie may think that Lane's darkest secret is trivial, but Lane's pretty sure that he has a lot more to lose. Three months in Lane's world translates to at least three years in Lonnie's, and that's being conservative.

"Either way: Nina's deal, it isn't illegal," Lane deflects. "It's a win-win. Or a win-win-win if you include me and Mia. And, I mean, let's be honest, this whole situation is driven by institutionalized homophobia. We're righting a social wrong."

"You still gotta be hella careful, my dude. You might think I'm paranoid, and I'm not saying *I* see it this way, but someone could say you're messing with conspiracy."

"Conspiracy's like Frank Sr. shit." Lane tries a smile, but his jaw is too tight.

Lonnie adjusts his posture. "Look, I know I'm only just trying to get my GED now, but I was a foster kid. Between that and my more recent entrepreneurial endeavors, I've spent a minute in courtrooms. And I'm pretty sure that if there's two people involved, it's conspiracy. This is like conspiracy to like commit bribery. Or, I dunno, deprive this chick of her legal rights. Coercion. Or some sort of abuse of legal process." He finishes his beer and lets out a long belch. "Defrauding her maternal rights? Is that even a thing? Maybe something with human trafficking or crimes with a minor if the prosecutor gets after it."

"You're getting your GED?"

"I told you that before."

Lane shrugs.

"I'm trying to, anyway. Remember: I quit dealing. Weed,

anyway. Coke's too goddamn profitable. Hoping to start at North Seattle next year."

"Community college?"

"Yeah, become a paralegal."

"Wow. OK. Congrats. But I thought you were on my side on this thing. Or, at least, on Nina's and my side. I mean, it's clearly"—Lane pauses again for dramatic impact—"clearly in the kid's best interest."

"I'm one hundred percent on your side, that's why I'm telling you this," says Lonnie. "And, yeah, it's probably in the kid's best interest. Like I told you before, my birth mom's a total loser, but there's a lot of research now that says kids still do better with their biological parent, even if those parents suck. And drugs alone aren't a reason to remand a child. A parent can get better."

"*Remand?*" Lane's not sure of the definition but would never admit to not knowing a word in front of an intellectual peer, let alone a guy who is struggling to get his GED a couple of years short of thirty. "Well, she wasn't just using. She was dealing. Which is way more messed up. No offense, Lonnie."

"Let me put it this way: It's a vast legal ocean out there, and you might be wading into unsettled law. That kinda shit goes all the way to the Supreme Court. And if there's one thing we should both know by now: if you give a cop a ledge, they'll climb that wall."

"So why don't you loan me cash to get back to New York? I know you got it."

"You're joking, right? You know how much I lost on your fake-ass weed deal? You're lucky I didn't beat it back out of you."

"Yeah, I was joking. Just now. I was." Lane collects himself. "This thing is a slam dunk anyway. There's no bribe. There's no conspiracy. I'm not trying to pull a bait-and-switch. I'm facilitating what she already wants. Like a mediator. I gotta maneuver past her hard shell, all that socially induced scar tissue; establish trust and then, you know, mediate what needs to be mediated."

"You're the Ivy League guy, not me. If anybody can make something good outta this, it's you. I mean, even eggs Benedict once came out a chicken's pussy, right?" Lonnie orders them another round.

AS WITH MOST EVENINGS OUT in Lake City, they wind up hanging out in a car. Tonight, it's Lonnie's truck: the Rimrock after party. Lonnie busies himself racking out lines on a Bone Thugs-n-Harmony jewel case with the edge of a Subway gift card and rolling up a ten-dollar bill over and over until he obtains optimal cylindrical tension. The cocaine gleams blue under the digital equalizer on the Alpine.

"When you were a kid, you never tried that foster-to-adopt? Like Nina?" Lane asks.

Lonnie waits to come up from his first line. "There was no cutoff then. No timeline for the birth parents, you know." He massages his nose between his thumb and forefinger, choking back the drip. "I drifted through like twenty foster homes while my mom was trying to get off smack. And once you're a teenager, you're outta the game. Done . . . unless you're like a hot sixteen-year-old white or Asian chick."

He offers the jewel case, but Lane keeps to his no-drugs pledge and passes. Lonnie puts up no argument and does the rest himself.

"Foster-to-adopt though, that's a pretty hilarious scene." Lonnie breathes through his mouth. "It's probably the only place on earth a bunch of gays and evangelicals all sit around in the same room and hang out, taking parenting classes and talking the finer points of child rearing 'n' shit. It's rent-to-own, so they're all looking for newborns from the worst, most low-down, nastiest family scenarios, 'cause those're the ones who don't get reinstated."

He runs his fingers over the jewel case collecting the fine dust. "Nina shoulda done a regular adoption or gone to the sperm bank or found some horny interstate truck driver or something," Lonnie says. "Hey . . . I mighta done her myself . . . for the right price, you know?"

"Yeah, you know she's got the loot to go the traditional adoption route. But she says the agencies are all homophobic. And her wife's a liberal do-gooder. Wanted to save a kid in need, you know, like getting an old dog from the pound." Lane half invents as he goes along. "But no good deed goes unpunished, right?"

He does know that Nina and Tracey brought Jordan home before he was a year old. The boy spent a few months with Inez, and then a few more with a foster family that was in it for the cash and avoided any level of emotional attachment.

"Do you know what that does to the human psyche?" Nina asked Lane as they drove back from Fred Meyer to her place.

"To have that kind of connection snapped clean off? And then denied in your neediest hour?"

He shook his head, not wanting to compare himself to a baby, but still felt like he could relate.

In order to ensure a sense of continuity, Nina and Tracey kept Jordan's birth name. Even though they'd wanted to name him Atticus, Milo or Henry, after Tracey's father. They battled to be certain that he felt like part of the family: He was on the Christmas card, Tracey got his name tattooed on her shoulder and they even sold the Belltown condo for the Green Lake house in order to create more space for the little guy. He was behind in every development indicator, except his weight, which was bloated with a diet of Ruffles and McDonald's hash browns. The poor kid screamed every time he was left alone in a room, even for a few moments.

For the first six months, they didn't hear a word from or about Inez. Didn't know much more than her first name. She and her baby daddy were both in jail for dealing, and she missed her first two supervised visits with Jordan after her release.

Tracey stayed at home with Jordan while Nina transitioned from software to real estate. They got Jordan's weight under control, improved his gross motor skills through toddler gymnastics, worked on his English—and Spanish too—and, with the help of a specialized sleep consultant, they were able to get him to relax, if not sleep, through the night.

Tracey incorporated leafy greens and root vegetables into his food in inspired, hidden ways. He got haircuts from the salon where the kids sit in Disney-themed chairs and watch their choice of age-appropriate DVDs. New clothes came next, including matching light- and dark-colored Patagonia jackets to go with different pants and hats for the colder months. And there were the shoes. Shoes for playing, shoes for the rain, rubber boots for the mud, shoes for the house, shoes for dress-up and shoes for playdates were purchased and purchased again in bigger sizes to keep up with his growing feet. That doesn't even get into the books. The books that poured out of his bedroom and into the hallway and were layered atop the furniture in the kitchen and TV rooms and playroom. They had to make up for his lost time, and it was essential that Jordan consume a steady diet of thirty thousand written and spoken words per day—minimum.

With the new Adoption and Safe Families Act's shit-or-get-off-the-pot deadline approaching, Nina and Tracey's lawyer drew up paperwork. They bought Tracey's parents a flight from the Bay Area to come to the adoption party they had planned at the Chihuly Boathouse.

One Tuesday afternoon, two and a half weeks before the adoption party, the judge was to sign off on the paperwork. Instead, he reinstated Inez's daytime visits. Now without supervision.

She had completed rehab again, sported a glittering Jesus piece around her neck and a caseworker was helping her get a menial job. And that was enough. Until that point, Tracey and Nina didn't have any notion that she was interested in Jordan or repairing the relationship.

Their lawyer petitioned the judge about ASFA, but His Honor upheld Inez's extension. There was no additional discussion. He made his decision and was on to the next appalling domestic scenario on his docket.

"There's only so long a kid can drift without family." Lonnie chews at the inside of his cheeks. "In the end, all you know is: alone. I know hella people, but none of them'd help me move or come visit me if I got sent to Walla Walla or even call me up and ask, 'Hey, Lonnie, how's it going?' without some ulterior motive."

Lane tries to put an end to the conversation. He knows where it's going. "Not me."

"I know, my dude," Lonnie says with a jolt of animation. "Let's go buy forties before the stores close. C'mon."

Lane pictures them drinking in the 7-Eleven parking lot and Lonnie ranting about fractional-reserve banking and the true fact that he can't meet any girls or maintain a romantic relationship. From there they'd end up at some random tweaker's apartment doing lines and drinking Mickey's until everyone is numb enough to finally stop talking about how the CIA created the AIDS virus, watch the sun come up, take some unidentifiable gelcaps to try to manage the descent and spend the next two days in bed dreaming up low-effort ways to commit suicide. In order words, an amplified version of how Lane's felt every day since he got back to Seattle.

"Can you drop me off at home?" Lane says, making minimal effort to dress it up as a request.

ELEVEN

BLINKING HOLIDAY LIGHTS AND PLASTIC garlands ring the cold cut display case. Christmas crowds surge the store, gorging themselves on everything from recliner chairs and pre-assembled holiday cold cut platters to electric brooms and sale half-racks of Red Dog lager. Eight minutes have ticked off the lunch break, and Lane's optimism stumbles. He searches for that synthetic confidence he's used to bullshit his way to an A– without doing the reading in undergrad seminars or to get across Seattle on an expired bus transfer.

After three different smoke breaks with Inez in which he wore down her outer defenses with free Parliaments but still didn't get beyond small talk and furtive eye contact, he spent two days strategizing for this first full lunch break together. He wrote out and rehearsed his messaging points but didn't account for not being able to find her, that such a small detail could threaten his whole plan. He swears under his breath as he speed-walks around the store, trying to look purposeful but not desperate.

She's not in the break room, now decorated with strings of Mylar snowflakes. He waits in the hidden smoking area. It doesn't last long. The wind burrows through his black Dickies, drilling into his femurs. He still has sensitive spots on either thigh from where he used to donate marrow at $250 a pop for hospital research. His old friend Robbie had turned him on to that one with the irresistible pitch, "Great cash but like the worst pain you'll feel in your life."

He asks after Inez in the Home Essentials and neighboring School Supplies sections. A middle-aged coworker removes his glasses and says, "She's probably busy convincing another sad bastard to loan her their paycheck."

"For what?"

"Whatever. Her son. Christmas. Some crap." The man cleans crust from his eyes. "Hard to refuse a cute chick with a young kid. You ever notice the ass on that one?"

Half of the lunch break has bled away. Lane runs out front to try to see if she's in the lot. The smell of the deep fat fryers greases the air, trailing him for the first ten paces out to look across the great expanse of pavement.

He returns past the Coinstar machine and the Toy Shoppe game with its mechanical claw dangling above a treasure trove of malformed teddy bears and hard Pikachus. No Inez.

Lane considers giving up and thinks about how to best explain this failure to Nina. How to convince her not to cut him loose. Not yet. On his way back to the deli, he spots Inez standing in front of the Washington's Lottery vending machine. The fluorescent lighting from inside of the yellow box washes over the curves of her cheeks and shines off of her dark lashes. In this light, he is able to distinguish the color difference between her pupils and her irises, as dark as her hair.

"Don't do it," he says. "Not during work hours." He's willing to bet that if she gets herself fired and that leads to her losing visitations, Nina will refuse to pay him.

"Lottery?" she asks. "No way, man."

"Fireable offense." He is not sure if he is lying or not. "Seen it happen before. More than once. And none of them won any cash either." Now he knows he's lying.

"Can you hook me with some lunch money then?" She stares deep into his eyes, piercing back to his brain.

He won't see his first paycheck for weeks, but he waves her over. "I got something for you. But we only have a few minutes."

As they walk toward the deli, Lane reassures himself that he is the one in charge and the unwelcomed racing pulse and tingling extremities he feels are because of the stakes of the situation. That and the tight time frame. That's all.

IF INEZ IS UNCOMFORTABLE WITH the metallic finality of the walk-in door bolting behind them, she doesn't let on. She blows into her clasped hands and watches the vapor burst from between her fingers.

"You sure you can't loan me some lunch money?" She feels the chill working its way around her collar and down her back. "Cold as balls in here." Lane yanks a Ziploc bag full of slicer scraps from behind the mayo drums. It's all shredded chips and trim from the ends of the turkey loaves. The seeds and stems of the cold cut universe.

"Personal stash." He smiles and passes her the bag. "I don't share this with just anybody."

She takes it in her arms, sits down on a crate of premade ambrosia salad and rips into the turkey, eating two and three slices at a time. He takes off his jacket and drapes it over her shoulders.

"Why you being so nice to me?" she asks through a mouthful.

He considers for a moment and decides to go for it. "You know you got all the guys here wrapped around your finger, right?"

"*Right* . . ." She rolls her eyes and digs back into the bag.

As Lane is about to ask her if she wants some cheese scraps, they both jump at the grinding clang of the walk-in door being unbolted from the outside. Inez hides the bag between her legs until they see that it's Bizarro Lane from the deli counter.

"Don't you know how to knock, dude?" Lane shakes his head, trying to build solidarity with Inez through mutual annoyance.

"Heck. Sorry, Biz," says the kid, who then turns to Inez. "Hey, I thought I saw you come back here."

She nods to him and smiles.

"How's your son?" he asks.

She swallows. "Great. Yeah. Bigger every day."

"*Son?*" Lane interjects, trying his best to sound surprised.

"Yeah, my little man. He's two. Two and change."

The clerk turns his shoulder to cut Lane out of the conversation and drops his voice. "Um, I'm not trying to, you know, pressure you or anything, but I was meaning to ask you, is there, uh, any chance you have that twenty bucks?"

"Yeah, for sure. But, remember, after Christmas." She starts searching the bag for the most intact remaining cold cut.

"OK, sorry, that's right. And your husband? He doing better?"

"It's been a hard year. With the accident and all."

"I thought he had cancer?"

"Well, yeah, but the accident, that's what caused it. But, either way, your help means a lot to my son. He loves Christmas so much." She turns on a smile with a humble charisma that Lane hasn't yet witnessed. "You're doing the Christian thing."

The guy smiles back. She's made his day even though he's out the cash. "Mars Hill? Sunday? I looked for you there last week."

"Weird," she says. "You probably didn't recognize me 'cause I dress real proper at church."

Lane edges back in the conversation. "You go to Mars Hill too?"

Inez nods.

"Cool. Me too. Great theological, um, approach," Lane continues. "Dude here and me, we've been talking about going together soon too. Right?"

The clerk doesn't say anything.

"Right, man?"

"Yes. Oh, yeah. Of course," the kid obliges.

"OK then . . . I gotta get back to work," Inez says. She covers a few cold cuts in plastic wrap and stuffs them in her pocket. She gives the clerk a quick hug with her forearms, maintaining a foot of distance between their torsos, and sends him out through the door.

She thanks Lane and goes to leave too, but he follows after her.

"Like I said." Lane nudges her in the shoulder.

"What?" She tilts her head in a way that Lane almost feels like she might be flirting with him.

"Wrapped . . ."

"The cold cuts?"

"No. Around your finger."

"It's not like that." She keeps moving.

"Your husband know it's not like that?"

She shakes her head. "You don't know what it's like, dude. When's the last time you got hit on at work? How about every day, from every direction by a bunch of old weird losers with dandruff and face scabs and long hairs sticking outta their moles like a fucking catfish."

"You mean that butcher with that gnarly thing on his neck? He totally looks like a catfish. That's so good."

They both take a moment to savor the agreement.

"Would I be hitting on you if I asked you out for a drink then?" Lane asks.

"Yes."

"Is that a 'yes' to the drink or 'yes' that I'm hitting on you?"

"You and Tom have some kind of bet or something? He asked me the same thing like an hour ago."

"And what'd you tell him?"

"That I'm married."

"OK, well, I'm making progress then."

"I dunno. Last thing I need is to be talking to another Fred Meyer—"

"Old weird loser?"

"Well, you're not *that* old . . ."

"Hey now. Easy. I told you, I'm here for the holiday." He pulls his New York State ID from his wallet and waves it in front of her. "We can go to church. Not go to church. Whatever makes you happy."

She shrugs, smiles and keeps going.

TWELVE

"TOTAL BULLSHIT." NINA'S VOICE CRACKLES through the deli landline. "Absolute, total bullshit. She's using that Christmas shtick to hustle lonely fools out of their cash. Probably to buy more meth."

Lane leans against the wall tiles in the back while talking on the landline. "No chance?"

"Are you kidding me? She can't care for Jordan for an afternoon, let alone the biggest holiday of the year. Last time he was with her for two hours. Two short hours and he came back covered with red bumps. I asked what in God's name was going on and that stupid bitch says—like it's nothing—'Oh, must be fleas.' And I'm like, 'From where?' and she's goes, 'Our pit.' A *fucking pit bull* that she forgot to mention. 'But he's a mix,' she says. And even worse, the caseworkers who were supposed to be doing supervised visits before didn't have a clue about it. Just missed the canine death machine in the corner there. This whole process, which will determine, oh lemme see, whether we can keep our son or not, is being conducted by inept, semieducated morons and mouth-breathers."

"I'm working on it." Lane tries for a tone of renewed conviction. "I'm building up to it."

"C'mon, use your brain. Use her retardo Christmas scam to your advantage. It sounds like hard work to hustle all that money. To dodge all those debts. You need to solve all her problems—all in one fell swoop."

LANE UNDERSTANDS DESPERATION. HIS FRIENDS J.C. and Robbie used to make jokes that Mia was his "one fell swoop." Or "Willy Wonka Ticket," as they called her the last time they all hung out before Lane told them to go fuck themselves, got out of Robbie's car at the stoplight and kept walking. Sure, the trust fund, the three-bedroom apartment, the connections . . . none of that hurts. Money and access are very real things.

But Lane knows he has dignity. Grace. Desperate or not, he is sure that he loves Mia for Mia. She's beautiful. Not too beautiful . . . People who've been too attractive their whole lives never build any other capacities, like a developing nation that's happened across massive oil reserves. Mia is worldly, whip smart and has a level of compassion he hasn't before seen in a woman who shaves her legs. Case in point: It was her idea to pay for Lane's degree. OK, that's also something she's doing for him, but, again, he never asked for it.

Mia knew about his drug conviction. She knew that it disqualified him from federal loans. She knew how hard he'd

worked. Knew about the socioeconomic factors that had con-
spired against him. He'd overcome a subpar education. A lack
of role models. A rickety family situation. He got good grades
but still didn't have the overall academic standing to receive
funding from Columbia itself. He may not have been accepted
at all if not for a well-timed call from Mia's godmother to the
dean of admissions, with whom the godmother shared a driveway easement in Bridgehampton.

Mia was inspired by Lane. He had the struggle and gump-
tion that she believed made people whole. The ingredient that
she felt missing every morning when she drifted between
dreams and wakefulness, reflecting on her purpose or lack
thereof.

And their relationship worked both ways. She wasn't close
with anyone else, kept people at a distance, didn't like to talk
about her past. She needed Lane. Consumed him. He was hers,
on her terms. He was a quick study and learned to steer clear
of off-limits topics of conversations: mainly stuff about the in-
ner workings of her family or her immovable positions on social politics. He knew how not to offend her, how not to hurt
her feelings. Beyond everything else, Mia believed that Lane
could be somebody, and she was going to be the one to make
it happen.

Lane knows that you don't stumble into that kind of situation. You forge the relationship through hard work. You earn it.

THE DELI PHONE RINGS AGAIN. Lane guesses it's Nina calling back before he picks it up. He cups his hand over the re-

ceiver, as Cheese and Rice is now sitting a few feet away in front of the walk-in, taking his fifteen-minute break and reading *Left Behind #4: Soul Harvest* in paperback.

Lane's supposed to be out front to cover the counter. It took Tom a matter of hours to renege on his promise, but Lane is still refusing and told the coworker that he has to keep any eye on the counter even while on break.

"The caseworker reassured me that the Christmas thing isn't happening," Nina spits through the phone. "But Inez, she *is* slated to start to get overnights. Fucking overnights. Then it'll be weekends. And I know what's next. I can read between the lines. You know what it is? Reinstatement. They're not saying it yet, but I'm sure of it. That's why you've gotta nip this thing in the bud. I've been thinking hard on this, and I need this done by Christmas."

"*Christmas* Christmas?"

"Is there another one I don't know about?"

"That's not, um, that's not possible."

"Tracey refused to get out of bed today. I need to be able to tell her some good news. To give her this as a Christmas present."

"Tracey? You're gonna tell her? About this?"

"Of course not. She can never know. Not the details. Only the end result."

"There're still a few steps." He notices Cheese and Rice looking at him. "It's gonna—"

"We got up at night with Jordan when he was little. Every two hours. Soothed him. Did the Five S's. Changed his diapers. While what? She smoked rocks. Snorted OxyContin. I worked my ass off to build up my real estate practice. While what? She sold meth out of the same trailer where Jordan lived? Do you know what it feels like to even think about losing your baby? And to people like that? People who will ruin his life. The most important things for a child are stability and consistent love. He's ours. Our child. That we've raised. Tracey always says: being a parent is about bonding, not blood."

"I'm gonna, you know, get her number on my next break," Lane whispers. "I'm making progress."

"You don't have her number yet?"

"It's . . . she's kind of a tough chick."

"Well, I'm a tougher chick. I'm fucking nails. She can't even fathom what I can do to—" Nina cycles through a series of deep breaths and dials back her volume. "You know what he does when he goes to her house? Watches TV and eats Hot Pockets. Have you ever read the ingredients list on that shit? It's like a goddamn book. Takes up the whole side of the box in like, I dunno, four-point type. That kind of lax parenting—or let's call it what it is: lack of parenting—is OK for some kids, but Jordan's in a fragile place. We are giving him the life he deserves, not the bare minimum requirements so he won't die."

The bell rings at the counter.

Lane motions with his head to the clerk: time to go up front. He points to the phone and mouths, *"Important call."*

"We are doing the right thing here. *You* are doing the right thing here," Nina continues. "I'm counting on you: Christmas Day, Lane."

As Cheese and Rice steps toward the counter, a man with

parted hair and an off-brand blue Gore-Tex jacket over a dress shirt looks at a photo and then at his face.

"Lane? Lane *Boosh*?" He leans against the outside of the glass case and hoists a manila envelope over the top. "These are official legal documents. Read them thoroughly, as you must respond to the court."

"No, I'm not . . . that's not me."

The guy returns to the photograph in his hand. "Sorry kid, we found you through employee records. Like I said: read them thoroughly as—"

"No, seriously. My boss Tom, even he says we look alike, but Lane's—"

The clerk turns to the back room in time to see a glimpse of the loading dock as the exterior door slams shut.

THIRTEEN

THE FIRST HALF IS MORE or less a competent fence climb. He straddles the top fringe of the eight feet of chain link. An inch of air and a thin layer of cotton between the galvanized steel-wire points and his scrotum.

He throws his other leg over—or he tries to—and that's when he starts to go down, ripping his Dickies from the knees to the ankle, plowing a red trough the length of his calf and then coming to a halt as the point snags the front laces on his right Rod Laver.

He hangs head-down from the top of the fence, writhing and twisting long enough to see Toby running his way in a crouch, as if approaching a landing helicopter. The shoelace snaps, and Lane drops face-first into the long grass swept across the mud.

Toby helps Lane to his feet. He evaluates the distance to the house and then to the side door to the garage. He throws Lane's arm over his shoulder, and they make a break for the garage.

They slam the door and catch their breath in the dark, afraid to turn on the single bare light bulb. "Some cheesecock came 'round looking for you," Toby says.

"Why do you think . . . I ran . . . ran all the way . . . from Fred Meyer?" Lane pants. He then clears the empty Coke bottles, cobwebs and an old toilet plunger out of the garage window so he can spot up along the side of the house to the purple Saturn parked on the street. "That him?"

"I think so. Yeah." Toby pulls a Rainier from the cooler, taps the lid, cracks it open and passes it to Lane. He grabs one for himself. They both take long drinks in silence. The can feels comforting in Lane's hand. The aluminum gives just enough as he drinks down the sixteen ounces.

He moves to the bench seat from his dad's old Ford Galaxy that still lives in the corner of the garage. He wipes mud and grass off his face and then rolls up his pant leg to examine the blood streaming from his calf. "What'd you say to him when he came to the door?"

"I told him I ain't seen you. You don't live here." Toby finds a rag atop the lawnmower and applies it to Lane's cut. "I thought he was a cop. Till I saw his pussyboy car."

"Holy fuck, that hurts." Lane yanks back his leg. "That rag clean?"

Toby sniffs the rag. "Yeah, it's got like a little gas on it."

"*Motherfu*—" Lane jumps to his feet. "You're gonna give me lead poisoning."

"We used diesel on cuts all the time up in Bristol Bay." Toby pulls down the waist of his jeans and boxers to show an inch-wide swath of scar tissue curving across the top of his ass cheek. "Was all I had for three days before we got back to port and could get real stitches." He hikes his pants back up and clears his throat. "What's dude then? One of them divorce-papers guys?"

"I told you like ten times—like a thousand times—all's good between me and my wife." He pretends to be collecting his emotions while he digs for an explanation. "That guy out there. He's IRS. No, SEC. You know the SEC?"

Toby shakes his head.

"Well, he's not interested in me. But what I know. He wants Mia's dad. Her family, I'm telling you, Toby, they're involved in big business. Like they don't really work. All of their income comes from assets and investments. Like they buy up smaller businesses for fun. They've got summer houses with helicopter pads and libraries and safe rooms. Stuff you can't imagine. Paints a huge target on your back."

IT WAS A MATTER OF days between Lane and Mia getting engaged and getting married at City Hall in downtown Seattle. They'd already been seeing each other for months and both knew it was right. That, and it was time for them to make some decisions. Mia's friend's project in Beijing was killed by Bezos and they were going to need to find a new place to live. As Lane's sights were on Manhattan, marriage was an obvious precursor to the move. Mia wasn't keen on New York but was battling her own mounting and unfounded anxieties that Lane would leave or cheat on her.

They got married in street clothes. Mia sprung for the two

plain fair trade silver bands. No precious stones. Diamonds were as evil as cigarettes. Gold wasn't much better.

The ceremony was over in ten minutes. There were no parquet dance floors. Nothing bespoke, handcrafted or artisanal. No "Come On Eileen" or "Wanna Be Startin' Somethin'." It was like getting a driver's license, except they kissed and then cried. Lane was creating a family, one that he could count on.

Lane's mom was the witness. He made sure that Mia would never see his house, and he signed off on his mom's outfit before she ventured out. She brought Mia a bouquet of yellow roses from Fred Meyer. And they all went out to Canlis on Mia's credit card. Lane ordered the safe choice of pan-seared chicken for his mom and gave her a lecture ahead of time about table manners. She was so intimidated that she barely spoke during dinner. She did enjoy the Willamette Valley pinot noir and nodded along when Mia was impressed with the hints of pine and green tea.

Lane and Mia plotted the coming months and talked of a long honeymoon in Central America: surf camp in Nicaragua, treehouse ecolodges in Costa Rica and open-water dive certification in Roatán (for Lane; Mia got her PADI Divemaster the summer after graduating high school).

But Lane insisted that they get established in New York first. He loved that Mia knew about literary quarterlies and private dining clubs and underground art galleries. He was sure that New York was full of other people like her. For Lane, New York would be as much of a homecoming as it was for Mia.

But he didn't want to move there and become part of the

idle rich. He didn't want anyone to ever think he was a charity case or a gold digger or not Mia's peer. He was going to be taken seriously. He was going to fulfill his destiny and earn a PhD from an Ivy League school.

Lane's teachers and guidance counselors had long ago made sure he understood that education was the surest form of upward social mobility. For a kid who'd forced himself to become a competitive student while his closest childhood friends were all smoking bowls and cutting class, a PhD from an Ivy League university was the equivalent of making the NBA—a version of the NBA where you had to pay hundreds of thousands of dollars to set foot on a court with no spectators.

More specifically, he had long dreamed of Columbia, even before there was any realistic chance of him attending the school. Columbia was where men of stature were mass-replicated. Diplomats, professors, presidents, Supreme Court justices. Boutros Boutros-Ghali. Hans Blix. Not to mention Franklin and Teddy Roosevelt. And there were the writers: Kerouac, Salinger, Upton Sinclair and even Hunter S. Thompson. It was the perfect balance of Ivy League exclusivity and urban sophistication.

Lane was perplexed by Mia's hesitance about moving back to New York. Wondered why she refused to return her father's calls. She suggested they rent an apartment in Seattle or Portland, someplace lower-pressure.

They got in their first real fight when she brought up an interest in Bellingham. Lane came close to losing his temper. It was as if they hadn't just had a thousand circular conversations about how Seattle was too provincial, how Portland was too monocultural, and now she wanted a one-horse town full of hippies and hikers a few feet from the Canadian border? Her response was to completely shut down. On the best of days, coaxing out her true feelings was like trying to pull trout from a stream with your bare hands. Lane was patient and picked his battles but would not yield on this one. She, in turn, warned him he was being a steamroller.

As Lane pushed, Mia's father opened the door for a grand return. Her dad offered the keys to her mother's apartment. The one in Gramercy where Mia's mom lived after they separated. The apartment that had sat empty since her death. Some other discussions happened between Mia and her father about money. Lane never learned the specifics, but a decision was made.

Lane looked forward to Mia's father taking him on as a son. He could be the father Lane never had. A father with whom he could share his ideas and ambitions.

But Mia's dad hadn't even heard of Lane at that point. In fact, he wanted Mia to come home because he feared that she'd make an impulsive decision, shack up with some lowlife like Lane and squander her inheritance.

TOBY SEARCHES FOR SOMETHING TO say. A half hour has passed in the garage. Maybe an hour. Hard to tell. Toby and Lane drink in silence. "You hungry, son?"

Lane prefers not to be called "son" but realizes he hasn't consumed anything but Rainiers since breakfast. Toby pulls an old Motorola MicroTAC Digital Personal Communicator from his jacket, flips it open, turns it on and calls Lane's mom inside the house. They talk for a moment, and then he hits the power button. "Gotta make sure the government can't track ya," Toby enlightens Lane.

Through the window, Lane watches his mom walk out the back door of the house with a watering can. She glances over her shoulder at the Saturn and slips through the side door of the garage. Inside the watering can she has microwaved Jeno's Pizza Rolls and La Choy chow mein in yellowed, flaking Tupperware that predates Lane.

They eat in silence, the red water in the pizza rolls scalding Lane's tongue and blistering the roof of his mouth.

When he's done, Lane and his mom dig through the boxes of his old belongings stacked in the back of the garage. His mom is somewhere on the spectrum between sentimental and a hoarder, and he finds everything from his grandfather's wooden fishing rods to short stories Lane wrote about Reganloaf the Bard, his top Dungeons & Dragons character back in elementary school.

Both Lane and his mom notice the Ewok Village, but neither says anything. His mom scraped to buy that plastic junk from Fred Meyer for that Christmas a few days after Perry died. "There it is." She pushes the nest of miniature tree houses to the side and brings down a cardboard box of Lane's Scout gear. He unpacks a dented aluminum canteen with a bit of water sloshing around the bottom that smells of paper clips and athlete's foot. Next is a dull survival knife with strike-anywhere matches inside the cracked compass-capped handle. And then he finds what he's looking for: a handheld plastic telescope, the kind you buy in the gift shop of an amusement park or children's museum. He wipes clear the dust-caked lens on the bottom of his shirt and approaches the window, hoping that the Saturn is empty.

Instead, he looks right at a pair of binoculars. Full-sized binoculars with gold-mirrored lenses. They're aimed at the front of his house, not back at him, but he ducks below the window anyway.

"Can I use your phone? To call into work?" Lane asks Toby from the floor. "I can't go in tomorrow."

"I ain't got too many minutes left . . ." He turns on the Personal Communicator and passes it to Lane.

"I need to be alone for a few." When Toby doesn't pick up on it, Lane points to the door. "I feel weird talking and people listening, you know?"

"Don't hold it right up against your ear," Toby points out. "Tumors . . ." He and Lane's mom gather their belongings.

"I'm gonna come right back with some stuff to put on that cut, Lane," his mom says as they head back to the house.

Lane paces the length of the garage, skipping to avoid bearing weight on his right leg, as he dials.

The call goes right to voice mail.

"Mia, it's me. You said—no, you promised—you'd wait. Please don't do this. I'm going to be there, in New York, in a week . . . or so. At the most. I promise. Let's talk about this in person. Me and you. Without your dad. Please, Mia." He battles to keep from stuttering. "I love you."

FOURTEEN

LANE CALLS INEZ'S HOME PHONE number. The one that's listed on her old pay stub. He can't give her a solid explanation as to how he got the number. Something about talking to people at work. She points out that nobody at Fred Meyer has that number. He mentions that then it must have been from someone at Mars Hill who suggested that they meet. Maybe Pastor Mark. Yeah, Pastor Mark. Before she can challenge him, he's already well down the road of his rehearsed story about how he cut his leg in the deli and won't be in for a while or, who knows, not at all before he returns to New York.

He'd like to hang out again before he leaves town. He wants to get to know her better. Maybe she can even come visit in New York at some point. He has lots of airline miles. This seems to turn the tide.

Lane suggests they meet up tomorrow evening at the Lake City public library. The one where he did all of his homework in high school and much of college. They'll start at the library and head out from there.

He selects the library because it is the most refined (and free) place that he can limp his way to though the network of alleys and not get spotted by the process server. He can guarantee that none of his old friends or any Fred Meyer employees will be there, as they're all repulsed by books and learning.

And he needs to go there anyway. He hasn't seen his email since he returned to Seattle, and he knows that the library has a couple of computers. There have to be messages in his Hotmail account from Mia. He is surprised he didn't think of it earlier.

He asks Nina for three hundred dollars in petty cash to cover the overhead for the evening out—etcetera. Operating costs, if you will. Nina drives down the alley with her headlights off and slips him two twenties out the driver's-side window.

"I'm not a math guy." He pulls his hand back across the blackberries and through a hole in the chain link. "But you forgot a zero."

"Her idea of a nice date is if the guy kicks in for the drugs. Or agrees to use a condom. Plus, I don't want you doing anything impulsive: like jumping on the next red-eye to New York."

"But, I'm, I'd never—" He wonders if the hospital still pays for marrow donations.

"Update me tomorrow night." She rolls up her window before he can respond.

LANE THANKS GOD THAT HIS mom got her act together and washed his clothes. He admires himself in the mirror, tucking and untucking his black button-down into dark jeans with the faint veins of bleach marbling. He steps into his now-scuffed black leather slip-ons, pulls on his jacket and adds a touch of the D&G cologne that Mia bought him. Then he sneaks out the back door and hobbles out through the garage.

A sense of hope heats his cheeks, his forehead, his gums. Of course: Mia's been emailing him this whole time and he hasn't thought to check. Maybe she hasn't been able to speak on the phone because her dad is there watching and listening. Controlling everything. Maybe the emails can explain this insanity. That her dad is pulling all of the strings. That he is holding her as an emotional and financial hostage until Lane can ride in and liberate her.

He walks through alleys, avoiding the mud and pooled rainwater that crowds out the middle while trying not to slip on twenty-foot-long stretches of moss along the sunless edges. He notes the variety of homemade compost silos. Old trucks and mobile homes up on blocks. Chicken coops. Recycling bins. Bulkheads made of creosote-soaked railroad ties that keep people's backyards from washing into the alley.

He imagines sitting across the table from Mia at Union Square Café. Three thousand dollars—or three thousand minus the cost of a one-way business-class flight to JFK—in his pocket. Actually, he and Mia would sit next to each other in a booth. Hip to hip. Thigh to thigh. His hand on her knee. The Lamb Chops Scotta Dita half eaten on his plate. He isn't worried about the other half; Mia taught him to eat until he is lightly satisfied, nothing more.

Then, of course, he'd pay the lunch bill. "No, no, I've got it," he'd insist. "You sure you don't want an espresso while we're at it? Biscotti?" If she was watching, he'd add in a twenty-five-percent gratuity. They'd walk across Union Square and up Irving Place toward their apartment, his arm around Mia, the white headphones with one in each of their ears for all passersby to appreciate.

THE MOMENT HE STEPS INTO the side door of the library, he's hit with the smell of old paper, binding glue and body odor. The buzz of the tube lighting. The horrible drop-down ceiling panels. The Formica dividing walls. His throat starts to get tight. He'd always found the place a bit depressing but, as a teenager, it was a fair tradeoff against the parade of his mom's wastoid boyfriends.

He flips up his jacket collar and pulls his chin down to his chest while standing in line at the front desk. Lane pens his first name on the clipboard and waits for his allotted fifteen minutes of computer time while a rancid homeless, or at least homeless-looking, guy (you can never tell in Seattle, he could be a Microsoft founder) downloads porn images on the desktop.

Dude is looking at soft-lit '70s stuff: big perms, big muffs. Lane guesses it's the porn of the dude's youth. Is porn like music? Do most people never move beyond their high school glory days? Moreover, is it the taxpayer's duty to continue to provide this guy with access to free masturbation material? Lane wonders what Hobbes—or whoever the appropriate role-of-the-state political philosopher is—would think, but he concludes that Hobbes would be too blown away by electricity and even more so by internet porn.

When Lane's turn comes up, he begins by wiping down the

mouse with his jacket sleeve. He gets online, prepares himself
for what her emails might contain and then waits some more as
his Hotmail loads.

When it appears on the screen, the email contains: nothing. Nothing from Mia, anyway. He checks again. Is it possible
that her father recalled her emails from his account? How om-
nipotent has he become?

Lane tries to log into her Hotmail account. He uses pass-
words that worked in the past. His name. The date they met.
The beach on Martha's Vineyard where she summered as a kid.
The name of her deceased cat. The name of her deceased cat
backward. The name of her deceased mother. The name of her
deceased mother backward. Nothing.

How can this be? Rather than focusing on it, he searches
"nina radcliffe realtor seattle" on Google. He finds a *Seattle Magazine* article announcing Nina as the year's top urban-lifestyle
agent with a headline about Silicon Valley hot meets Seattle
cool. Other links declare her a new member of the Chamber
of Commerce. A $25,000+ Supporter of the Intiman Theatre
Festival. A ninth-place finisher, after a local weatherman and an
obscure former Seahawk, in a golf tournament to raise money
for children with a disease Lane had never heard of.

Lane opens the site of her eponymous real estate company.
As the page loads, it triggers upbeat piano and acoustic gui-
tar music. The kind of thirty-second stock instrumental track
that's named "Never Give Up" or "The Best Is Yet to Come."
The music builds to a crescendo that brings to mind Nina, alone
in a field of clipped green grass, a Steadicam spinning around
her, the Seattle skyline below: her dominion.

The site reveals more headshots than property images. She looks younger. Blonder. Sunnier than in person. The houses on offer are all new constructions. Townhomes. Condos. None of the charming, problematic Seattle Tudors and Craftsman homes that are so much a part of the city's traditional character with their collapsing pipes, asbestos insulation and poorly positioned windows that don't open.

He clicks on the ABOUT tab and is hit with that same smiling photo of Nina, Tracey and Jordan that Lane found in her purse. The caption names them as her wife and son. There is another photo of her talking on a headset phone with a Stanford pennant on the wall behind her. There's an overindulgent multipage bio that he skims. Stuff about LA and Bay Area business triumphs. An aside about moving to Seattle to spend more quality time with her wife and now their young son. Standard Pacific Northwest red meat about enjoying the mountains and kayaking. How she's wildly successful but, otherwise, just like the rest of us. She's also—in her own words—a regarded coach and mentor who challenges both herself and other agents. She turns talent into performance and believes that relationships are more important than sales.

Lane googles himself. Nothing. Nothing except a pay option to search criminal records for Lane Bueche. He doesn't know how Mia and her father could do this to him: let him fall this far.

He considers googling Bray but thinks better of it. It would be poor form to commit suicide right here in the public library before his date with Inez. Instead, he sets about opening a

Hotmail account under the name Sara Christensen. A girl he dated for a couple of months during his junior year. Mia would recognize the name from tales Lane told in the first weeks of their relationship, when it was still fair game to compare romantic backstories.

As soon as the account is functional, Lane writes to Mia as Sara, saying she is crazy for letting such a good man almost slip through her fingers. He writes that Sara has never gotten over Lane and wishes every day that she could have such a man in her life again. That she hears he is back in Seattle for a few weeks and that tons of women are vying for his attention. Sara signs off saying that she is sorry to bother Mia, that she knows it isn't her business, but she doesn't want Mia to make the same mistake she did.

As Lane contemplates a PS to explain how Sara could have gotten her hands on Mia's email address, the same homeless man from before pushes up against Lane, his single large dreadlock and multilayered sweatpants stabbing Lane's nostrils with spikes of ammonia.

"My turn," the guy says. "Fifteen minutes."

"Hold on. Gimme a second."

"Says fifteen. You had fifteen." He motions to the sign. "Why doesn't nobody care about rules no more?" He starts to pull on the back of Lane's chair.

Lane stands up to confront him. "I said hold on, man."

"Don't you got no respect for a vet?"

"Listen, dude, I was in New York when—"

The homeless guy darts, moving rather fast for an aging alcoholic, and tries to claim the swivel roller chair with his ass.

As he sits down, Lane kicks the base of the chair, and it shoots back toward the wall.

On his way down, the guy manages to grab the keyboard, pulling the whole computer off the desk along with it. The monitor lands atop him on the floor with a meaty thud. The screen goes black. The man rolls onto his side, moaning. "Help. Assault. Help."

Lane's throat gets tighter and tighter. Everyone is staring at him. He tries to justify that it's little more than librarians with patchy facial hair, gnomish teenagers and a coterie of homeless and mentally ill people using the place as their heated rain shelter.

"Assault. I'm gonna sue." The moaning gets louder, as if Lane were twisting his heel into the man's kidney. He turns and hobbles as fast as he can out the door, and wants to keep going all the way to the airport and get on that business-class seat to JFK and return to normal.

HE HIDES BETWEEN THE OUTSIDE brick wall and the bushes on the far side of the library. As soon as he sees Inez arriving, he'll head up to the front door so they get there at the same time. He's keeping it together. Keeping it strategic. Minimum exposure.

"Somebody call 911." Inez surprises Lane from behind with a stiff index finger to the ribs. "Nerd rapist in the rhododendron."

"Shhh—" He almost stutters again and regroups. "This isn't what it looks like."

"Like you're creeping in the bushes at the public library?"

She wears a black dress remarkable only in that it is not sufficient for the December cold, her legs are bare down to her cheap heels and she's overdone the black eyeliner. He notices details that eluded him while at Fred Meyer: her strong chin, her nose that's almost squared off, contrasted by the soft curls of her hair.

"That's not even a rhododendron. And I told you about rape jokes, it's not—" He sees the homeless guy come out of the library. Lane spins to face Inez and crouches to the ground. He pulls up his pant leg to show her the homemade bandage of a piece of old white T-shirt and masking tape. "Tommy's lucky there weren't any witnesses or I'd sue the shit outta Fred Meyer. Totally unsafe work environment."

She doesn't look impressed. "What's up with the *library* for a date?" she asks.

"Who says we're on a date?" He leads her by hand to the alley, avoiding his friend in the doorway. "It was . . . it seemed convenient. What? You antibooks or something?"

They make their way through the backstreets and tangle of old one-story wood buildings to dart across Lake City Way and into the next alley.

"I read."

"Books?"

"Graphic novels."

"I don't even know what that is. What about real books?"

"The Bible."

"The Bible?"

"You ever read *The Celestine Prophecy*? That book changed my life."

"Isn't that about an Aramaic manuscript left by Mayans in Peru?"

She nods, unsure.

"You shouldn't need a gringo to tell you that the Mayans were in Central America. Peru was Incas. On top of that, Aramaic was . . ." Lane catches himself and turns his focus down the length of the alley where he admires how decrepit and sad everything is. He's supposed to be brokering a deal with Inez, not evaluating the compatibility of their cultural tastes. He needs to keep on task. Alcohol will help all of this. He pushes open the back door to the Rimrock. Holds it for her like a gentleman.

"I can't go in there." She put her hands on her hips.

"Too fancy?" He nods through the door to his friend with the eye patch and wheelchair at the bar.

"Man, you know how to turn up the romance. Got another plan?"

FIFTEEN

"THE GREATER GOOD?" SHE LAUGHS, revealing dimples and a slight gap between her front teeth. "I don't even know that that means. I mean, I understand the words, but . . . as what you do? For work?"

"You know. The greater good is like using your knowledge, your expertise to make the world a better place. To help out humanity. To give back." They enter the teriyaki place a few doors down the alley. Not the library. Not a dive bar. Middle ground.

"You know what's the greatest good? Making cash." She's confused by the menu but, with his coaching, settles on chicken teriyaki. Once the food arrives in polystyrene clamshell containers, Inez puzzles over the chopsticks. She tries to spear her chicken with the point.

"Anyway . . . must be nice to have choices," Inez says. "I've been putting one foot in front of the other since I was like fifteen."

"I started working at fifteen too." He starts to regurgitate his life spiel. *Lane Bueche: A Primer.* "Used to do the morning shift in the meat department, hosing it down before school."

"No, I mean, I left school. My mom needed help so I— Can I get a fork or something normal?"

He gets up and grabs her a plastic fork and knife. Throws in a Dixie cup of tap water and a paper napkin for good measure. Not a gentleman; a consummate gentleman. She continues: "What do you do in New York to be able to do all this charity and stuff?"

"I go to Columbia."

No response.

"The university, not the country. In Manhattan. I'm a PhD student."

"But what do you do for money?"

"That is my work."

She focuses on turning over a piece of teriyakied thigh meat with a plastic fork.

"Why didn't you tell me you're not into teriyaki?" he asks.

"I don't like Oriental stuff." Then she puts her paper napkin in her lap, adjusts her posture and considers for a moment, digging for an insightful question. "You gonna be like a teacher?"

"A professor? I mean, I'm in the social sciences in an interdisciplinary field, so it's hard to know what the path looks like as a professor. Plus, with tenure like it is these days, young professors get shuffled around on one-year contracts. It's Duluth this year, Spartanburg next year." He's never liked answering the career question. The height of banality. He falls back on modified language from his PhD application essay. "I feel that, considering where I came from and the obstacles I've overcome in achieving this level of academic success, coupled with my personal insights regarding the underprivileged, it's my calling to choose the path that will give back and impact the greater good."

"You're like the Mother Teresa of Lake City Way?"

He tries to maintain a positive, if not neutral, expression, but he's annoyed by her oversimplification. "I like to think I'm more like the— By the way, people don't say *Oriental* anymore."

"Chinese?"

"Teriyaki's not Chinese. It's Japanese originally. See the sesame here? And the garlic? That's American. It's more of a Hawaiian thing that got reinvented in Seattle."

"It's still Chinese to me. They reek of garlic."

"Teriyaki?"

"No, Orientals. I don't like to sit next to them on the bus." She pinches her nose.

He doesn't know how to respond.

"I ain't racist, if that's what you're thinking."

"I'm sure you've actually got a lot of Asian friends."

"No, none. But I hate everybody equally. People suck."

"Uplifting way to look at the world."

"I'd work for the greater good of dogs." She sweeps her hair back with her hand, showing the whorl of hair on her neck to Lane. "No dog ever screwed me over."

LANE AND INEZ SMOKE CIGARETTES as they wait at the Metro stop for her bus to come. They laugh about people at work. Tom with his dumb mustache and baseless swagger. The tall married guy in the fish department and the obese cashier who don't think anyone knows they're fucking. The lady at the Customer Service desk who manages to never shut up while never saying anything. Inez steps closer to Lane, closer than strangers would stand, but they don't touch.

They could have walked the other direction to a different stop. But Lane wanted to come here, to the bus stop that was the site of his first heartbreak. The one he could compare in magnitude to that of Mia. He brings it up to Inez. Nonchalant. Like he didn't remember until this moment. "Hey, you know what? I think this is the same place where . . ." The perpetrator was his girlfriend for all of ninth grade, his first love, the girl he almost slept with dozens of times (maybe once or twice), but they were suspended between childhood and adulthood and didn't know how to transition from taking clothes off to having intercourse—or, at least, he didn't. She was the girl who worked with him to almost cure his stutter.

Back then, he'd believed that if you were honest and invested love, your efforts would be rewarded. That relationships failed if the guy was a deadbeat or an asshole. It was at that bus stop where she detonated not only his emotional well-being but his concept of love and relationships. And control. She told him the breakup was necessary for them to grow, that it was a good thing.

Four days later, Lane found out that she was already dating his former best friend. The best friend who'd said he was too tired to talk when Lane called him in tears. The friend who already turned sixteen and whose dad had bought him a used Mitsubishi with a car stereo connected to a Discman.

Rumors spread through school that his friend let slip in woodshop that he'd slept with Lane's girlfriend even before she'd had the crushing conversation with Lane at the bus stop. That same bus stop where Lane stood weeks later in the rain while his ex-girlfriend and ex–best friend stopped at the red light in his car, singing along to a Queensrÿche CD.

If anything positive came out of it, it was that Lane got serious about school. It was the same time that he first saw Clinton's "Hope" ad. He couldn't afford a used Mitsubishi, or a Discman for that matter, but at least he could get better grades and become a more important world citizen than that traitorous fuck.

Lane would become better than him. And better than her. Better than his mom's boyfriends. Better than all of Lake City. And now, after years of work, these goals were within Lane's reach. No, they had already been in his hand. But, all of a sudden, he has nothing to show for it.

He doesn't tell Inez the whole story, preferring to focus on the parts that make him a sympathetic protagonist. He doesn't admit that he stuttered for a week straight and was unable to be emotionally available to a woman again until, well, perhaps until he met Mia.

"You still never told me your kid's name." He tries to turn the conversation back to her before he hangs himself with too much detail.

"Jordan."

"That Biblical? Like the river?"

"Like the shoes."

"OK, I see . . ." He has to pretend to be someone else,

perhaps Bizarro Lane, in order to not shit all over that bit of information.

She stares back at him: flat.

"How do you say it in Spanish? Hordan?"

"The fuck should I know?"

"Oh, I thought you— Where're you from?"

"Here."

"OK. Here. I know that. But you speak Spanish?"

"I love how white people never say nothing direct. You trying to say I look Mexican?"

"No, I wouldn't—"

"I never knew my dad, but his family's all Yakama. From the rez."

"Eastern Washington?"

"Yeah, I got a grannie out there I'd like to visit again someday, but I always lived with my white trash hippie mom. She means well—or used to mean well before she became a full-blown alky—but the path to hell is paved with good intentions, right? I mean, quartz crystals and astrological charts don't put no food on the table."

"And your son, he lives with you too?"

"He's my son. Why wouldn't he live with me?"

"I don't know. I thought his dad could be—"

"His dad?" Her laugh rattles away like a pebble ricocheting down a well. She regroups. "Well, it's complicated. There's these two Richie Rich dykes, 'The Aunties' as the caseworker makes me call them, who—"

Lane spots a purple Saturn over her shoulder. He jumps back into the bus stop shelter, pulling her with him.

"What the?" She looks straight into his eyes again.

He doesn't know how to explain and, instead, leans in for a kiss.

She counters with her forehead. "The hell, dude?"

"I dunno." He opts to go down swinging. "I like you."

"You for real?" She turns away. He feels her insecurity for the first time.

He sees that he can get his fingernails into the fault lines below her surface and pry them open. "Yeah, I like that you say what's on your mind. The way your hair curls along your neck. The little gap between your teeth."

He's not sure but thinks she is a little embarrassed.

"No. Look. I got one too." He shows her his teeth. "It's coming back in style. Nice to have a few flaws. Makes us human. I mean, not that it's a real flaw or anything."

He leans back in for a kiss. This time she accepts. Slowly. Not opening her mouth. He keeps one eye open, looking for the Saturn, but doesn't see it again.

"You were telling me. Some Richie Rich Aunties. The situation with your son—"

The bus pulls up to the stop and opens its folding doors. Inez jumps aboard and turns to Lane as she climbs the stairs. "Next time, let's eat someplace American."

SIXTEEN

"YOU USED UP ALL THIS time to do what? Find out she's a racist? A homophobe?" Nina shouts through the phone. "What are you gonna tell me next? She's a liar?"

Lane pulls the quilt up over his feet. His mom's space heater has gone out again. He presses the landline to his ear while watching another end-of-year TV special about September 11 with the volume off. He flips the channel: same thing, different network. It seems that they are starting to brand the whole tragedy as "9/11."

"Crazy how the legal system works." Lane comments. "Lesbians are bad. But racists are OK."

"Only a straight white guy would be surprised by that."

"Easy now, c'mon, I'm not— I've studied a lot about the effect of patriarchy and white entitlement in our society. And there's a whole other discussion if someone of Native American descent can be racist and not just prejudiced within our power structure, but my point is—"

"No, the point is: Try to imagine what my son will be like

if he grows up with her and whatever pedophile relatives and rabid dogs she lives with. Where will he end up? It's theoretically possible that he'll overcome all of that ignorance, all of those obstacles and still make a decent life for himself. But it's not probable. In fact, it's massively improbable. Jordan's already lost the attachment to his biological mother—I can't even bring myself to say her bullshit name anymore—and he lost it or never had it with the other foster family. He'll forever feel those breaks. I mean, even though Jordan's bio mom is a stranger to him, she's already inflicted incalculable pain on him. That's why attachment parenting is so important to Tracey and me. Jordan needs to heal that scar, not be forced to accept another, deeper cut."

"The timing, it wasn't right tonight," Lane says. "But I'm getting close."

"You better be close. Tomorrow's Christmas Eve."

THE FIRST FEW TIMES THE process server disappeared, Lane hoped the guy was giving up. Or at least calling a truce and taking a few days off for the holidays. Doing the decent thing. The compassionate thing. But he always came back. It was a siege. He was orbiting, waiting for Lane to give up or slip up.

Lane spent enough time watching the guy through the toy telescope that he gave him a name: Brett. And a backstory: Brett was from outside of town. But not too far. Edmonds. Shoreline. Someplace unambitious. He had three kids with his high school sweetheart. Either way, she left him because she could no longer stand his complaining, his negativity about that fact that nothing ever happened in his life. He not only had to do this process server work out of pure desperation to pay his alimony and child support, but he got his satisfaction from visiting on others the same pain he felt himself. It was Brett's little bit of revenge against the world for failing him. For failing his dreams. He once imagined a career in the FBI, as a PI or even as a regular cop, but ended up as a glorified delivery boy. He's a sad man who eats a solitary dinner of mini-mart burgers and instant coffee while bathing in his own farts in his purple Saturn, his single remaining possession other than his stupid blue rain jacket that's not even a real North Face or Patagonia. Not even a Columbia.

As Lane studies Brett, he starts to wonder if the dude knows Mia's real motives. Maybe he's seen something on one of the legal papers. Something about how Mia's father was able to put her up to this. Some bit of essential information that could be used to turn all this around.

Lane wants to march out to the car and demand that Brett tell him why Mia, why her father, are going ahead with this. Mia told him—almost every day—that she would only marry for life and never split like her parents did. She had been so wounded by her parents' separation and what it did to her mother. Mia's dad kept the main apartment. Traveling for board meetings. Occupying his free time with high-end Ukrainian escorts. Dating women Mia's age, never for more than a couple of months. While her mom turned in on herself. She was the outsider in the extended family, but she didn't have the skills to live outside of the family. Mia was sent off to a New England boarding school, and all her mom had left was her charity. She had started it years before and not done much with it. Mia couldn't explain in under ten minutes the purpose that it served. Something about sustainable global art parks for peace for children. All with like a Rolfing, Esperanto or Feldenkrais element to it.

Why divorce? Why go the same route as her parents? He was a good person who wanted a chance to love Mia as a committed companion, to become his best self and to give back to her and others. Was it such an indelible stain that he was born poor? Why not give the marriage a chance?

If Brett understood this, maybe he would help Lane out. Save him from a life like his own. But, no, Brett was another hurdle, another bit of interference between Lane and the life he was supposed to live with the woman he was supposed to live it with.

"IT'S GORGEOUS," LANE'S MOM SAYS, picking up the purple reading pillow with both hands and cradling it as if it were her first grandchild. "I don't remember the last time you gave me a Christmas present."

"You mean *such a nice* Christmas present?" Lane smiles to Toby.

"No, a present."

"Put it under the tree, Ma. Christmas isn't until tomorrow." Lane motions to the plastic tree cocooned in tinsel. "And sorry, Toby, didn't get anything for you, but you know how it is."

"No worries, Lane," Toby says. "But as I was trying to say

before, me and your mom, we want to talk to you. About your plans."

Lane's mom trains her eyes on the ground.

Lane starts to walk to the TV room. "I have an important call to make. Maybe tomorrow." Toby brought this up a couple of times already. Some sort of parental come-to-Jesus chat, even though Lane thinks of Toby as closer to the random dude sleeping on the couch than a parent. Lane had hoped the preemptive pillow present would be enough of a distraction for today.

"Can we please talk now, son?"

"Man. What's your problem?"

His mom steps in, her eyes still following the floorboards. "Please, Lane,"

"Fine. This is ridiculous because you already know my plans. I'm home . . . for vacation. To see my mom. A little longer than usual, but, you know, some pretty crazy shit went down in New York. Maybe you've turned on the TV or seen a newspaper in the last few months? And then, after the holidays, like everybody else in America, I'm going home. Home to be with my—to be with Mia."

"You sure?" Toby asks.

Lane's mom redirects for him. "She's such a nice girl. So pretty. So smart."

"What do you mean 'You sure?' Of course I'm sure. I said I was going, didn't I?"

"That's great news because Dottie and I, we got some news too," says Toby.

Lane hasn't heard his mom's first name in ages. "Please tell me I'm not gonna have to call you Dad."

"No, but, well, since a little before you got back—"

"I'm gonna be a big brother?" Lane laughs.

"No, nothing like that. Your mom and me . . . we're heading south for the winter. Becoming snowbirds."

"Congrats?" Lane imagines his mom in a bedazzled sweat suit, loading up on fake turquoise and nachos at a Tempe road stop.

He would not be sharing this with Mia, whose father flies select friends and family down to Mustique for New Year's Eve. But Lane is fine with it, overall. At least he'll have the house to himself for a few days until he gets his cash from Nina.

"We're gonna drive my camper rig to Nevada. Come back in June," Toby says, putting his arm around Lane's mom. "We're so done with Pacific Northwest rain. I've put in about fifty too many winters here already."

"Vegas, huh?" Lane asks. He's never been but has always looked down on its crass materialism and tacky hedonism.

"Laughlin," Lane's mom beams. "I've never been south of Portland."

"A friend has some grounds work for me down there," Toby says. "We were planning to go in early December, but your mom wanted to stick around a bit longer once you showed up."

"I couldn't leave you." His mom's voice trails off.

"Yeah, you coulda left me here, Mom. I'm a big boy. And if—for any reason—I end up staying for a few extra days in January, I can hold down the fort then too."

"See, that's the thing." Toby clears his throat and gauges Lane's reaction. "Can I get you a beer and then we talk about this, Lane?"

"No, tell me 'the thing.'"

"The thing is that we rented the house," says Toby. "My nephew and his family from Nome, they're here starting in January."

"January? Like when in January?"

"Like next week in January," Toby says. "January first. Can I get you that beer now?"

SEVENTEEN

CAMBODIAN TEENAGERS IN KOBE JERSEYS call each other *negro* while smoking by the garbage cans at Dick's Drive-In. Inez weaves through the crowd and then steps out from under the shelter of the awning. She runs through the rain to the passenger side of the old Dodge truck with the Winnebago camper in its flatbed. Lane argued that it was too tall to park close to the awning, but she's confused as to why he picked the furthest corner of the lot.

She runs her penguin sprint with a bag full of steaming fast food under her arm, the contents creating a swirling grease fractal on the white paper bag. The side door of the truck is locked. She pounds on the window but doesn't see Lane inside.

"Come around," he shouts from the little back door atop a stepladder. "There's a table."

By the time she gets the paper bag to the tabletop, it's disintegrating from the rain and grease. They tear it open and pour out the goods. Two cheeseburgers. A Deluxe. Two shakes.

Strawberry for her. Chocolate for Lane. And one thing of Dick's fries, with the potato skins still on.

His pager buzzes again in his pocket, but he ignores it.

She clears her wet hair from her face, tries to get it back into her ponytail. "This is pretty, what'd you call it? Plabby?" she says, running her hand along the carpeted walls and the foldaway table covered with a fake wood veneer.

"Thought you'd like it," he says as they toast with the milkshakes. "Merry Christmas . . . Eve."

He's right. She couldn't be happier. And he has to admit, as the rain pounds on the roof of the camper, that he is as comfortable in his own skin as he's felt in a while. A profligate serving of fat and salt, deep-fried carbohydrates, melted cheese and red meat in their own little bit of borrowed space. The heater runs hot and smells of burning dust. The benches are overstuffed couches bolted to the Winnebago's floor. They flip between classic rock on KZOK and KISW. It proves Lane's long-held theory that either Zeppelin or Heart is playing on at least one Seattle station at any given point in the day.

Toby was OK with the idea of Lane borrowing the camper. He was open to driving it past Brett with Lane hidden in the back. The trickier part was convincing Toby to let Lane continue on with the camper while he then walked home in the rain. But Lane didn't have to work too hard once he leveraged the profound betrayal of his impending eviction.

As they finish eating, Inez turns off the radio. Classic rock is her mom's music, she complains. With additional noise muffled by the carpeted walls, Lane feels like he's in some sort of hillbilly sensory deprivation tank. They both become aware of the silence, look at each other and share a short, awkward laugh. He averts his eyes, then studies the musculature of her forearm, a few stray moles, the light black hair down to the smiley scars on her hands and realizes that their shoes are touching under the table. "Sorry." He moves his foot away. In a different world, he thinks. Different life. Different universe. Different everything. He needs to get on with the business at hand before things go in a different direction, but he's not sure how to open his pitch.

Inez makes it easier by coming around his side of the table, squeezing up alongside him. Her hand finds its way to his thigh. He breathes to steady his nerves and clears more strands of wet hair from her face with the back of his hand. They kiss, her tongue entering his mouth. Then she pulls back.

"I want to talk to you about something." She half smiles. "But I feel like it's kinda soon."

"I think I know what you want."

"You do? How?"

"People at work. They talk."

"Well, I haven't known you that long, but, shit—I'm embarrassed . . ."

"It's OK: Christmas. Your son. You want me to . . . you know, help you out."

"Seriously? You heard that at work?"

"Well, maybe just a good guess, I guess."

"So, that's a 'yes'?"

Lane presses his lips up against her hair and inhales. She doesn't smell of the bargain perfume he imagined. He ignores the traces of tobacco and focuses on the scent of rain and sharp winter air. It cuts through the fog of the food and musty carpeted interior, triggering a narcotic drip in his brain, a sort of creeping contentment followed by impulses that push him to go further, to consume more with no thought to the past or future. "Yes, of course. Of course." He scrambles to recover, pinching the soft skin on the inside of his elbow. "But I have a better idea, an idea that can help you to—"

The pager buzzes again. They both curse it under their breath. He uses the distraction to rehearse one last time in his head. He'll say he can come up with a little money for her, but the real money, the long-term solution lies with Tracey and Nina. She should talk to them. No, wait—and it's key that he make this seem spontaneous here: He can do it. He *will* do it. Do it for her. Right away. To give her a better life. And Jordan too. All of her problems—in one fell swoop.

"Wait . . . before you say anything else . . . I have a special request." Her fingertips make their way toward his belt. His hands run down her sides, skirting close to her breasts. "Can you . . . I feel silly, but can you dress like Santa?"

"For what?"

"For it. You know." She kisses him harder.

He looks her up and down. "To, like, what? Hook up?"

"No, you fucking perv." She scans his expression for signs of sarcasm or insanity. "For tomorrow. Dress like Santa tomorrow. For Christmas. With Jordan. And I need you to be there early, like ten. At the latest."

"Help you out . . . *at your place?*" The moment bleeds back into his broader reality. His ears and neck prickle with heat. His scalp crawls. His vision sharpens to the point of an exaggerated high definition. Lane examines the creases around her eyes, the creases that shouldn't have arrived for another decade. "You mean help with Jordan? In person?"

"He needs male role models. You're not seriously gonna say 'yes' and then back out like two seconds later, are you?"

The pager buzzes again.

"Can you answer that thing or shut it off," she says.

"OK, gimme a second." He pulls the pager from his pocket and conceals it in his shaking hand so she can't see the screen.

It reads, SHE GOT HIM 4 XMAS?!?! WTF???

"Lane?" Inez waves her palm back and forth in front of her face. "Lane, you gonna leave me hanging?"

EIGHTEEN

"LAST CALL," CONNIE ANNOUNCES. LONNIE, wearing a Santa hat, orders a round of room-temperature well vodka shots for him and Lane. He thinks a moment and doubles the order. Adds in a beer each. There's little more pathetic or more fun than last call on Christmas Eve at the Rimrock.

"This GED class is killing me," Lonnie says to Lane, turning back from his empty pint of Rainier. "No direction without a regular teacher. And so much stuff to memorize outta books. It must be hella hard to keep all that shit in your head to get into a good-ass school."

"Yeah, I mean, in college, a lot of things work more in the realm of abstract thought, you know," Lane answers.

"What's that all about?"

"It's hard to explain." Lane rotates the base of his glass on the bar while he searches for an example. "Like for my admissions interview, the guy asked me, 'How many hands do you have?'"

"Two. That's easy. Unless he had his arms behind his back or something."

"Yeah, two. But then he asks, 'Is that more than or less than the average number of hands?'" Lane smiles. "Dude even had me for a second. A split second."

"What'd you say?"

"More than. Right? You gotta figure that not an insignificant number of people are born without a second hand or lose it in an accident. Almost nobody has three hands. So the average is less than two. Worldwide, you know."

"Abstract thought . . . huh?"

Lane nods.

"I thought abstract meant that it didn't have like a physical part. That sounds more analytical than—"

Lane cuts him off. "It's OK, Lonnie. Don't sweat it too much."

"How about, did you ever realize that by the time you die, you will have made a dick—your dick but still a dick—orgasm like a thousand times more than any pussy? All guys are like that. And that's if you're lucky. Some of us'll be like ten thousand or more. That's some abstract shit to think about." Lonnie adjusts his Santa hat and returns to staring at his empty beer glass in time for the new round to arrive. "One thing I do know that's simple street smarts, though: If now you ain't sure about this Nina thing, you gotta step up and take the divorce with Mia."

Lane watches the Rainier carbonation bubbles hang on to the side of his new pint glass for as long as they can, then peel off and rush to the surface where they dissolve into the great ocean of nothingness. "Nah. No. Fuck, no."

"Mia is being forced to go through with it. You said so yourself."

Lane shrugs and takes an inordinate amount of interest in the three-foot silver plastic tree at the end of the bar.

"Suck it up and take a settlement. Then get back to New York. And when the timing's better, set things right with her. In person."

Lonnie does have a point. With enough money, Lane figures he could be working toward his degree while he plots how to win back Mia. Even if that takes a while, he could continue to look for future funding options for his PhD.

"Who knows, you could end up meeting a different rich chick while you're at it." Lonnie toasts Lane with the warm vodka shot.

"I don't want another girl."

"Does Inez know that?" Lonnie's mouth curls at one corner.

"I told you nothing happened. Nothing real anyway."

"Nina's gonna totally believe that when you break the news to her."

"I haven't decided anything yet." Lane massages his face with both hands, trying to take some of the tension out of his jaw. Nina must have paged him a dozen times tonight. Lane pleaded with Lonnie to meet up and talk it through before he calls her back. After all, Lonnie got him into this shit in the first place. Since they've arrived at the Rimrock, Nina's tried Lonnie a couple of times too.

"For conversation's sake"—Lane puts back his shot, almost

barfs, struggles to regain control and continues—"if I were to consider this idea, do you know a lawyer here in town who'd do it pro bono?"

"Do what?"

"The settlement. The—" He pauses to be sure he can get the word out. "The . . . divorce."

Lonnie stretches, revealing Mickey's hornet and Marvin the Martian tattoos on one forearm and a crude weed leaf that looks like it was done stick-and-poke style with a needle and Paper Mate ink. He busts out laughing. "Even if you had coin for a lawyer, you'd be taking a knife to a gunfight. No, you'd be taking a limp pecker to a nuclear war. And you already got a record. Dude'll destroy you."

"I'm so glad I asked for your counsel."

Connie slides them a couple more vodka shots on the house. "Early Christmas present, boys." She winks.

"Again, common sense. What's more valuable to rich people than a few thousand dollars?" Lonnie asks.

"A few million dollars?"

"Think: what do they really value?"

"Tax shelters. Cuff links. I dunno . . . walk-in wine refrigerators?"

"Appearances, son, appearances. You're a wart on this motherfucker's nuts. He can have you frozen or zapped or whatever. No doubt. But the power you got is to be nice and go away first so he don't have to spend the money or time and especially not have to make an ugly, painful scene to get rid of you."

"Did her dad put you up to this?" Lane takes his second shot. "I'm starting to feel like Inez right now."

Now both corners of Lonnie's mouth rise. "Inez had ... let's say *has* a chance of winning."

THE PAGER LIES IN THE middle of a small pool of drying vomit on the TV room floor. The buzzing wakes Lane up. He clears the regurgitated Dick's Deluxe off the screen with his thumb, almost throwing up again.

The time on the pager says 9:52 A.M. Even if he sticks to his word and goes to Inez's house, he's going to be late. He did get Lonnie's Santa hat, which is a start. The pager's screen reads CALL ME OR ELSE.

His mom catches him on his way to the bathroom to grab a towel. "Merry Christmas, honey."

"Merry Christmas, Ma." He gives her the longest hug he's allowed since he returned home. She feels warm in her pink bathrobe and slippers and is short enough to fit under his armpit.

"Mom?"

"Yes, sweetheart?"

"Can we talk about this Nevada thing?"

"Isn't it exciting?"

"Maybe. I guess. But I—"

"I'm so happy for you that you'll be back with Mia again soon."

He knows he can get her to change her mind. "It's that ... I wanted to say that I'm not sure ... I don't think that this—"

The phone rings. "Hold on," she says, doing a quick about-face and heading to grab the phone in the kitchen.

He grabs a towel out of the bathroom and returns to the TV room. He covers his mess with the towel and steps on it, grinding his foot in small circles.

"Lane, phone," his mom calls from across the house. "It's for you, Lane."

"Who is it?" he asks as he reaches the kitchen. "Why'd you say I'm here?"

His mom shrugs and hands him the phone.

When he puts the phone to his ear, all he can hear is light breathing. Mia, he hopes. No, too heavy. His hands tremble. "Hey. Uh, Merry Christmas?"

"The fuck've you been?" Nina screams. "You know what kinda stress this whole thing has caused over here? I'm hoping, I'm praying—and I'm an atheist—I'm praying on my knees that you've been busy tying this up with you-know-who."

He swallows and then waves his mom and Toby out of the kitchen so he can have some space. He rolls back his shoulders and offers, "I don't know how to say this . . . but I'm not sure this's gonna happen. I don't know if I can do it."

"Oh, yes, you can. You *will* do it. We've been ambushed by a shameful, felonious, homophobic judge, and you want to what? Up and walk away?"

He lowers his voice. "I have a suspended sentence. And this whole thing, it isn't what I thought it was. What you said it was."

She raises her volume as far as he's dropped his. "It's exactly the same. She's playing hard to get. She's trying to negotiate from a stronger position, and you want to cut and run at the first complication. Typical loser mentality."

"I don't know."

"That's right. You don't know. You don't know shit. This morning—Merry Christmas by the way—I had to take my son to the state social services drop-off point so he can spend the holiday in a dilapidated trailer park. With a bunch of junkies. Do you have any idea what it's like at my house right now? Do you know what the conversation is gonna be like over the roast beef at dinner? Not too fucking merry."

"I'm not saying that it's right. I'm saying that it's not so black-and-white."

"Did you fuck her?"

"No, of course not. I'm not taking her side. It's that I can't be on the wrong side of the law right now."

"Wrong side of the law?" Nina scoffs. "How about the wrong side of right? What is it that you study again? Social justice?"

"Social policy. But I don't want any side of this. I don't want any of this at all. I just want to go back to my wife—" He presses the button to hang up and places a collect call to Mia without ever taking the phone away from his ear. He has to remind himself that he needs to start breathing again. When the operator records his name he pleads, "Answer me, Mia. Please."

He's greeted with a *doo-dah-dee* tri-tone and a canned voice explaining that the number has been disconnected or is no longer in service. It's OK. No big deal. He'll handle this with her father. He'll go straight at the fucker. That was what he intended to do anyway. The call to Mia was to give her fair warning, he reassures himself. He's done hiding. It's time to negotiate a solution.

He marches past Toby and his mom in the living room. They're drinking their Sanka and packing. "Merry Christmas, Lane. We got you a present." Toby hoists up a bottle of pinot noir that Lane recognizes from the Fred Meyer discount wine shelf. It has a shiny bow stuck on it.

Lane keeps going. He opens the front door of the house and spots the Saturn across the street. He walks right at it. Nina doesn't know what she's talking about. He's got more potential than any of these people. More than Nina. And he's smart enough to make the tough short-term decision for the long-term victory. He and Mia's relationship is of incalculable valuable, and her father is going to have to make it worth Lane's while if he's to take even a temporary step back without making a huge, disgusting, low-class and very public scene. And no matter how well he compensates him, it would just be a pause. There's no finality unless he decides there is finality.

Lane taps on the driver's-side window of the parked car. Brett is sleeping inside: the hood zipped all the way up on his jacket, manila folders stacked on his lap, his mouth agape. He is not as startled as Lane hoped, but his eyes blink open and he rolls down the window.

"Merry Christmas, Brett," Lane says.

"Huh? Um, oh wow. Lane? Lane *Boosh*?" He straightens in the seat and checks his watch twice.

"Bue-*shay*." Lane nods. "Give it to me."

"Hot damn. I bet my boss that today was the day." Brett hands the legal envelope through the window. "He owes me a footlong."

"Now get the fuck outta here." Lane turns and starts walking back toward the house.

"Those are official legal documents. Read them thoroughly, as you must respond to the court," Brett drones after him while starting up his car.

"Hope you're proud of your stupid little life," Lane says as he continues toward the house.

Lane's mom and Toby watch him through the kitchen window. Lane tears open the envelope and nods to them as if he's accomplished something worthwhile.

He reads her name. Mia. His name. He scans for the word *divorce*.

He flips to the additional pages: sees a list of medications. Latinate names she's never mentioned. Prescriptions he's never heard of. She left Dartmouth to do inpatient treatment in Minnesota. Never showed up. He reads the word *bipolar*. Reads it again. Sees it in a few different places on the page. He's having trouble getting air to the bottom of his lungs. He takes another step toward the front of the house and stops.

He returns to the cover page, and his eyes focus on the boldface word he'd avoided before: *annulment*.

Petition for Annulment of Marriage.

NINETEEN

DURING THE HEIGHT OF THE Perry Bueche era, the family went out to dinner every month or so. They'd head to Dick's, and Lane always had a Deluxe and a chocolate shake in the back seat of his dad's Galaxy. Perry wore his best gray Kangol flat cap to cover his bald spot for these special family occasions and got Dick's little plastic cups of diced onions for a nickel to sprinkle on his burgers. Combined with a steady intake of Pall Malls, the onions made Perry's breath intolerable.

While his parents bickered about whether it was worth the price of going out to dinner or not, Lane watched the stray seagulls dive-bomb for lost fries and bun fragments. Even young Lane knew these birds were stranded too far inland. But they were surviving. Thriving even. Using their wits to out-angle the crows. They'd evolved eating Dungeness crab and juvenile coho salmon but learned to suck down trash as well as any Lake City pigeon. They did what they had to do until they could make it back to where they belonged.

Before Lane's dad's grand finale in the Bill Pierre sales lot,

Dick's was the family standard for a night on the town. But on a few extraordinary occasions, when Perry had a good run selling used Fiestas and beater Ranger pickups, Lane's mom would put on lipstick and they'd all go out for pork chops and buttered mashed potatoes at the Jolly Roger.

The pink stucco art deco building with a three-story turret that flew a skull-and-crossbones flag was the unofficial gateway to Lake City. In fact, before the area was absorbed into Seattle, the roadhouse sat a single, strategic block north of the city limits. Originally called the Chinese Castle, it had been a speakeasy, a casino and a brothel.

Lane has no idea if it is true or not (he thinks he might have made it up himself), but it is rumored that Jack Kerouac once drank at the Jolly Roger in 1956—the year before *On the Road* was published—when he was an alcoholic nobody who drifted through to see where his idol Gary Snyder, a.k.a. "The Poet of Lake City," grew up.

By the time Lane's family was going to the Jolly Roger, it was little more than a faded diner with roped-off rooms and septuagenarians hunched in cracked vinyl booths, gumming down soft chicken potpies, ham steaks and rib eyes. The city proclaimed the Jolly Roger a historical landmark, but it burned down in the late '80s. The owner was seen wheeling out his file cabinets the day before. It became the Shell station, and since then its only claim to fame was that someone found a dead newborn in the bathroom wastebasket.

Neighborhood legend holds that the Jolly Roger's turret was a lookout for the cops so that patrons were able to escape via an underground tunnel running under Lake City Way to the wooded ravine across the street.

This is the same ravine that Lane now descends into on a switchback dirt trail leading from the guardrail on the street down through the maples, nettles, blackberries, ferns and cattails. Deep in the thicket, he spots the remnants of an old wooden shack, not much wider than a phone booth.

He's known about the University Trailer Park for years. Sure, it's an affordable place to live in an ever-more-expensive city. But Lane considers it the unmentioned herpetic lesion on the nether regions of Lake City. He had seen a little bit of it from its car entrance when Robbie drove by to try to score acid from an hard-faced old hippie who used to live there, but he never knew about this trail until he and Nina saw Inez exit from it.

He sizes up the little shack and wonders if it's the door to the tunnel, or what used to be the tunnel. He'd love to tell his Lake City boys, especially J.C. and Robbie, that he'd found the mythical passageway. If he weren't avoiding J.C. and Robbie, that is.

Lane steps off the trail and wades through the thicket toward the structure. Using his bottle of Fred Meyer pinot noir to keep the thorns at bay, he makes it to within a few feet of the shack. He pushes the waterlogged Santa hat back off his eyes and observes a pile of empty Bud Lite cans, a pair of men's tighty-whities—soiled?—and a splintered wooden pallet in the entrance. He unscrews the wine bottle's cap, takes a few long drinks and bushwhacks close enough to the shack to peer inside. As his vision adjusts to the dark, Lane realizes he's looking into the eyes of an older man squatting on the ground. Maybe he's resting. Maybe he's defecating into a earthen hole. Lane assumes the worst as his default position for everything in University Trailer Park.

"Who you supposta be? Santie Claus?" The old-timer sips something out of a sixteen-ounce disposable foam cup.

"You mean the hat?" Lane pushes it back up off his face and shrugs. "Yeah, something like that."

"Well, you look like shit." The old-timer laughs through missing front teeth.

"Not much of a costume, I know."

"No, you." The man traces a circular motion toward Lane's face with the piece of newspaper. "*You* look like shit."

"DARK PONYTAIL? I DUNNO, I think I seen her out back in the Annex." The old-timer's weathered facial skin looks tougher than the bottoms of Lane's feet and remains motionless as he talks. Lane wonders how the hair in the man's steel muttonchops is able to push its way through such rawhide. The two of them emerge from the woods and step into the main loop of the trailer park.

Dude waves his cigarette toward a one-lane dirt road that leads out the far end, disappearing further down into the ravine. "I don't go back there. Too much drug dealin' 'n' wife beatin'. Not to mention them Guatemalans movin' in now."

Lane looks up the rear road, trying to discern the outlines

of another row of trailers through the pines and light rain. He thinks about Inez's call. He was crying on the couch in the TV room when his mom told him to pick up the phone. "There's a little boy here who's been sitting by the door for two hours— waiting to see Santa," Inez said. The whole world can let Lane down over and over again. But he's not the kind of guy who lets down a kid. *I rise above. I fucking rise above*, he repeats to himself.

Lane takes a bitter slug off his wine bottle. He's desperate for a few hours without thinking about Mia, about the annulment, about that embarrassing flurry of collect calls he made to every number he could find for her dad.

"Can I get summa that, fella?" the old-timer asks, eyeing the wine.

"The wine? Yeah, OK." Lane goes to pour some into the foam cup, but the guy grabs the bottle out of Lane's hand and takes it straight to the head. He then wipes his mouth and whiskers with the back of his forearm.

The old-timer proceeds to enlighten Lane on the finer aspects of the North Seattle lawn-aeration business. It was good work until he got undercut by the Central Americans and outclassed by the big landscaping companies with their legions of Toros and Husqvarnas.

Lane remembers he's late. He says goodbye to the old-timer and starts to walk up the road.

"But, your wine." The guy waves the final third of the bottle at Lane.

"Keep it."

"You sure?" He cleans the mouth of the bottle with his palm.

"Nah, man. Merry Christmas."

ON THE OLD-TIMER'S SUGGESTION, LANE walks around the back of the loop so as to avoid the one little house in the middle of the trailer park, the cinderblock shed where the super, That Bastard Doug, monitors any dogs, foot traffic or cops coming into the park.

Most of the mobile homes don't look like they're mobile. They're ensconced in cocoons of blue plastic tarpaulins, plywood and sheets of corrugated plastic that function as rain protection and perimeter walls to fortify the core living space. There are garbage bag windows. Tinfoil over glass windows. Paper over glass windows. And the popular particleboard windows.

Each trailer is a mini-fiefdom packed up against the next. There is a central dumpster overflowing with trash, but a lot of the garbage is piled high in front of the houses. Some looks like it's been burned in shallow pits.

The Annex reminds Lane of camping. Not that he's ever been camping. But he did go to his mom's old boyfriend's place out at a lake to go fishing once or twice when he was a kid. Both places give Lane a feeling of being hidden away in the trees and muck. Except in the Annex you can hear cars disregarding the thirty-five-miles-per-hour speed limit on Lake City Way, and when you look up you can see the back rooms of Talents West, Frank Sr.'s stripper recruiting and bookkeeping headquarters, cantilevered off the embankment above. The single road through the Annex is full of mud puddles in the ruts of tire tracks. The number of cisterns hints at a lack of reliable water or perhaps the lack of reliable drainage. Lane sees a few carcasses of old propane tanks. Half-working strings of Christmas lights show that there is at least some electricity.

Lane has her address on the same bill he used for her phone number. But it seems that there are no numbers on the actual trailers. He searches for some sign of life among them. Most of the windows are papered over. He can hear the thumping of bass but isn't sure where the music comes from.

Lane does see kids' bikes leaned up against the steps to one trailer, a six-foot plastic basketball hoop in front of another. He knows he needs to reconsider his prejudices. Yes, Lane's pretty sure that this is the shittiest of Lake Shitty. But just because these people are poor, because they've suffered historical grievances or didn't win the lucky sperm lottery, they are not necessarily unfit to raise children.

Seattle is now home to the richest man in America—with a few others nipping at his heels. From 1986 to 1996, Microsoft stock soared a hundredfold, creating three billionaires and some twelve thousand millionaires in a sleepy city of less than half a million people. That's like a millionaire per block.

Then Amazon and Starbucks also went public in the '90s, continuing the metamorphosis. Even as the bubble burst, the city continues to price out its older, poorer and non-tech younger residents. Lake City is the leaky, yellowed fridge in a remodeled kitchen of granite countertops and fresh stainless steel appliances. And this trailer park is the unidentifiable leftovers in the back of the fridge's crisper. But Lane knows that compared to elsewhere in the world, it's still not terrible.

Lane imagines that there are conditions like this all over developing countries and those places are teeming with kids. Many of them very happy and healthy, or at least that's what he's been told. He's read about and learned to respect the noble poverty of Bolivians and Nepalis while hating the shortcomings of his neighbors. Gary Snyder might not have had regular electricity when Lake City was all lumber camps, dairy farms, and a brick factory. And he became Kerouac's idol and a Pulitzer-winning poet.

Standing in the middle of the dirt lane, Lane spins around a few times. He stares at a tree and starts to forget why he came here. Then he sees it: the blue trailer. Inez's blue trailer. But then he sees another. Both have Seahawks posters in the window. There's another one a little further down that's also blueish, and it has Christmas lights and a Seahawks poster. As he goes to knock on the door, he sees another one with a dream catcher and a plastic Rudolph in the window. And a Big Wheel on the porch.

He steps around some big rain tanks under the front gutter, walks up the path past a sad attempt at a flower garden, a few empty pots and wet, hard dirt in a wooden pen. He raps on the aluminum storm door with his knuckles, and it reverberates a metallic rattle.

There are a few deep barks. The internal door opens, and the snout of a pit bull pushes the storm door open and growls right at Lane's crotch. If he had a lower blood-alcohol level, he might have jumped, but he still floats backward down a few steps. The dog has a good set of teeth, a solid bark and a pigeon-like chest that it squares up to Lane. It pushes through the door, picks up speed and continues right past Lane and on down the road.

"Daisy. Stop, Daisy." Inez grabs the screen door before it closes and sticks her head out. She turns to Lane. "Made it, huh?"

"Said I would, didn't I?"

Jordan appears behind her. He has inflamed eyes and a T-shirt with its factory creases still in it that reads SANTA'S FAVORITE LITTLE HELPER.

"Merry Christmas. Santa's here," Lane announces to the kid, swaying unevenly.

"No Santa," Jordan says with a note of recognition. "You mommy friend."

"Yeah, I'm your mommy's friend," Lane responds, with a nod toward the door and Inez beyond. He had no idea the kid could even put two words together.

"No, *mommy* friend," Jordan insists.

TWENTY

"DAISY. C'MON, DAISY, YOU BITCH." Inez pushes past Lane onto the porch, calling the dog back in with a shrill, two-fingered whistle. Lane has always been envious of people who could pull that off. Whistling—even better with one hand—and knowing how to snap, change a tire, drive a stick or roll cigarettes. If he were honest with himself, he'd admit he is lacking in practical skills. But now is not the time to be honest. Especially with himself.

Daisy isn't as impressed by the whistle, and Inez has to take off after her in bare feet.

"Mommy friend," Jordan repeats.

Lane takes a step further into the trailer and stares at Jordan as if telling him, "Easy now. You're confused, kid." But it's lost on the toddler. Lane's expression starts to harden into "You know what happens to snitches?" until he is distracted by the prodigious disorder inside the aluminum and plywood rectangle that is Inez's home.

Various styles of driftwood sculpture clutter every space

capable of supporting them. The walls are draped in oil paintings of bears, eagles and wolves, often accompanied by the ghost outline of a pensive Native American shaman. There are Jesus votives. Saints figurines. A chain pharmacy version of a Bob Marley poster. Piles of rubber bands. Twist ties. Layers of plastic grocery bags pillow the floor under the coffee table. Belongings are packed into milk crates and cardboard boxes. A green glass globe wrapped in yellowed macramé is suspended from the ceiling. Lane watches as it refracts the dust-flecked slivers of daylight that sneak in around the edges of the foil on the windows. He hears the crackling of a frying pan on the hot plate and smells the butter cooking a thin breakfast-style steak.

To be fair, Inez has made a yeoman's effort to add a Christmas-like veneer to it all. There is a small tree, or more like a branch harvested from a tree, draped with a single strand of blinking lights. There are also a few presents wrapped in newspaper under the branch, and there's even a Spider-Man push-bike that Lane recognizes as a Fred Meyer Christmas special.

The blazing sound of a TV on full volume dominates the room but is nowhere in sight. Lane determines that it's coming from the aft cabin as the wall doesn't reach to the ceiling and the door is made of a colored plastic bead curtain.

Inez steps back in the house holding Daisy so tightly by the scruff of her neck that her front paws skim above the floor.

"I'm not a dog owner," Lane suggests, "but a collar might—"

"You really gonna give me advice right now, dude? I've got enough—" There are a couple of quick popping noises and smoke starts to fill the trailer.

"Shit." She runs across the room and rips the pan from the hot plate, burning her thumb in the process. She jams the pan into the sink full of fouled dishes and tries to open the tap, but the water sputters and the smoke turns black.

"Mommy friend," Jordan announces.

Lane tries to help by opening the door and fanning out the smoke.

"Shit," Inez says a second time—less frustrated than defeated—as Daisy bolts back out the door. Inez turns to Lane, battling back tears.

"Mommy friend," Jordan cries.

"Santa's everybody's friend." Inez tries to smile and then turns to Lane. "It's so rare that he calls me Mommy."

"What's he call you then?" Lane asks, as Inez starts out the door and after the dog.

"He's confused." She slows down long enough to shrug, the smile no longer backed by any genuine emotion. "Watch him again for a minute, huh?"

THE SANTA HAT LISTS TO the side. Lane pulls the hat back down over his eyes and tries to recapture Jordan's attention. "Do I look like Santa now?" Before the kid can answer, Lane turns to Inez. "I know . . . Not much of a costume. Best I could do on short notice."

Jordan mumbles, bursts into tears and lies facedown on the couch. Inez runs over to pet his back with her unburned left hand until he stops.

"*Kids.*" Lane winks to Inez as if he knows something about

children. "So what do you want me to do here exactly? You know, with him and all. I'm having a bit of a tough day. Plus, I gotta get home soon."

She encourages him to be Santa. To watch some football games with them on TV. "Between his father and those—" She checks her thought. "Either way, he's a boy. He needs some positive male role models."

"Between his father and those *whos*?" Lane asks.

Inez ignores the question. "Anyway, all we got is me and his grandma here now." She nods to behind the beaded curtain where Lane can hear what sounds like QVC at top volume. "There's no man in his life. Not one worth nothing, anyway."

Lane looks between the beads of the curtain to see Inez's mom laying prone on the bed in sweatpants and a T-shirt. Her arms spilling over the edge of the mattress. A white roll of her stomach webbed with blue veins crowds out the top of her pants. She appears to have spent more time in that bed than walking or doing anything else in the last few years. He nods to her. "Merry Christmas."

No response.

Inez pulls the curtain to the side. "This is my mom. Wanda. Mom, this is Lane."

"You got something to drink?" Wanda asks.

"I brought you a bottle of wine."

She continues to look at him, unblinking, waiting.

"Some dude up at the front part of the trailer park . . . he took it."

"Who?" she raises her voice over the TV.

"Some old-timer. He got talking to me about lawn aeration—you know, like when they pull all those little dirt plugs out of the grass?"

"That look like goose shit?"

"I guess so, yeah. Anyway, the whole conversation got kinda like technical and complicated, and I spaced about your wine." Lane looks down the length of Inez's mom, and his eyes keep on going once her legs stop. There are no feet. No shins. The sweatpants are filled to the top of the knee or so, and the rest looks like a used condom or a deflated balloon.

"I'll take one a them Icehouses from the Shell station then. The big ones," she orders.

"Doctor said no more drinking," Inez jumps in. "And, anyway, Mom, he's here for Jordan. For Christmas. Not to get you drunk."

"No respect," Inez's mom says.

"You're an expert in respect," Inez says. "A black belt."

"Let me get some of that steak then."

"What's the magic word?"

"Fuckin' abracadabra. Listen, I'm a goddamn diabetic, and all I eated today was like six Cheetos."

"*Ate*, Mom." Inez cringes. "*Ate*."

"No, I said six. You never listen."

"DO YOU WANT TO SING some Christmas songs?" Inez asks Jordan, who is facedown on the couch. She motions to Lane.

"Uh, yeah, that, uh, sounds like a great idea." He takes the cue and tries to conjure some enthusiasm.

Jordan looks up long enough to jut out his lower lip and puff his cheeks.

"How about Rudolph?" Inez announces. "OK, Santa. Let's do it." She fishes the plastic Rudolph the Red-Nosed Reindeer out of the front window and holds it within inches of Jordan. "Look. Look, Jordan. Look, Jordan. Look. It's Rudolph. Rudolph the Red-Nosed Reindeer. Don't you want to sing the song. C'mon, Jordie. Jordan?"

Lane is in a fine state to ignore what's going on between Inez and her mom but providing entertainment to an upset child is quite another matter.

She gives him another hard stare. Pushing.

"Rudolph . . ." He works through the dehydration and cottonmouth. He tries to swallow and then starts again off-key, "Rudolph the Red-Nosed Reindeer . . ."

". . . Had a very shiny nose," Inez continues.

". . . And if you ever saw it," they sing together. Inez returns to the kitchen and tries to resuscitate the cold, charred steak in black, congealed butter. She pries the plastic spatula under it, pulling up a layer of flaking Teflon. ". . . You would even say it glows . . ."

The house phone mounted on the wall rings. Daisy is alerted and paces, her tail between her legs.

Inez lifts the receiver, its plastic surface swirled with brown smoke stains. "Is that you?"

It's quiet for a minute. She holds her hand over the phone.

Lane retreats over to Jordan and places his hand without moving it in the middle of his back.

"Uh-huh, Merry Christmas to you too then. Yeah, I hear you. But you know what the answer is."

She turns to Lane, puts her palm out toward him in a cross between a surrender and stay-on-that-side-of-the-room, and mouths, "*Sorry.*"

"Yeah. No. That's not up for discussion." She busies herself with trying to clear something out of the rug with the toe of her shoe. "You're not supposed to be here. You're not even supposed to call. You've got us in enough trouble as is."

"Is that Kevin?" her mom calls from the other room. "Tell him to come over."

Inez put her hand over the receiver. "Quiet, Mom."

"Quiet, you," her mom says. "You don't know how to treat a man. With respect."

A thunderhead builds behind Inez's temples, pushing out the veins on her neck, forcing her eyes forward in their sockets. It reminds Lane of watching the TV reports of the rock dome swelling on the side of Mount St. Helens. On that morning that it blew in the spring of 1980, Lane's dad took him to Maple Leaf Park, one of the highest points in North Seattle, where they could see the mushroom cloud on the horizon.

Wanda continues, "I got a present for Kevin."

"How about a present for me? Or your grandson?" Inez shouts at her mom.

Almost there, Lane thinks. But, instead, Inez surveys all of the Christmas decorations in the room, her son, her visitor, and then as fast as her rage comes on, it blows itself out.

"You are not welcome here." She metes out her words into the phone, hangs it up and returns to the kitchen area to work on the steak.

"Mom? Can I use your microwave?"

"You know I don't approve."

"Of me using the microwave?"

"Of how you treat Kevin."

"Remember what I always tell you about him, Mom?"

"That he's got a huge cock, 'specially for a white guy."

"Uh, no," Inez's face flushes red. "That he brings more problems than he— Look, it doesn't matter. It's my decision, and he's not coming."

TWENTY-ONE

"HO, HO, HO, LITTLE MAN." Lane nudges Jordan and sees if he can get him to roll over. "You having a good Christmas?" Lane certainly isn't. At least Jordan is getting attention and presents from Inez. An old drunk wiped his bacteria-infested palm on Lane's sole present. And he's been cut loose by his wife, who's denying that they were ever married. He's been redacted. Everything that happened between them—meeting at the party, living on the houseboat, their plans, their drive across the country, coffee in Gramercy Park, their favorite South Indian restaurant—it was all the impulsive episode of a troubled young woman off her meds.

He was her mistake. Or she made a mistake and he was the outcome of it. He was less significant than the outcome. He was a detail in a series of her missteps, and her father taking the reins of her life was the outcome. He's like the D that she got in French back when she was full-time pulling bong hits, cracking nitrous and dropping acid second semester of freshman year at Dartmouth. The D grade that inspired her dad to call up a dean and play the alum card and the donor card. He got the class retroactively dropped. He turned two other classes into pass/fail courses so those Cs became passes and she finished the semester with a B average: a B, two passes and a dropped credit that she could make up with a summer class at some point. A respectable enough 3.0.

Maybe he was destined to be low-class all along. The universe was somehow determined to make sure that nothing good happened to him. That he never got any breaks. He could work hard, but he'd never improve his lot. Except for a few outliers, the American Dream is for immigrants with ambitious parents who are unwavering in their support of their child's academics but are also consummately practical and force them to become dentists, engineers and lawyers. The American Dream is also for upper-middle-class people who later reminisce about roughing it in low-paying summer jobs but who were already born within striking distance of success and with the safety net to take risks.

At least Lane believed in himself. He had that going for him. Or he used to. Most of his peers never even had that. It's not like Lane or his friends grew up knowing a single person who was successful. He'd seen Frank Sr. at the Italian Spaghetti House. And Frank Jr. walking out of Talents West a couple of times. But he didn't have any tangible role models. There was nobody in Lake City to give him advice or show him a career path. Or any path, for that matter.

To make things worse, he knew that if he didn't re-up at Columbia this January, his pre-felony undergraduate school loans would come out of dormancy and he'd be buried under an avalanche of debt. He could struggle all he wanted. It was a fool's errand. He was already an indebted sharecropper. Running in place. If only he'd ignored all of those academic voices in school who told him he was smart, to think of other people and learning and the state of knowledge, epistemes, and what the fuck, the greater good. He should have majored in accounting. Or at least something like marketing. He realizes now that his problem is that he is too intelligent for a country of money-hungry philistines. Too intelligent and too nice. Too humble. Or at least too thoughtful about his fellow man. If he were a little less academic and more ruthless, he might have found his way into communications or business or something with a real-world application and a financial future rather than all of this bullshit. At least after six figures of debt he'd be able to get an entry-level job somewhere.

He found it unfair that no matter how hard Mia tried to mess her life up in her quixotic pursuit of authenticity, she had never fallen that far. It was as if she stepped outside of the evolutionary struggle and existed as a free-floating life form unencumbered by the rules that governed the rest of the universe. Had she been born into Lane's family, she wouldn't have made it to adulthood.

The microwave beeps in the bedroom, and Inez returns with a hard shingle of burned steak and a lump of semifrozen peas, and starts divvying them up onto disposable paper plates. Inez hands a plate to Lane, puts a plate in front of Jordan and stands up with the third plate. He sets about sawing at the steak with a plastic knife.

"A million bucks says Jordie ain't gonna eat that," her mom

shouts from the other room. "You shoulda made my casserole:
the one with them tater tots, cut-up hot dogs and Velveeta.
Nice 'n' soft. You loved that as a kid."

Inez feigns gagging herself on her index finger.

Her mom goes on. "And what about me? You want your
own mother to starve on Christmas?"

"I'm coming, Mom. You know I got you." She takes a plate
into Wanda's room without so much as a thank-you in return.

Lane tries to keep Jordan occupied in the meantime. He
picks up a plastic Santa Claus on a motorcycle and revs the
engine. It lights up and plays "Jingle Bell Rock." Lane thumbs
the MADE IN CHINA label of a kid's scarf knitted with HAVE
A TOTALLY AWESOME CHRISTMAS.

"The hell?" Inez yells at her mom. "Where'd you get that?"

She comes out of the room with an empty plastic pint bottle of gin and throws in in the trash. She shakes her head. "Fifteen minutes. Tops. Watch . . ."

Jordan refuses to eat a bite of the dinner. He screams and
cries as if Inez were trying to feed him spoonfuls of fiberglass.

LIKE CLOCKWORK, WANDA IS DOWN for the count. Inez
pushes her way back out through the beaded curtain, carrying
her mom's television set with both arms. Lane knows he should
help her, but he lacks the motivation to get up right now. She
walks at a hunched angle until she's able to set it down on the
floor. After plugging in the set, she adjusts the antennae and
pushes the buttons one after the next.

"You know what channel the game's on?" she asks Lane.

"What game?"

She laughs as if he were joking. Lane doesn't like to let on that he doesn't understand the rules of football. That he's not sure what a down is. Or a rush. Or a safety. It's something he feels compelled to lie about. This cultural illiteracy is not masculine. Not American. Lane knows he's different, but in Lake City he's always needed to be careful to not come across as too different, too bookish. He was teased into giving up all of his Dungeons & Dragons stuff in middle school. He grew up during the binary years of the Cold War, after all, and ran the risk of being pegged as a Commie or other dangerous nonconformist. He feels the same pressure to pretend that he likes bullshit like pancakes, a tasteless vehicle for syrup; driving, more stressful than useful, and *Peanuts*, the aggressively humorless comic strip, not the legume.

Inez revisits one of the earlier channels and places a piece of rolled tinfoil between the two antennae. The game comes not into focus but into enough of a semblance of an image that they can make out the lower-third score graphic and the shapes of players through the snow and distortion.

"Who you think's gonna win?"

"Those guys." He motions to the team with the ball. "Yeah, they're solid this year."

"You hear that, Jordan? Those guys. Who are they, Lane?"

He tries to make out the Seahawks logo but is at a loss. "Uh, New York?"

"Yeah, New York is gonna win. Uncle Lane says so." She turns back to Lane. "You think you could explain the rules to him?"

"He's too young, I think. It's a complex sport. Lotsa strat-egy, execution." Lane stretches out and feels his joints start to melt into the floor. Once he's down, he's down. The announcer goes on about Indianapolis taking the snap.

"Who're the Indiana team?"

Lane's eyelids are hot and thick. He rolls on his side and make sure she can't distinguish the words of his mumbled answer.

He thinks back to that first winter right after Perry died, when they kept the heat off and took to burning cardboard and scrap wood in the fireplace for warmth. For Christmas, his mom pawned her television so that she could get Lane the Ewok Village. She did whatever she could to make him happy and became so close with the lady who ran the toy department at Fred Meyer that she'd get a call when the new Kenner ship-ment arrived. He wonders if he could find an elusive vinyl-cloaked Jawa or a blue Snaggletooth in his old toys. Maybe he could turn a buck on eBay.

"C'mon, dude. Pull it together." Inez shakes him back awake. "I'm gonna put on some music. Whatdya like?"

"It's your place," he punts. "What kind of music're you into?"

"A little bit of everything."

"Lamest answer ever."

"OK, then. I used to listen to local, you know, grunge, like everyone else. But now I'm more into underground stuff. Stuff you never heard of." She flips through a Case Logic of burned CDs labeled with a Sharpie all in the same handwriting.

He's been to new places opening up in old mayonnaise factories in Williamsburg. Even a warehouse party in Red Hook. "Underground, huh?"

"I admit, I dabbled in trance, when I didn't know any better. And even some embarrassing happy hardcore shit," she says, then realizes she swore in front of the kid and covers her hand with her mouth. "My ex is a DJ. Or he used to be. Got me into the Jungle scene around town."

"Uh-huh." Lane's not sure what she's talking about. He surveys clothes in a couple of small cardboard boxes and tries to change the conversation. "Where's your room?"

"You're pretty much looking at it," she says. A cat walks right under Daisy's nose—the dog doesn't move from her rest. There is a milk crate full of thin, glossed booklets.

"Jordan's too young to read, right?" Lane isn't sure when kids learn to read, let alone walk or talk. "You been reading comics to him?"

"Those are graphic novels. A bit too much sex and violence for a two-year-old."

Lane tries to sit up, fighting against increased gravity like the spinning cage ride at the Puyallup Fair that speeds up until you're plastered against its interior wall. "Like anime stuff, right?"

"*Anime* means animation. TV or whatever. Manga is books. You ever heard of *shojo*?"

Lane doesn't want to admit to not knowing this many things in a row. He pretends he didn't hear the question.

"I think *shojo* means girls, but it's like also a kind of manga aimed at girls." She searches under the comics and finds a couple of books by an author named Yuu Watase.

"And you're into this stuff?"

"They're all fantasies about characters with special powers. I've got some other *shojo* stuff here too." She starts to rummage for other books under the plastic bags and worn clothes on the floor. "Like *X/1999* by Clamp—Clamp's two people, I think— and some more out-there stuff you never heard of like *Mai, the Psychic Girl* and *Battle Angel Alita*."

"I thought you didn't like the Orientals?"

The relevance of the question is lost on her.

The phone rings again. She starts toward it but then opts not to answer. Wanda shouts from the other room, "Pick it up, huh? I'm tryin' to sleep."

Jordan starts to cry. When Inez cradles him in her arms, he intensifies to hysteria. She can't figure out how to sooth him. She tries everything. Petting his back. Smoothing his hair. She gets Lane to make funny voices. They rev the moto-Santa in his face. They try to dance for him. They turn on the TV. They search for cartoons. They turn up the volume. Lane is no help. Childcare is outside of his areas of expertise.

"Check the kid's goddamn diaper," Wanda yells from bed. "Jesus Christ."

Inez holds Jordan down and rips open his diaper. She sees the viscous contents suspended in midair for a split second as she regrets that she didn't first check the interior. Rookie mistake. It splatters all over her hands, the front of her pants and the floor.

"Who am I fooling?" Inez holds the screaming child on his back and tries to stabilize his legs while pulling down his pants. Jordan responds as if he were battling off a prison rape.

"Get me a roll of toilet paper," she commands Lane. "Right now."

He enters the bathroom, which reminds him of something he'd see on a Greyhound bus but with more shag carpeting, Christian iconography and a padded toilet seat. He snatches the roll of the back of the tank.

"Holy f—" Lane says returning from the bathroom.

"Hey. Watch the language," she responds.

He needs a moment to gain his composure. He had no idea a toddler could produce anything of that grandiosity.

Inez was caught off guard too as the toilet paper smears the soft feces, leaving tracks down the child's thighs and up his back. Jordan kicks it into the pants around his knees and onto the carpeting.

Daisy starts to bark as loud as she can, and Inez bursts into tears.

"Shush, Daisy," Inez shouts, and wipes her face with the back of her hand. "Lane, can you wet this paper down for me."

The dog continues and runs laps around the trailer.

Lane moves as fast as he can to the kitchen sink, almost tripping over the fleeing cat. The sink spits rusty drops that disintegrate the rough one-ply.

"I got . . . the paper it—" He holds it out toward her in his cupped hands like a dead baby bird that fell from the nest.

"Find me a real rag from the kitchen then, dammit. Something. Anything. The sponge . . ."

Between a wet dishtowel and half a roll of toilet paper now stuffed into the plastic bags from under the coffee table, they are left with the beshatted clothes, smeared carpet stains and the barking dog.

"Hand me a new diaper. I'll wash his pants later." She steadies her emotions.

Lane looks for the diaper, scanning the room. Sweating.

"C'mon, man. The unopened pack. Right there in front of you." She screws up her face at Lane, studying his mannerisms, evaluating his sobriety.

He passes her the plastic pack of diapers, which he must admit were right in front of his face. She tears open the bag while still holding down the miserable kid and wrestles the diaper on him. But she can't close the tabs at the hips. Not even close. "Fuck." She chokes back her terror, confusion, embarrassment and overall sense of loss of control.

"I told you them diapers was for little babies," Wanda shouts from her room and goes back to sleep.

Inez turns away from Lane, but he can see her back heaving as she cries in silence.

TWENTY-TWO

IN THE GRAMERCY APARTMENT, THERE was a garbage chute right out the back of the kitchen. It was past the sink. Over by the maid's quarters, which they used as Lane's home office.

He was lazy about brewing coffee in the apartment, as their espresso maker was an elegant yet multistep salvage piece from a Florentine restaurant. It had too many knobs, buttons and tubes that gave off steam. Mia had an account at the café on the corner where they could get coffee delivered to the apartment (and meals, as neither of them had time for cooking). This was essential during long reading and study binges. And, then, when Lane had finished his double, sometime triple Americano, he could wheel his desk chair to the door, lean out and chuck the to-go cup, sleeve and lid right down the chute. No need to even stand up.

Now he finds it very uncivilized to have to walk all the way across the trailer park to get rid of a diaper. Not many Americans are without garbage collection in the twenty-first century, but he has managed to find one.

After the diaper meltdown, Jordan cried himself out and fell asleep bare-assed on the couch. Inez and Lane sat on the floor watching football with the volume off—while Daisy licked at the stain. Inez put her head on his shoulder, and they lay back. She loosened her ponytail, and he buried his face in her hair. She put her lips against his neck. He reached out and held her hand for a moment while Inez pretended she wasn't crying. But the more she tried to tamp it down, the harder it came, her tears collecting in the collar of his T-shirt.

She covered her face, rolled away and told him to please take the bag with the diaper out to the dumpster. He wasn't too keen on it. But she kissed him on the mouth. With need and potential behind every nerve ending in the soft tissue of her lips. He knew they were crossing lines but felt for a moment that he wasn't a horrible, putrid troll. A feckless loser. An embarrassing detail.

HE USES A TWO-FINGER PINCH to carry the plastic bag with the diaper in it all the way to the dumpster. At least he manages to keep his other eight fingers clean. He isn't into carrying the thing; he doesn't want to think about it too much. If he did, the burning liquid in his stomach would push up his throat like mercury in a hot thermometer and tickle right at the base of his gag reflex.

The dumpster is overflowing with all sorts of garbage. Is that a dead dog rolled in a bathroom rug? Chicken bones crawling with maggots? A plastic grocery bag full of raw sewage? Lane's not sure. But, either way, it's tough to take.

He finds himself wanting to get back through her door and to the comfort of the floor by her side. He wants to feel taken care of. Close to her. He knows the situation is complicated, but he can't be bothered to care too much right now.

When he reaches the trailer, there's a bike parked in the front. A scooter with a BMX bungeed to the back. Lane tiptoes up onto the stoop and puts his ear to the door. Daisy is barking. Jordan is awake and crying again.

A male voice shouts, "Rent. And bus fare. And to get my scooter fixed. And how am I supposed to get a present for Jordan, anyway?"

Inez tells him to lower his voice.

"It went to my classes. The ones I'm gonna take," he continues. "They're an investment in our future. In Jordie's future. And, you know, I have debts. If you don't hook me up, all of that falls apart."

"Are those new Nikes?" she asks.

"Stop looking for a way to criticize me. You think you're all smart and shit. But all you're doing is standing in the way of me improving my life. For us."

Lane realizes that he might have to confront this guy. Not fight him, per se. But insert himself into the dispute. Be the bigger man. Tell the guy to leave.

As he evaluates the situation, he considers how this is not unlike the study of economics. You can plan to talk him down. You can plan to turn the other cheek. All of that is great in theory but assumes you are dealing with a rational actor. Inez's meth-head jailbird won't-take-no-for-an-answer baby daddy doesn't fit Lane's profile for a rational actor. All planning goes out the window. It is more than possible that Lane will end up getting his ass beat and left in the dumpster next to the dead dog and chicken bones.

And Lane was never much of a brawler. He had bigger and tougher friends who had his back when necessary. Sure, he'd been in some scraps and he could, more or less, handle himself. He knew that most street fights last a single punch. His grandfather told him, "Even if you think you might get in a fight, hit him in the nose or kick him in the balls." He figures that it's better to win on a sucker punch than be bitching through a broken jaw about how it wasn't a fair fight.

However, Lane knows that he could never beat someone who has nothing to lose. He is too precious. He cares about his life. His future. His face. At least, he used to. Lane thinks of the one evening when he made the mistake of taking Mia out with J.C. and Robbie. At a commercial hip-hop club full of North Seattle heroes dripping in TJ Maxx's finest factory irregular Abercrombie gear and a few half-naked chicks who'd carpooled down from Lynnwood. J.C. and Robbie—both with their gel-spiked hair bleached to a near white, both claiming they'd had the idea first—competed to impress Mia with stories of the sand-filled beach-themed night club they were going to open or how they were about to write and sell a combined sequel to *Top Gun* and *Cocktail* called either *Top Cock* or *Cock Gun*.

Between beers one and eight, J.C. and Robbie were on a good run. They riffed off each other, imitating the voice of the trashy parents back in Lynnwood coming to terms with how their poor parenting had affected their daughters' lack of attire for the evening. Both Mia and Lane were crying from laughing.

And then, as it always did, things went downhill.

The night culminated at the Denny's at 3 a.m. with Robbie doing a line of crank off the plasticized menu, jumping atop a table and threatening to stab some swing dancer kid with a butter knife. To be fair, the swing dancer started it and Robbie was bluffing: he lived for moments like shouting, "Step back or I'll cut ya," in front of a captive audience. After the dude splashed a double-fudge milkshake across Mia's suede jacket and they were all tossed out by the night manager, Robbie continued to yell in the parking lot that the swing dancer had "a tiny cock" while the guy shouted back, "I'll fuck you in your fucking ass, faggot."

As things calmed down, Robbie made his way through the gathering crowd at a speed that seemed too slow, too casual to be threatening and dropped the guy. Knocked him out cold with a single right overhand to the eye.

But Lane's not that guy. He's nervous, or as nervous as someone can be with his present combination of hangover and alcohol intoxication. He keeps listening through while watching what looks like a crow try to pick the head of a dead rat out of a mud puddle, the gray daylight passing through the back of the rat's open jaw.

The boyfriend yells something about how he could go back to jail. "Why don't you trust me? I trusted you when you needed it. No wait, I get it: You hate me. You know what? I hate 'me' too. I'm a piece of shit. Nobody'll help me. Not even you. I think I'm gonna kill myself. It doesn't matter because it's gonna happen sooner or later."

Lane takes a step toward the door and positions his trembling hand above the aluminum handle. He counts downward from five.

"And you owe me too. If I hadn't— Why do you keep looking at the door?"

As Lane arrives at number one, he hears, "Who's out there?"

Lane doesn't stop running until he's dodged all five lanes of traffic across Lake City Way and hides behind the dumpster at the Shell station where he takes a knee on the wet pavement until his lungs stop burning.

TWENTY-THREE

THE GUY IN THE EVINRUDE hat is up on his feet to greet Lane as soon as he comes through his mom's front door. Lane doesn't want to speak to anyone, especially not some redneck in mom jeans with a '90s goatee masquerading as a chin. But dude springs out of the old rocking chair like he means it, shifting his tallboy to his left hand so he can offer Lane an eager shake with a broad, calloused palm and four and a half fingers with blood-blistered nails. Lane doesn't introduce himself and doesn't listen to the guy's name. All he can think is how J.C. and Robbie used to debate whether that kind of dense goatee is best deemed "prison pussy" or a "dick target."

He continues past Toby and his mom on the couch, leaning against the TV-watching pillow, and on toward the TV room.

"Lane. Lane," Toby calls out. "This is Chaz that I told you about."

Lane swings open the door and is a couple of steps into the TV room before he realizes that there are two pimple-faced teenage boys and a younger kid, around ten, sitting on the floor and couch. One teenager stashes a magazine between the cushions before Lane can see what it is. They have some sort of video game console plugged into the TV and are hard at work on a shoot-'em-up game.

Lane's entrance startles the game player, and his character gets killed. "What the?" the eldest-looking of the kids pouts. "You ever hearda knocking, dick?"

Lane takes in the smells of body odor, flatulence and semen in the room and beats a hasty retreat.

"Who was that?" he overhears one of the kids ask the other.

"Some weird old guy," the teenager responds.

"This place sucks," says the other.

LANE DOESN'T ENTER THE LIVING room so much as stand in the doorway and flag his mom over to him. Toby keeps talking with Chaz about sockeye salmon smoking techniques when Dottie gets up.

"Anybody call for me?" Lane asks his mom.

She shakes her head.

Lane motions toward Chaz with his jaw. "You said after New Year's."

"That's when we're leaving."

"And?"

"Hotels are outrageous over the holidays."

"That's their problem."

"Toby invited them. We can use the money."

"Toby. Come here, please." Lane waves him into the hallway too.

Toby was already keeping tabs on their conversation and is out of his chair before Lane finishes waving.

"I don't think this is a good idea. You guys going out of town and all," Lane starts before Toby even gets there. "Don't think I don't I see what you're up to."

"What I'm up to?"

"Renting her house out from under her to bankroll your travel plans."

"Listen, son."

"I'm not your son. How many times do I have to tell you that?"

"OK, Lane. Look, your mom and I, we've been planning this for a long time. And if you could talk to us and tell us what you need, we coulda better . . ."

"Mom, I think these people need to leave. I want those strokers outta my room. This whole thing—it's not in your best interest."

His mom stands in silence.

Toby begins, "Dottie—"

"I asked her, not you." Lane places his hand on his mom's shoulder. "This plan is crazy. Say it, Mom: you tell us what *you* want and I'll do it. I'm sure that Toby will honor your wishes too, right, Toby?"

LANE GETS COMFORTABLE IN TOBY'S trailer, parked in the driveway of dirt, gravel and weeds running alongside the house. He brings the foam cooler with him and locks the door from the inside. "I'm on to you, motherfucker," he repeats to himself.

He can't believe his mom. How could she stand by while Toby told him some obvious lie about how they came up with the idea to go to Nevada last spring while they were digging razor clams on the peninsula? That they worked together to find him a job down there? She never leaves the house and goes places. That's not Dottie Bueche. She doesn't spend money or take risks. Her idea of a good time is watching *Days of Our Lives* and clipping coupons that she'll never use because she doesn't like the crowds at the store. She hasn't even been up to play bingo at the Tulalip in almost a decade. She gets carsick at anything over twenty miles per hour.

Both Toby and his mom assured Lane that Chaz and the kids are supposed to stay in the living room until they head down to Nevada. But Lane decided to make a point. He wanted his mom to see the impact of her decisions, the effect on her only child versus whatever chump change Toby is wringing out of this.

When Lonnie shows up, Lane's mom sends him out to the trailer. Asks him to talk some sense into Lane. Before Lane can tell Lonnie that the divorce settlement plan exploded before liftoff. Before he can tell him about going over to Inez's house. About the psychotic boyfriend. About the losers colonizing his house. Lonnie busts into the trailer, hyperventilating with "dudes" and "mans" and "I got crazy news."

Lane knew it. Lonnie figured something out for him. That pro bono lawyer? Here it comes:

"I met a girl. Last night. After you left. At the Rimrock. A girl."

"Oh. Cool." Lane slumps.

"I thought I recognized her for the longest time, then *she* . . . came up to *me*. Says, 'Ain't you in my GED class?' We started macking, and that was that . . ."

"GED . . . nice," Lane nods. "Beer?"

LANE RUBS HIS HANDS TOGETHER for warmth. He and Lonnie drink Rainiers at the folding table strewn with cans and listen to the radio. He finds both Zeppelin and Heart. Simultaneously on different stations.

When Chaz comes out and knocks on the door, Lane quiets Lonnie. "Watch this . . . Dude wants another free beer," Lane whispers. They hold their breath until he leaves.

Lane cracks another Rainier and gives one to Lonnie to make up for last night's tab, but he is counting how many are in the cooler and calculating how long that will last him.

"Listen, you think I could stay with you for a few days?" Lane asks.

"That's the thing," Lonnie says. "This girl. She's still at my place. I came to ask what I should do. We had this crazy night— didn't get much rest, you know—and she's like still asleep."

"What time is it?"

"I dunno. Late . . . dark again."

"Tell her to go. Wake her up and tell her. You gotta be direct with people. Don't be too 'Seattle' about it."

"I'm not sure."

"Tell her you already told your friend he could stay there."

"She doesn't have nobody else. It's Christmas. And, I think—I know—I like her. She was a massage therapist, but now she wants to go to Pilchuck, study glass-blowing, you know. She's very spiritual too. She knows about like Buddhism and shit."

"She's probably crazy." Lane tries to stretch out on the couch, but his legs butt up against a cabinet. "And, speaking of crazy, Nina was right about Inez. I mean, she's not *crazy* crazy—she's charming in her own way. But the chick is crazy fucked up. Not the right situation for a kid to grow up in, for sure."

"Did Nina get ahold of you? I know she was calling a lot."

"Don't say anything to her. OK? You promise?" He waits for Lonnie to nod. "And can you find out about Inez's boyfriend for me. What's his story?"

As Lonnie shrugs, Chaz knocks again. "Seriously?" Lane makes an effort to sound exasperated and unlocks to door to find the Alaskan packing a dip and wiping his hands on his jeans.

"Some chick called you," Chaz says as he swabs tobacco grains from his front teeth with his stub of an index finger. "Two of 'em. Yo, you got a spitter in there?"

"Really? Who?" Lane's cardiopulmonary system goes on pause in anticipation of the answer.

"She was pissed off. Izzy—"

"Inez. Yeah. OK. Who's the other?" He passes his empty beer can to Chaz.

"Name ends in an 'a' or 'ia' or something."

"Mia?"

"Yeah. Something like that."

Lane's vision tightens. He's going to pass out, but then he

is saved by doubt: his most consistent companion over the last months. "Wait, Nina?"

"Maybe. What was the other one again?"

"Mia. What'd she say? Why didn't you get me?"

"I came out and knocked."

"Well, you shoulda told me what it was about." Lane tries to pace in the space around the bench and folding table, his head cocked to the side to avoid the ceiling. "What was it about?"

"Guess she wanted to say hi." Chaz twists and ratchets the opening tab to gouge out a hole in the top of the beer can. "It's Christmas, right?"

"Great insight. Did you get her number?"

He shakes his head as he spits a brown bead of saliva into the aluminum.

"Well, *fuck*. Is she gonna call back?" He leans out the door within a foot of Chaz, close enough to smell the wintergreen in his dip.

Chaz shrugs.

"Why are you even answering the phone at my mom's house?"

"They're out . . . walking around the neighborhood, lookin' at Christmas lights or something."

Christmas lights? Lane's mom's lost her mind. He retreats back inside the mobile home, punching the top of the folding table. It collapses, scattering the empty beer cans across the floor.

All three stare at the mess.

Chaz then reaches into the trailer and grabs himself a beer from the cooler. "You mind?"

Before Lane can answer, he says, "A little bit of advice from a guy who's been around longer than you: Don't never sweat a chick. Fuck her. It's her loss. Move on. Look at me. I came back from Prudhoe Bay and my old lady ran off with a goddamn podiatrist. Dude plays with feet for a living. *Feet* . . . think about it. She says he's gonna take her to live in Anchorage—dinner at Sizzler like two nights a week and all that. She left me with three kids. I'm pretty sure one isn't even mine. You think I'm crying about it? Lotsa fish in the sea, kid. You got no idea how much trim I get now."

Lane looks Chaz up and down from his Evinrude hat with the tunneled brim to his beer gut and the tobacco stains on his jeans. He grabs the door to the trailer and pulls it shut.

TWENTY-FOUR

LANE ISN'T LISTENING. HE'S WATCHING Tom use his bottom lip to suck the sweet drips of orange Crush from the tips of his mustache. How the off-center part in his lip hair rises and falls as Tom enunciates, as he becomes more expressive, more convinced of the wisdom he is imparting on his unwilling protégé.

"You see? You gotta sell it, Lame-o." Tom talks at Lane. "I know you got this 'I'm too good for this' college-boy attitude, but you gotta charm 'em. Think about it like you're hitting on a lady, not any lady but a ten, or at least a six, at like one a them wine bars. Let yourself go. Feel it in the moment like 'Ladies and gentlemen, check out the ultimate chip-and-dip experience. A goddamn explosion in yer mouth. Eye-fuck 'em a little bit. Reel 'em in and then—*bam*—Big Dipperz." As he holds the bag of giant tortilla chip shovels in front of Lane's face, Tom jabs Lane in the ribs with two rigid fingers. When Lane flinches, Tom fakes to hit him in the nuts with the back of his hand.

And then, as Lane realizes he isn't about to be overcome by a wave of groin pain and allows himself to breath again, Tom is gone.

Lane finds himself alone. Alone as he's ever been. Exposed in the middle of the store with nothing more than the waist-high stand with the fluorescent-yellow Big Dipperz sign. Vulnerable from all sides. A rudderless ship in open water awaiting the U-boats.

He spreads out an array of the oversized corn scoops with a pallet of processed factory versions of guacamole, beans, cheese and salsa, all in identical plastic containers and all with machine-blended consistency, in different yet uniform colors: greenish, brownish, yellowish and reddish.

Tom was incredulous about Lane's work accident and abrupt disappearance. He let him come back after four unpaid days, but not without taking his pound of flesh.

Lane knew he shouldn't have complained about his initial reassignment to the hot case. Yes, he hated it. He came home with a patina of oil and fried animal fat covering his head as if he'd been swimming down by the public boat launch at Matthews Beach and surfaced through a rainbow swirl of spilled diesel. And while he had to serve people at the counter here and there, running the risk of encountering old friends or enemies, he spent much of the day off to the side cooking chicken pieces and strips, Pizza Stix™, deep-fried burritos, corn dogs, fish sticks, jalapeño poppers, mac and cheese, Ragin' Cajun rotisserie chickens and such.

Beyond the onslaught of chicken drumettes, the main part of the hot case job was hustling out jojos. These regional delicacies found in supermarkets and public school cafeterias throughout the Pacific Northwest consist of precut frozen potato wedges doused with a Northern mass-production take on Cajun seasoning and fried in the same oil as the chicken. They're supposed to be a side dish, used to round out deep-fried poultry scraps into a calorically satisfying meal. But jojos, by themselves, are a favorite of broke teenagers and every stripe of late-night drunk who can't swing McDonald's or Dick's.

Lane was tasked with putting a half dozen jojos in each foil container. He added two ketchup packets, wrapped the foil in plastic, weighed, priced (after removing the tare weight of the container, assuming that he was motivated to do the extra step), stickered and loaded scores of these containers under the hot lamps throughout the day.

All he had to do was spend some extra time plastic wrapping, pushing buttons on the fryers or examining the thermometers and he could avoid the counter.

The real problem was that Lane knew that the hot case was a journeyman job, that the hourly should be much higher for overseeing all those deep fat fryers, the ovens for the baked chicken breast and the premade mac and cheese and the full chicken rotisserie. That was like a ten-dollar-or-more-per-hour job. Maybe twelve. Not only did he still not like the feeling of getting ripped off, but he would have liked to make that extra cash that he justifiably earned for his hard work. And he was sure that the union would agree with him. Cheese and Rice wasn't going to say anything to Tom or advise the union. But Lane was no pushover company man, and he needed to stick up for labor, for decency and fair pay.

"You know what? You're right." Tom said. "Instead, I'm gonna give you a new position as my 'personal assistant for special projects.'" He started Lane off hand-scrubbing the vents and duct work above the deep fat fryer. Lane swears that he found a dead rat encased in an amber brick of congealed fryer fat, but it could have been a dust ball too. After that, Tom told him to wear a chicken suit and spinner sign to advertise rotisserie chickens out in front of the store. Fortunately, the costume seemed to have been sized for underaged labor, so Lane was reassigned to floor displays.

"CARE TO TRY BIG DIPPERZ?" Lane asks Inez as she walks up to him at the display stand. "They're an explosion—"

"Thanks for nothing," she says, twirling her hair in a ring around her finger, unrolling it and doing it over again.

"—in your mouth ..."

She glares at him. "I wanna explode my fist in your mouth."

"Uh." Lane leans in. "Remember your crazy boyfriend or husband or whatever?"

"So what? You scared? I can't be messing with no guy who's a pussy."

Lane's not sure how to answer. He crushes a Big Dipper in his hand and tries to talk himself down from stuttering. He reminds himself that she is embarrassed and being defensive and does not believe that he is a pussy.

"You let me down. You let Jordan down," she says. "On Christmas. How was I supposed to explain that to him?"

"I think you'd better look at yourself and the guy you chose

to procreate with before you start blaming me for letting anybody down."

"What's your real story? I don't think you're going back to
New York. Did you make that up? I don't know if you ever even
been there."

"What? How can you say that?"

"I heard you begged for this shitty job back."

"Who said that?" he asks, but then lets it go because he
knows it's true. "Look, I don't want to fight with you. I have
a lot going on in my life right now, and I can't overcomplicate
things any more than they already are, you know?"

"Biz," Cheese and Rice shouts from the deli. "You got a
call, dawg."

He abandons his post. "Sorry, Inez. It's my, uh—whatever.
Keep an eye on it for a second?" He's off before she can refuse.
"One second. I swear."

He grabs the wall phone in the back of the deli.

"It's me."

"Who's me?" Lane feels a flutter in his chest and running
up his neck. He thinks for a moment, hopes for a moment. But
he knows better, recognizes the smoker's huskiness of the voice.

"You look ridiculous out there selling nachos."

"They're not nachos . . . Nina."

"I'm in the Home Entertainment department. Come
find me."

"You been watching me?"

"I'm only here for five more minutes. I'll make it worth
your while." She hangs up.

He hides in the back, stubbing his toe over and over against the baseboard. He peeks out of the back to see Inez standing at the display stand, still wrapping her hair around a finger and staring off into the distance.

"Dude." He beckons Cheese and Rice. "Tell Inez I'll be right back."

"I'm taking care of the—"

"Do it, man. C'mon." He pretends to tie his shoe so his head is below the level of the display case and then slips out the far side of the deli.

NINA KEEPS HER VOLUME NOT far above a whisper. "I'm gonna make you a deal."

"I dunno." Lane shifts from foot to foot.

"It's not for you to know or not know, Lane. I'm telling you what's happening."

He noticed her black leather jacket before anything else. Nina stood with her back to him watching *Toy Story 2* on a Westinghouse TV with a built-in VCR. The jacket appears to be more expensive than any of the electronics in the department.

They stand side-by-side pretending to watch the characters on the screen. Lane checks over his shoulder again.

"Did you know they were already monitoring her as a parent—when they got busted for drugs?" Nina asks.

"For some reason, she didn't tell me that part of the story."

"It all started with pink eye."

"Do I have to hear this now?" Lane slouches.

Nina keeps watching the movie. "When Jordan was a little baby, she brought him into a walk-in clinic with his eyes crusted shut. They gave her antibiotic eye drops. Standard, right? Then they brought him in again: same shit. A third time: more of the same. When a caseworker paid Jordan a visit two weeks later, the kid still had it. She says she was confused by the directions. Eye drops. I don't think she can even read."

"I'm pretty sure she can read."

"Read, not read. What's her excuse, then? General incompetence? Total negligence? Point is: She's a disaster. Can't figure out eye drops but knows how to sell drugs. She knows how to run a hustle when it benefits her. That's about it."

"OK, so you think she's a horrible person. We've determined that."

"And she either slept with this judge or made some sort of homophobic church pact with him. It's preposterous. Look: I don't give people a second chance. But, considering the timing and that I'm in a bit of a sunken cost dilemma, I'm gonna see this through with you. You have potential, Lane, but you need more spine. I can help you with that."

"OK, so she has problems, but this situation, it's complicated. And I'm not trying to screw anyone over. Or break any laws."

"You seem ready to screw me over. Me and my wife, and let's not forget the most vulnerable of us all: little Jordan."

"You know how many problems I have right now?" Lane turns to leave. "I don't need this."

She presses an envelope into his hand. "Yes, you do."

He works his index finger in under the corner of the flap and tears along the top of the paper. Lane pulls back one side of the envelope to see a check made out in his name for five thousand dollars.

"Five . . ." He reads it to himself and asks, "Who's ABC Holdings?"

"Shell company. Pretty much untraceable."

"Is it real?" He's never received a check with three zeroes on it before.

"'Course it's real. See the bank name on the check. Lake City branch'll cash it."

He swallows hard.

"It's postdated for next week. You can buy a flight for the day after you cash it, go first class if you want," she says. "Take it. Finish what you started. Get back to your wife. Your life."

He stands in silence, holding the envelope.

"We're gonna take a new tact."

"It's *tack*. Like in sailing. *Tact* is more like 'sensitivity in social situations.'"

"Shut the fuck up, Lane."

"Sorry."

"I'll be in touch later today. But remember: you mess with me and I'll cancel that check before you can say 'squandered potential.'" She snaps her fingers, backs away from the TV and leaves.

"WHAT THE—" INEZ STANDS WITH her mouth open. "You used up like my whole break."

"Bathroom emergency, you know." He stands to the side of his Big Dipperz stand, waiting for her to vacate it for his return. He reconsiders and then ventures, "Thanks."

"Thanks? You're lucky I was here to cover your ass when

Tom came around. I had to flirt with that nasty old bastard to keep him from losing his mind. Disgusting."

"I appreciate it, but, I mean, you coulda told him I'd be right back." There's a long pause, and Lane swears he can hear the buzz of the tube lighting overhead. "So I, uh, I got it from here."

"That's it?"

"Yeah. I appreciate the backup. I mean it."

"Cool. Yeah, cool." She starts to walk off, emotionless. But then she pauses. "I don't even know why I'd help you."

"What? How about: because I helped you." He starts to organize and clean the lids of the different dip containers. "I helped you a lot. Or at least I tried to help."

She laughs. "Really?"

"Yeah, really. What do you mean, really? Fucking *really*? Did I come over on Christmas? When I was having one of the worst days of my life? I showed up at your—"

"Take it easy, you two. Customers, customers." Tom hushes them and motions toward the soft contours of a sweat-suited shopper on a Lark motorized scooter.

Tom puts his hand on Inez's back, stroking between her shoulder blades. "You better be nice to her, Lane. She keeps playing her cards right, you'll be her assistant too by this spring."

Lane forces a choke. "I'm not, you know— I mean, it's cool that you let me come back through New Year's and all, but I'm not gonna be here too much longer."

"Sure, Lame-o." Tom laughs. "Whatever you say." He pulls Lane aside, turning his back to Inez.

"Listen, kid. I know you're fragile and think you're going

through a rough time or whatever. But you can't be bringing that drama into work."

"I'm fine." He blushes, worried that Inez can still hear the conversation.

"As my personal assistant, I want to give you a little guidance. Give you some wisdom. Listen, you know what I do when I'm feeling down? I grab a ten-dollar bottle of wine and the biggest box of Magnum XXLs off the shelf. Then I wait until either the finest or the ugliest female cashier is working. I like that foreigner one too, with the rag-thing on her head. Anyway, I go buy it all from her, real slow-like. I don't say nothin'. I just make eye contact the whole time."

"Let me guess," Lane deadpans. "Then you're cured?"

"There's no way she's not imagining it, am I right? I get days of material outta that. Sometime I also throw in something random, like a tub of margarine or an electric back massager."

"Thanks for the guidance." Lane is mortified by the thought that Inez heard everything. "I have a lot to learn from you, Tom."

"Best part is: I return it all later for a full refund," Tom whispers. "Do that with a different cashier, though."

TWENTY-FIVE

LANE PICKS A LOOP OF black hair out of Toby's Old Spice and admires it under the bare bulb in the bathroom. Toby and his corny ponytail and beard are all white. Salt-and-pepper, at best. Lane doesn't want to think too much about the body hair of the old dude who is getting naked with his mom, but it does raise the question of whether Chaz or the teenagers are using the deodorant too.

That'd be wrong: all of those puberty hormones jumping from their armpits into the Old Spice and then getting transferred to Lane. Those kids are like some sort of black mold, creeping over every square inch of the house with their stank tube socks, sharp little Fritos crumbs and wadded-up Kleenex. Now this. Nothing is off-limits.

Lane does his best to avoid all of them. He's taken to pissing in the side yard in the tall grass along the fence and blackberries. And his mom brings his dinner out to the trailer and knocks on the door, but she's been inconsistent with breakfast and lunch. When forced to go inside to grab a meal, he makes sure to protest. To show his displeasure. And takes his frozen lasagnas and microwaved pizzas with him back to the trailer. He walks slow in front of his mom, eyes cast downward.

"Did she call again?" he asks Toby, Chaz and his mom, fishing to find out if Mia gave him a holiday courtesy call or if something more is at play. "I think she might be in trouble, is all."

"She ain't in no trouble, man. I toldja: Do yourself a favor. Let it go." Chaz contorts his face into a joker grin so he can drop a new dip between his bottom lip and gums.

"Wait, who are you again and what are you doing in my mom's living room?"

"Chaz. Remember?"

"Well, you don't know what you're talking about. We're not in Buttfuck, Alaska. And this isn't even about me. I'm looking out for her."

"All right, kid," Chaz says. "When you get older, you realize that most everybody's got different versions of the same problems. The trap is thinking that it's all about you."

Lane doesn't *think* he's special or unique. It is a proven fact that he's both special and unique. At least while swimming in the small pond of Lake City.

OUT IN THE TRAILER, HE gets dressed for his meeting with Nina. The little plastic bubble windows are beaded with condensation from his breath. As he looks for clean socks in his piles of clothes on the table and bench, he thinks about his trips to the library and his attempts to contact Mia by email. She may have quit Hotmail and started one of those Yahoo! accounts, but he doesn't know the address. Perhaps her father is even keeping her offline. Lane wouldn't put it past him.

Lane finds everything he needs but a pair of clean pants. He will have to go look in the TV room and brave the savage youth.

He knocks on the door. No one answers, but he can hear gunshots and explosions emanating from the TV. He opens the door an inch at a time. The kids look up and then go back to playing and watching the screen, its light flickering off their faces, casting inverse shadows of their chins up and across their faces.

"Just grabbing something." He steps over the youngest and busies himself digging through his mom's newspapers, the kids' dirty hoodies and pieces of *Maxim* magazines to find his rumpled pants on the floor.

On his way out the door, he turns back to the kids. "Why don't you guys go out sometime or do something?"

"Like what?" asks the older one.

"Go meet some girls. Or at least—I dunno—read a book. Watch a decent movie. You're rotting your minds."

All three of the kids laugh.

"Funny, huh? Video games aren't gonna get you anywhere."

"So what? We can be like you?"

Lane starts to respond but fights back a stutter.

"Books are creepy old-guy shit."

"How old do you think I am?"

"Old. Like twenty—maybe—twenty-three?"

"I've gotta go," Lane says as he backs as fast as he can out the door. "Important meeting."

NINA COMES DOWN THE ALLEY in the Mercedes and honks her horn. It's raining and her fog lights are on as then sun sets in the late afternoon. Lane jogs out through the garage door, his chin on his chest, brow furrowed and cheeks hardened to shield his eyes from the rain.

He pauses so that the kids can see him getting into the car. Only one is facing the window. And he's not sure if they can see that it's a Mercedes through the blackberries. But it's better than nothing.

Nina steps on the accelerator and flies out of the alley without slowing down to look for oncoming vehicles. "The judge. The caseworker. Inez. They're all in it together. In the same cult: Space Mountain or Strawberry Hill or some shit."

"Mars Hill."

"That's it. Like Jesus and the God of War had a lot in common, right? They think homosexuals should all be stricken with AIDS by God and men rule women."

"Yeah, they're some sort of New Calvinists who say *dude*, train kids in digital marketing and proselytize online," says Lane. "They're like our own homegrown megachurch."

"Sound like nice people." She pulls into the Shell parking lot and looks in the rainy evening at the darkness of the trailer park. "We have to stop them."

"Wait. I didn't agree to 'we' anything exactly. I didn't say 'I'm back in.'"

She ignores him. "They're all a bunch of hypocrites. You think a regular person dedicates their life to preaching this kind of intolerance? They join these cults because they can't stop looking at kiddie porn or when they get out of gambling rehab or need to stop beating their spouse. And then, out of the blue, because they've made right with Jesus Claus, they have some sort of moral authority. What kind of moral authority does she have over me?"

He imagines he could use Spinoza or maybe Nietzsche here but can't back the name-dropping with an explanation of either of their philosophies. "I dunno. What does anybody really have over anybody?" He looks out the window.

"We're gonna take a more proactive approach. Aim for her weak point."

"Which?"

"Drugs. Obviously."

"She doesn't even drink."

"*Doesn't drink* . . . For how long? A month? Two months? She's a convicted drug dealer. An addict. It's a matter of time. And then what? Wait until Jordan is back with her before it all comes apart at the seams? Once my wife has already been destroyed by this. Once Jordan is triple-fucked and has to start this process all over again with a different foster family. Why doesn't anybody else see this?"

"Can't people get better?"

She shakes her head.

"No?"

"One in a hundred. No, one in a thousand. And those come from good families or already have some sort of structure or bright spot in their past that serves as an anchor. Fucked is fucked."

"I don't think that's fair."

"Fair? What's fair? I don't believe fair exists . . . I don't even respect fair. People get what they get. It's a combination of hard work and luck. None of us deserve anything."

Lane shifts in his seat, exaggerating his movement enough to let her know that he doesn't agree without having to say it and provoke additional conflict.

"I know you're a liberal arts guy and one of these Seattle idealists who think everyone has the potential to be good and rational and get along if they become better educated and more enlightened," she says. "That if people open their minds and read enough books they'll find some sort of consensus based around progressive values and the world is gonna be OK. But it ain't like that. That's not how it works. We're not all destined for some sort of just and better future."

"You got it all figured out, Nina."

"Yeah, I kind of do, actually."

Lane gives up on his Pacific Northwest restraint. "You think you're the first Californian to move here with a bit of cash and think you know better than all of the locals? Truth is, you—and everybody like you—are just another type of utopian. You think there's no history here. That it's all a blank slate and you can show up and bully your way into creating a life on your own terms without accepting any realities of anyone else out here in this lost little corner of the country."

"Locals? Really? 'Cause some white trash, fishermen and hippie burnouts found cheap land here for a generation or two?

You all took it from the Indians in the first place. And none of you'll be able to afford to live here in ten years anyways. Maybe in Lake City. *Maybe* . . . The rest of you will be renting up in Lynnwood. And nobody's gonna remember anything about the past of this place. Such is progress, my friend." Nina lights another smoke. "Speaking of locals, you know what's your greatest cultural contribution?"

"Me personally? Well, as a student of—"

"No, Seattleites, dumbass."

"I dunno . . ." Lane stutters for a moment but deflects. "Tom Skerritt? No, wait, I don't think he was born here. Adam West? Kenny G?"

"How about bikini baristas? Or, even better, drive-thru bikini-barista shacks? Seattle coffee culture in a head-on collision with Lake City sleaze. Our girl Inez used to work in one up along north Lake City Way. Optimal mom material."

Nina tells Lane everything she knows about Inez from before she was pregnant, when she was standing around all day in nylon lingerie smudged with coffee grounds, getting harassed for subminimum wage plus tips by construction workers commuting into the city in their F-150s. Her boyfriend, Kevin, had long been a dealer, hustler and smackhead. He washed up from the peninsula or the islands or someplace unimpressive.

Inez got pregnant, and they dealt with it the way they knew how to cope with stress and the challenges of life: cutting corners, breaking laws, escape through addiction, playing the victim. "Poor life choices. Over and over again." Nina shakes her head for emphasis. Kevin and Inez started selling drugs out of her disabled mom's trailer, and the rest is history.

Nina cracks her knuckles and clears her throat. "Look, she's having a tough time. She needs to cut loose. Needs to relax. To have some fun. You should go over there and be a comforting friend." She hands Lane an amber plastic bottle with a few round white pills in it and the prescription sticker picked off. "Make absolute sure she feels better. And then you can get on with your life, as I deal with the next steps."

He holds the bottle between his thumb and index finger, giving it a little shake to see the shape and size of the pills. "Prozac?"

"Try OxyContin."

"And if I don't?"

She pulls out a photo of her, Tracey and Jordan in some sort of a government-looking building of cheap brown office chairs and Formica. The kid is small, bloated and curled in on himself. "This is when we adopted him. Not adopted, but started to foster, you know . . ."

She pulls out another. "This is now." The photo shows Nina and Tracey reading a book to Jordan in a home office with a glass desktop. They're sitting together as a happy family. Nina is wearing a gray Kangol flat cap and laughing. The same Stanford pennant and rows of bookshelves fill the wall behind her. Jordan has grown, slimmed and his smile overtakes his cheeks. "You have an opportunity here, Lane. An opportunity for you. And for Jordan. To do the right thing. To change a life."

Lane looks over the photo again and again. "The right thing. Yeah. OK. But—"

"Think about who in this equation has a future. Including yourself. I know you're gonna make the right decision."

TWENTY-SIX

LANE IS NO STATISTICIAN AND despises academia's drift toward an overreliance on data and quantifiable research. He was never a numbers guy. But he's skilled at the participant-observation technique he cultivated by watching the scroll of would-be stepdads parade through his childhood home and later refined in his anthropology and area-studies coursework. He knows he has no hard proof, but after years of witnessing cold cut consumer behavior, Lane is certain that sliced turkey is the most popular lunch meat in America.

People consider it to be the ideal deli meat. It doesn't challenge kids' taste buds. It's good for busy adults with a vague sense of nutrition. Goes great with mayo and soft bread for seniors. It was the first fast food that sold itself as being good for you. None of the visible gristle of a sausage and without the ethnic pungencies of traditional deli offerings. No shame about fat or calories. Just a blemishless, inoffensive source of all-American white protein.

But Lane was always confused as to where such a piece of

meat came from. That's the point, right? Like a boneless, skin-less chicken breast under cellophane, it is many steps removed from the unmovable fact of being a dead flightless bird.

Many people, like Tom, are happy to believe it is simply sliced from the roasted breast of a large, healthy turkey, and they refuse to believe any different. Lane had seen few real tur-keys in his life but still had trouble imagining one large enough to yield that sized piece of intact meat.

When one of the purveyor's sales reps stopped through the store to see their product in the wild, Lane asked him to ex-plain. "It's all made outta milky meat jism," the guys said. On the next visit, he loaned Lane his copy of the company training VHS tape.

Lane watched as different bits and pieces from any num-ber of different turkeys were mechanically separated, bleached and thrown together in a vacuum tumbler, which he thought looked like the rotating drum in a cement mixer. Steel paddles inside the tumbler, plus a sizeable injection of salt and phos-phates, pummel protein and cellular debris out of the blood cells in the turkey parts. This soup of milky meat jism is called exudate.

The pieces, now swimming in liquid poultry, are heated and pressure-molded into metal casts. The exudate fills out any holes and joins the meat scraps together into an amalgamated loaf of random bits of turkey muscle.

This consistent white Jell-O is yanked from the molds, plastic-wrapped, shipped and then thin-sliced into chewable units by sandwich artists and slicer jockeys like Lane. Sure, it's another sausage-making process. But it doesn't render a sausage. The end product is the perfect guilt-free choice for your diet regimen or to stick in your children's mouths.

But be careful. Get it down fast, don't think about it too much and move on. If it stays in your fridge for a few days too long, the meat jizz will start to leach back out of the turkey and remind you what it's really made out of.

LANE STANDS IN THE OPEN door of the loading dock, breaking down cardboard containers with a box cutter and his foot. He razors the packing tape end-to-end, kicks in the middle of the box with his heel and heaves the flattened remnants onto a pile outside the door. Depending on the quality of the cardboard and the width of the tape, he sometimes skips the blade and goes right to putting his foot through the back of the box. It's rather cathartic.

He's done it enough times that he can intuit the optimal approach based on the box dimensions, which signify the former contents. The jojos and jalapeño poppers boxes are easier than ones that held tubs of macaroni or ambrosia salad.

Lane hears a female voice above his head. "So what's up? You don't talk to me no more?"

He finishes slicing the back of a box and looks up to see Inez standing over him in her work attire, her hands on her hips.

"It's not like that," he says, drawing the blade back into the box cutter.

"Not like what? I toldja you think you're the shit. That you're too good for me."

"I was gonna come talk to you."

"To what? Apologize?"

He shrugs. "I dunno, I was thinking I'd—"

"Do you even know how to apologize?"

"Yeah, of course."

"OK, I'm waiting."

He stands as if to face her and then busies himself with a box of fried chicken drumettes. "I know you're feeling embarrassed because—"

Her cell phone rings. She looks at the number, answers, "I told you not to call me here," and hangs up.

"New cell, huh?" Lane asks before she can return the Kyocera pay-as-you-go burner to her pocket.

"Bought some minutes, is all. Got a raise, you know."

"Raise?" Lane starts to pace. "How?"

She ignores his question. "What were you saying to me before?"

Lane shrugs. "Doesn't matter. How'd you get a raise?"

"Whatever, dude. You dipped on us on Christmas. Ditched me doing your job at work. I thought we had—thought we were moving toward something." She turns and walks off.

"Toward what?" He follows after her.

"WHAT ARE YOU DOING UP here? You don't even smoke. Not for real," she says as he trails her into the secret smoking section and sits atop the milk crate. There's a condom wrapper in the coffee can, mixed in with the cigarette butts. Lane is relieved that the spent prophylactic is nowhere to be seen. "Why'd you invite me up here that first time, anyway?" she asks, and she lights her cigarette.

"You seemed nice."

"That it?"

"Yeah. Something wrong with that?"

"You know what I think? I think you wanted to fuck me but you're not man enough to handle that I have a kid. Or that I'm not as fancy as you think you are."

"No. You're right. That's it. You got me pegged, sister."

"You ain't better than me."

"I never said I'm better than you."

"Well, you judge me."

"No. It's your boyfriend or your ex or whatever he is. It seems like you still have loose ends."

"Kevin? You think I want him showing up at my place like that?" she says. "You're scared of him? Aren't you?"

Lane laughs.

"He was gone in five minutes. I sent his ass home. But you ran away first."

"That's your opinion. It didn't happen like— I don't see it that way. At all."

"You're the hero in your own little world, Lane. But you only know how to look out for you."

"How can you say that? I gotta look out for myself right now, yeah. How else can I avoid getting sucked down into this morass? But, I told you, I'm dedicating my career to the greater good."

"The greater good of Lane fucking Bueche. You know what? I can't believe I started to let myself . . ." She trails off.

"Let yourself what?"

"Never mind." She flicks her cigarette off his chest. The ember burns a gray spot on his black polyester tie. "But I was right . . . you're a pussy."

"Hey. Wha— What the fu-fu-?" He wipes the ash from his chest. "I could get you in deep shit for that."

"My point." She marches off and shouts again. "Pussy."

LANE PUTS HIS HEAD BETWEEN his hands and his elbows on his knees. He's simply misunderstood. Like he has been throughout his life. New York was the one place he ever felt like he was approaching his true self, his potential. At Columbia. With Mia. He breaths the cold, wet air and thinks of her. None of this was necessary. They could've been figuring out which New Year's party to go to. Or planning to get out of town for a few days and stay at a bed-and-breakfast in the Hudson Valley. In between all of that, Lane should be gearing up for his second semester. Scanning the syllabi and buying books. Filling out the bookshelves in the Gramercy apartment.

"Where's Inez?" Tom jogs into the smoking section. "Some jerkoff with a moped is downstairs looking for her."

"She ain't here." Lane doesn't take his face out from between his knees. He finds the tone of the moped comment to be a bit rich considering that Tom doesn't have a driver's license.

"Somebody said you two headed up here together."

"Somebody who?"

"Blake."

"Who?"

"The guy who looks like you. The one in the deli."

"I can't believe you hired that guy."

"Yeah, he's pretty much retarded. She, on the other hand, she's not half bad, huh? Trouble though . . ." He nudges Lane with his knee. "You banging her?"

"No. C'mon, man. Don't be vulgar."

"*Right* . . ." Tom stares at Lane, keeping him on the hook, watching for a tell. "I think you should steer clear of her."

"Why?"

"Don't 'why' me, assistant. You get my sloppy seconds, not vice versa. And, anyway, this was your last chance, guy. I gave you the benefit of the doubt, and it was my ass on the line. You can't walk away from your job to come up here to hit on chicks."

"What does '*was* your last chance' mean? You firing me?"

"Wish I could. Need an airtight reason these days with all of these bullshit PC rules to protect losers and Al Qaeda foreigners who don't deserve to be here in the first place." Tom takes out a hard box of Camel Wides and starts packing them on the butt of his left palm. "Go on, man. Get back down there."

"Wait, can I have a second—"

"Get outta here, Lame-o. Lame-as-fuck-o."

Lane heads off before he stutters in front of Tom.

"NO, YOU DON'T NEED ME, Kevin," Inez says, her voice stern but heading toward a crack. "Everybody I know needs me. What about me? I need me too."

As Lane cuts through the refrigerated aisle, he bumps right into Inez and a man, about his age or a few years younger, arguing in the transition area between orange juice and the cases of domestic lager.

Assuming this guy is Kevin, he is not as tough as Lane imagined. He's not tough at all. He strikes Lane as a BMXer. A graffiti artist. A burner in oversized pants, an Adidas track jacket and a large backpack slung over a lean frame. Lane's still not willing to admit to himself that he was afraid of Kevin. Or even that he ran away. But perhaps he did misevaluate things a bit.

As a matter of fact, Lane is pretty sure he's met this guy before. He thinks Kevin used to hang out with Robbie. Or J.C. Maybe they went to middle school together. Or rode the bus. All of that said, Lane doesn't feel like trying to prove his masculinity right now in a public place. He'd rather avoid the whole dispute. But Inez sees him and Kevin registers her change in demeanor.

Lane fixates on his wrist as if he has a watch. He heaves his shoulders to feign exasperation like he's just realized that he's in a huge rush to be somewhere that isn't here. Somewhere behind him. He attempts a quick turnaround. An about-face. He's not far from the end of the aisle. But, at the edge of his field of vision, he sees Tom starting down the opposite end, nose down in his shift-schedule clipboard.

Inez turns toward Tom and then toward Lane and back to Tom.

"Kevin?" Lane grabs the guy by the arm and pulls him around the corner of the aisle before Tom looks up.

"Who the—"

"Holy sh— That you, Kevin?"

Kevin gives Lane a hard eye. "You the dude hitting on my girl?"

"You remember me, right? You used to spin downtown with my boy Robbie. Robbie from Lake City."

"I dunno. Nah."

"You don't remember me?" Lane shakes his head and laughs. "MDMA . . . shit works every time . . . Well, listen, I'm trying to help you out here." He keeps pulling Kevin by the arm, but he resists.

"Leggo a me, homo." Kevin twists out of Lane's grasp and starts back into the top of the aisle as Tom approaches Inez.

Lane grabs his sleeve again. "Trust me, dude. That guy . . . he's a cop."

"Cop?" Kevin does a shuffle step and starts to walk with Lane.

"Plainclothes. Like a special kind of cop. He's been waiting for you. Faster, man." Lane speeds him along.

"I saw him before, and he didn't—"

"He was IDing you. Checking you out. Gonna arrest you now for sure."

"What for?"

"Shit, man, you know better than anyone else . . ." Lane keeps Kevin moving out through the door and out into the parking lot. "Keep going. Run, man. Run."

TWENTY-SEVEN

LANE SITS ATOP THE CLOSED toilet lid with Toby's cell phone to his ear. He has a few minutes to make the call before Toby comes back from taking the garbage out. Lane could have asked to use it, but he didn't want to give Toby the satisfaction of feeling like he helped. In any way.

After working through multiple dead ends and answering machines in the Columbia University phone tree, he finds his way to a monotone-voiced lackey in the bursar's office who is holding down the department through the week between Christmas and New Year's. He asks when is the latest he can pay for second semester. Lane wants to know if he can delay until later in the term, until Mia comes back around or he lines up some sort of private scholarship. If he can stay in the game long enough, some opportunity might still present itself.

The receptionist goes to look up the file status. Lane chews at his cuticles and bounces his knees while he waits. The longer she takes, the more certain he is that she'll tell him that he's already been withdrawn. That there is a freeze on his enrollment.

"You're all sorted," she says with the emotional outlay of someone taking tickets at a movie theater or bagging groceries.

"Sorted? What do you mean 'sorted'?"

"Tuition's paid through the end of the year."

Lane is not sure if he wants to scream with excitement or ask her to double-check that it's not a mistake. He gives an abrupt "OK. Thanks. Goodbye" before any reaction can betray his surprise, if not the error of it all.

He runs through the permutations in his head. All he can figure is that, in the chaos of Mia's dad taking over her finances, he forgot to pull the money back out of Columbia. Or he didn't know Mia had paid it in the first place. Or she was still protecting him. Whatever the reason, Lane isn't going to question it. One shouldn't poke and prod that kind of serendipity.

He turns off the phone and slips it into Toby's jacket pocket.

BACK IN THE TRAILER, LANE puts his feet up on the cooler and stares at his check. He rotates it over and over. He thinks about the flight he could buy with it. The date. The departure time. The arrival time. The destination: JFK. Then he digs all the way to the back of the built-in cabinet to extract the amber pill bottle. He holds the check in one hand and the OxyContin in the other.

This whole hustle can't be that hard. Not on someone with a predisposition. A history. It's like surprising a former serial adulterer with a prepaid escort at his hotel door at midnight. He has to make it available, that's all. She'll do the rest herself. Like she'll do sooner or later, regardless. And he'll be off to New York, back on track to a brighter future. Lane's only challenge is to dig into himself to find the nerve. He has it. He knows he does.

There's a light rap on the door.

"Hold on." Lane scrambles to hide his escape package in his pockets. "What is it?"

There's no answer. Probably that Chaz redneck again. Lane opens the door to tell him to leave him alone but finds his mom standing outside in her pink terry cloth bathrobe. It's the first time she's come out to visit him for non–meal delivery purposes. He's still wielding the silent treatment against her, letting her know how very hurt and betrayed he is. And she's not the type to push.

"You OK?" she asks.

He doesn't answer at first but looks around at his circumstances. His world. The collapsible table. The mini-fridge. The hot plate. The crawl space bunk. He wants to let it sink in. "With a couple of sleeping bags and, if I wear socks, then I can sleep—a few hours at a time."

"She came to see about storage space." Toby arrives behind Lane's mom. "Tell him, Dottie. We need to see if we can fit her sewing machine and my WeedWacker back here with enough room for us to sleep at night."

Lane exhales with a dramatic display of his frustration, making sure his mom notes his discontent.

"You gotta stop guilt-trippin' her, son," Toby says. "You're tearing her up."

Before Lane can jump all over Toby, Lane's mom diverts.

"If you want to try to get an apartment up north in like Lynn-wood or something, you could—"

"Lynnwood?" He has trouble saying the name. "That's not even Seattle."

"Yeah, if you save up, you can get something up there. With roommates or something. And you can use my car while I'm gone."

"I'd rather you run over me with your car."

His mom tries to sweeten the deal. "My car's so old. I never drive it. And Toby's got his pickup. You know, Lane, you can keep using it even when I get back."

"It's pretty beat up. And I'm not planning to be here long. Plus, you shouldn't be planning on Toby's car for the future. Who knows how things will, well, you know . . ."

"The car runs, Lane," his mom offers. "And rent is cheaper up north. Out of town. Up where Toby is. A car'd make that possible."

"You should say 'thank you,' Lane," Toby interjects. "I could sell it for her for scrap. Make a few bucks."

"Bet you'd like that, Toby. Why don't you two come back later? I need to organize my personal stuff—move somewhere, like out to the garage, before you start throwing WeedWackers and sewing machines in here with me."

"C'mon, Lane," his mom says. "Please don't be like that."

"Hey, almost forgot to tell you," Toby adds. "A girl called for you."

"Mia?"

"That Inez girl," Toby drawls. "Told me to tell you to call her back. About New Year's Eve or somethin'."

TWENTY-EIGHT

"WHERE'D YOU SAY YOUR MOM is again?" Lane asks Inez as he lets the aluminum door slam with its metallic rattle.

"Dialysis." She is wearing her black dress again, same as their first date, and lighting candles and incense around the mobile home. "It was scheduled for early January, but she's in bad shape. Had to go in early. Stay a few days."

Her shoulder strap slides down, revealing the curve of the top of her breast. She pulls it back up as she stands, pretending that she didn't catch Lane looking.

"Sorry to hear that," he says, setting a mid-priced bottle of champagne on the few square inches of available counter space next to the sink.

"Happens all the time. She doesn't listen to me. Doesn't take care of herself."

"And Jordan?" His left hand finds its way to his pocket, where he holds the pill bottle between his index finger and thumb, spinning it over and over again.

"I don't think I ever, you know, fully explained it to you.

But he spends some time with his . . ." She takes a moment to consider her words. "'Aunties.' I'm pretty sure I mentioned them before. They're like these long-term babysitters he got to know while I was going through a tough stretch."

"For New Year's Eve?"

"It's complicated. A, uh—a deal I made in exchange for Christmas." She slumps a bit and then looks at the bottle of champagne.

"C'mon. One drink. Special occasion," Lane tries.

"I dunno."

"To new starts. A new year."

She thinks for a moment. "Yeah, OK. Screw it. I'm in the clear now."

"Nice. 'Cause I stole it from the state liquor store, special for you." Lane pretends he's joking.

"First Kevin at the store. Now this. Such, what do you call it?"

"Chivalry." He pulls two plastic tumblers out of the sink, washes them with the nub of a sponge, shakes off the water and fills them with champagne. They clink cups, making the extra effort at eye contact, and Inez tosses her whole cup back in one go.

She slides a Converse All-Star box out from under the coffee table and opens it to reveal a stack of photos. They pour another drink and sit next to each other on the floor and look at pictures of Inez and Jordan at the hospital when he was born. No Kevin in sight. She follows with a photo of her on Lake City Way as a teenager wearing ripped and faded 501s tucked into knockoff fourteen-hole Doc Martens and a blue-

and-white plaid with a black motorcycle jacket. She smokes a cigarette in front of Video Time Movie Rentals and crosses her eyes for the camera. Although she's trying to look wild and hard, her youth and innocence are what strike Lane. He thinks she's beautiful in the photo. Looks like someone who could make it out of the neighborhood. Like someone who might have a future.

She flashes another photo with her and a girl working the Chicka Latte stand in a gray, wet parking lot. She's in a bra and panties and is still clinging to a rebellious sneer. Lane sees her exposed midriff and the low drop of the front of the panties. He feels his heartbeat start to race and he becomes more aware of his physical proximity to her, but she moves on past the photo, mumbling about how he wasn't supposed to see that one.

The next is a photo of her holding Jordan—no longer a tiny baby, but not as big as he is now. She describes it as "the day I got back." Jordan is crying, and Inez has a nervous smile shot through with disorientation, relief and a bit of sadness. He's not sure why she showed this photo either. It's not the kind of picture that one keeps and displays as part of the curated visual narrative of her life. A milestone, yes. But one with enough dark undertones for it to live separate from the rest.

They pour another drink and are already chasing the bottom of the bottle. He wants to get to the point and get this all over with but is even more nervous than he anticipated. Lane thought the champagne would get his confidence up, but it's nowhere near enough. Good thing he has a backup plan.

She starts rummaging through her CDs, looking for something to put into the dented Discman attached to small Coby speakers. "Who's your favorite Seattle band?" she asks. "Please don't say Nirvana."

"I dunno. Hendrix?"

"Safe choice. Predictable. But classic," she says.

"You know I went to middle school with Hendrix's nieces?" he says. "Gorgeous girls. Family didn't have a pot to piss in. All of the money was going to some label."

"The family didn't get nothing?"

"The dad did, eventually. After a lot of legal fees. But he still cut out Jimi's brother and nieces. Said the brother was a druggie." Lane starts spinning the pill bottle again in his pocket. "Jimi partied himself to death by my age—and the grown brother doesn't get any of the inheritance because he does drugs. Can you imagine that? People are too hypocritical about that shit, huh?"

"Yeah, I dunno. Depends what he was doing, I guess." Inez pulls out a burned copy of the Alice in Chains *Sap* EP and puts it in the player. They listen for a moment. "My ex sees Layne Staley around. Buying smack and shit. It's not doing him any favors. Dude's a rock star but lives in some crappy condo down by Kinko's on Forty-Fifth."

"I figured he was in Hollywood these days." Lane pours them a final round of champagne.

"Yeah, but fuck Nirvana, you know. Fuck Pearl Jam too while we're at it. I was always more into Alice in Chains and Soundgarden anyway. They're real Seattle."

"I saw Soundgarden at my first concert. Bumbershoot in the late '80s."

"You serious? I was there," she says, and high-fives Lane, but their hands stay together, clasped. "With the Posies, right?"

"Right. Yeah, right. The Posies got booed." They continue to hold hands.

They avoid facing each other until she leans in for a kiss.

LANE GETS THE LAST DROPS of champagne out of the bottle. He can feel the pressure shooting the alcohol right through his blood-brain barrier.

"Man, it feels good to drink." Inez's volume starts to rise. "This is like the first time I've felt happy, like actually happy, in forever."

Lane can see the clock on the microwave in Wanda's bedroom. "The countdown to midnight is gonna start soon."

"What's your New Year's resolution?" she asks.

"I don't believe in all that. You?"

"Yeah. First time in a long time that I got one. I'm gonna do more for me. For me and Jordan."

"Like what?"

She pulls up the corner of the rug and digs out a small roll of one- and five-dollar bills. "I've been saving. It's only"—she flips through it—"like two hundred and eighty-three dollars now. But I want to give me and him a fresh start. I want to make his life better, not this . . ."

Lane tries to be encouraging, but a train of anxiety barrels through the fog of the alcohol. He rolls his head and looks toward the floor.

"*What?*" she asks.

"Nothing." He maintains his focus on the ground. "That's a great idea. Really. I'm excited for you."

"You OK?" She reaches a hand out to his knee.

"Yeah, of course."

"I mean, I know I have a shitty life here and it's not much compared to what you're used to."

"I didn't say that. I just have a lot on my mind."

"You have a lot on your mind? Like what? At least you're not worried that you're a horrible mom. That you don't have what it takes. That you have too much of your own failed mother in you."

"I don't know what to tell you. The parenthood thing looks hard. I mean, I don't know that I could ever do it." He starts to panic; time for the backup measure. "I need to go to the bathroom."

"What about the countdown? It's"—she cranes her head to look for the clock—"in less than like five minutes."

"I'll be right back." He thinks of Mia. The millennium. Of Columbia. That he never has to come back here. Inez's situation is fucked. And it will always be fucked. No matter what he does. No matter what she does. Right? He must remember that. He can fix his life; that's all he has control over. Him. "One second. I promise."

THE BATHROOM IS SMALLER THAN he remembers and even more overloaded with trinkets. While urinating, Lane digs the pill bottle out of his pocket and sets about opening the child-proof lid. He needs to kill the anxiety. Blunt the nerves. Then he will be able to follow through and do what needs to be done.

His hands are shaking. Sweating. He struggles to open the bottle. He knows he waited too long and won't have time for the pill to kick in after he swallows it. Lane decides he's going to have to crush it up and snort it. Maybe he needs to scrape off the coating with his thumbnail before crushing it. He's not sure. How difficult could it be? J.C. doesn't know how to write half of his lowercase letters, and he's capable of putting a number of pills up his nose per day.

As he pries the top off of the bottle, a couple of the pills fly out, ricochet off the sink top and disappear. He is too distracted by the fact that he's pissing all over his pants to see where they land.

"What're you doing in there?" she asks through the door.

No answer.

"Last deuce of oh-one?"

"C'mon." He dabs at his wet underwear with toilet paper. "Don't be crass."

"Crass? Isn't that like an old punk band?"

"It means— Never mind."

She downshifts. "You don't think I'm very smart, do you?"

"Why would you ask that?"

"'Cause you go to an expensive school and I, well, you know ..."

"No. Of course not."

"I don't believe you," she says. "Ask me a question. Let me see if I can get it."

"Like what?"

"Like something smart. Like what does *crass* mean? Wait, I'll tell you: it means gross and stupid and . . . *low-class*. Ask me something else."

"I dunno."

"C'mon."

"OK, um, how many hands do I have?"

"Two."

"Would you say that's more than or less than the average number of hands?"

"Is this a trick question?"

"It's abstract or, like, analytical."

"See, I'm dumb."

"No, you just gotta know how to look at things in a different way—an expansive way—in academia."

"Yeah, I'd embarrass myself with some stupid question like 'Do pregnant chicks count?'" She trails off to little above a whisper for her final words.

"Why would you ask that?" He laughs with her, at her.

"'Cause then a person can have four hands. Six hands with twins. Even more. There's a lot more pregnant ladies out there than one-handed or no-handed people."

"I'd never thought about— Yeah, that doesn't count." He backs out of the conversation, forcing his attention to a stack of Mars Hill pamphlets on the back of the toilet. "So how into Mars Hill are you?"

"That stuff in there's my mom's."

He does up his pants and starts thrashing around the bathroom floor, searching for the pills.

"You can tell me, Lane. Are you rubbing one out in there?"

"Caught me."

"Come to Jesus?"

"Something like that. Tell me more about the Mars Hill thing."

"I didn't lie exactly, but I exaggerated before. I don't go to church that much. Or ever. That doesn't kill your vibe in there, does it?"

"I'll manage."

"It's like my wedding ring at work. People think they understand you better."

He picks his way through the rug and finds a pill mixed in with a bird's nest of animal fur and pubes at the base of the toilet. Lane's not going to have time to crush it up, so he blows the hair off it and pops it into his mouth. At least it will help him with the emotional aftermath. He gags, chokes it down without water and then starts running a finger along the tiny gap between the edge of the carpeting and the wall.

"Hurry up, Lane," she says. "I'm trying to get a clear image on Channel Five. We only got a minute till the fireworks."

"I'm coming ... wait, which people understand you better?"

"Parole officers. Bosses. Coworkers. I also gotta look proper for this legal situation I got with Jordan."

"With whom? The state? No, wait, those 'Aunties' you mentioned before? You trying to make a 'children deserve a mother and father' point to the judge? Evangelical family-values stuff?" he ventures.

"What'dya think this is? The '80s? Alabama? The judge already hates the Aunties ... They're Californians."

"Californians?"

"Yeah, they brought up a lawyer from LA or wherever. Musta paid a ton of cash. The judge—he's old-time Seattle, and I have no idea if he's religious or not—but he took one look at all that tanned, frost-tipped, bleach-toothed California bullshit and ruled for me."

Lane gives up on his search. He's not sure there was a second pill in the first place. Back to the business at hand: he grips the pill bottle.

"I'm worried about my mom, that they're not taking good care of her. That all of the doctors are off for the holiday." Inez raises her voice over the sound of Lane flushing the toilet. "For all of her faults, I still feel guilty when she needs me and I'm here having fun. Breaking my sobriety."

"Family . . ." Lane says, looking at round pills through the side of the plastic cylinder. He reaches for the door.

"My mom and Jordan. I wish I could give them so much more."

He pulls his hand back from the door handle and wipes the sweat from his palms onto the front of his jeans. He should have taken the pill before he went to her place. He'd been too optimistic. Too confident in his ability to follow through. He wants to pace the bathroom, but it's too small. He takes another breath, squeezing the bottle until its sides start to buckle.

The host on the TV starts counting, "*Twenty, nineteen, eighteen . . .*"

"C'mon, dude," Inez shouts. "You're hella slow."

He starts to leave the bathroom again, then stops, turns to the sink and shakes out all of the pills into the drain as he fake-washes his hands. The water carries them down past the chrome ring and away into the black pipe below.

As he steps out of the bathroom, he bumps right into her. "I'm happy you came over tonight." She smiles, then closes her eyes and gives Lane a long kiss on his mouth. He doesn't react, not externally anyhow. She turns to the TV screen for the countdown. The host gets louder and louder: *"Four, three, two, one . . . Happy New Year."*

Inez throws her arms around Lane and tries to jump up and down, but he stands flat-footed, anchoring her to the floor.

"I'm—I'm sorry to do this. It's for the best. You're gonna have to trust me." He kisses her on the cheek and walks out the front door.

TWENTY-NINE

"WHAT'S YOUR RESOLUTION THEN, BIZ?" Cheese and Rice asks, tucking his blond bangs up under a hairnet and spraying the countertops with disinfectant. "You know, for New Year's."

Lane loads chicken-strip-and-jojo combos into a line of six foil containers, readying them for the lamps in the hot case. He doesn't answer. They've discussed the nickname too many times. He's been asked about his New Year's resolution too many times.

And he's still riding the Oxycodone Express. His brain feels as if it has a cool rush of extra cranial fluid lifting it up off the hardpan of his skull. Like those Japanese trains that levitate on reverse magnets. His wrists radiate a tingling, soothing heat into the palms of his hands.

"What? No resolution?" the kid tries again.

Lane wants to tell him that although some sixteenth-century pope decided on the Gregorian calendar, there's no real reason why the year starts January 1 and not on the Summer Solistice. But the greater point is: he doesn't need some marker to announce to other people about how he plans to re-invent himself, to make himself a better person. Lane wants to explain these simple truths to him, but he's sure that kid wouldn't understand. Or maybe he just doesn't care. He adds two ketchup packets to each of the foil trays and makes sure they're all straight, the logos all facing in the same direction.

"Anyhoo." Cheese and Rice faces Lane, inching toward his personal space. "I was thinking, I know what Lane should do . . ."

Lane stays focused on his work. He snaps off the grease-slicked latex gloves and shrink-wraps the containers with plastic film. He gathers the plastic in a wad on the bottom of the tray and melts it to the point where it seals and doesn't burn on the hot pad.

"You should go to college," the clerk states. The result of some spectacular deli epiphany.

"Thanks. Great idea, dude." Lane overheats the plastic. It contracts too much and holes yawn open where the film meets the foil corners.

"You seem like a smart guy. It's never too late to seek out God's path for you."

Lane promises to think about it. He tries to put an end to the conversation, but the kid won't let it go.

"You see, that's my resolution. I want to show people that there's a plan for them to—"

They both pause as the phone rings in the back.

Cheese and Rice picks back up. "God has a plan for you to—"

"OK, you know what?" Lane gives in. "I'm a fucking PhD student at Columbia."

"That's super cool, bro. The F-bomb is totally unnecessary but . . . Columbia . . . That's like down in Oregon?"

"No."

"OK, 'cause I went to a Bible camp in Prineville once, and my dad drove me across the Columbia River to get—"

The phone continues to ring.

"Can you get that?"

Cheese and Rice keeps talking.

"Get the goddamn phone, you fu—"

"I'm serious, though. Let me know if you need any other like advice or anything," he says, jogging into the back. "And I still want you to come with me to the Hill. It'll change your life—or not 'change' because all is predetermined—but you know what I mean."

Lane leans against the counter to shore up his balance and considers sticking his head into the deep fat fryer.

"It's for you, Lane." The guy shouts from the back.

"Who is it?"

"Hold on." Cheese and Rice spends a few more moments on the phone and then comes back up front. "Somebody named Mia. Super nice. Says you know her."

"HOW'D YOU, UM, HOW'D YOU get this number?" Lane labors to get each and every syllable off his tongue and into the Fred Meyer deli phone.

"Some guy at your mom's house. Charles?" Mia says.

The words hit him like seagulls into plane engines. He can't believe that she knows he's working as a near-minimum-wage employee in a superstore deli. She has to know.

"Can we start this conversation over again? Please, Lane," Mia asks, her voice familiar again, comforting. Almost. "How about: 'Hi. Happy New Year.'"

"Is it?" he asks.

"A New Year? Yes, last I checked."

"But is it happy?"

"I don't know. You tell me."

"Not my finest. You?"

"Well, if it makes you feel any better, things are still challenging here too," says Mia. "I've had a tough few weeks. My dad's been—"

"Tough, like mental health stuff?"

Mia tells him that there's some truth to it. She's not proud of it and she had always wanted to tell him, but she didn't want it to define her. Didn't want it to scare him off. She hasn't seen the legal paperwork, but she assumes that it's made to sound worse than it is.

"But do you want it?" Lane asks. When she doesn't answer, he adds, "The divorce. The annulment. The whatever it's called."

"I—I don't know. My dad, you see, he's having some— he doesn't want me to make any mistakes. He's worried about my inheritance. For my own good. For the long run. Until I feel better. But I do feel better. So—"

"Buy me a ticket to New York."

"He's keeping me on like a tight allowance. I don't even have my own— I'm calling you from someone else's phone."

There is a pounding on the loading dock door.

"Hold on," Lane shouts to the door as the person pounds again.

He stretches the phone cord as far as it will go, leaning to unlatch the door.

Nina stands in the doorway, picking through her handbag. "And?"

"Hold on a second?" Lane asks Mia, placing his hand over the receiver to be sure she can't hear.

"I can't. No," Mia says. "I've gotta go. I'll call you back."

"What? Wait." Then he turns to Nina. "Can you hold on, then? Gimme a minute?"

"No, I need to talk to you right now, Lane." Nina leaves no room for negotiation. She drops her voice to a whisper. "Who's that? The crackhead?"

"No. Nobody. Please, hold on. Two minutes. Please, this is important."

"Nobody?" Nina walks up to him and disconnects the call.

"DONE DONE? LIKE TOTALLY DONE?" Nina lights a smoke as they step out into the loading dock.

"Done done. Totally done." He drops his voices and tries to straighten a stack of flattened cardboard boxes with the toe of his shoe. "You didn't have to hang up my call like that. You coulda—"

"C'mon. Give me the details."

"I don't want to talk about it. Not here. It's not— I'm not proud of it."

She tells him that he should be proud. That he did the right thing. Especially for Jordan. Successful people are not afraid to fight for what they believe in. To make a hard decision. To overcome their doubts.

Lane asks for a favor in return. Not a favor so much as the completion of an earlier promise.

"I don't know how or when you're planning to do what's next," he says. "But I need you to wait a few days. Until I'm out of town. So she doesn't know it was me. You gotta take me at my word that I did it. And let me go."

"Take you at your word?"

"I gotta get back to school. I can't be waiting around here for half of January."

"Second semester doesn't start until January 19. Columbia's schedule is on its site."

"Yeah, but you said—you promised—you'd take care of the rest when I was already back, figuring out my life or whatever. That was the deal."

"The deal . . ."

"I left early. Left school, I mean. Because of 9/11. One of the greatest tragedies in American history. Remember? I have to get back to tie up loose ends. Be ready for the beginning of the semester."

Nina tells him what she does know. That he went over to Inez's last night. That she saw him enter the trailer. Saw his cheap-ass bottle of champagne. She knows that they were hanging out until midnight. Everything short of seeing Inez violate her sobriety and probation.

"I'm feeling—how shall I put it?—guardedly optimistic."

She stubs out the cigarette butt and lights another. "But I don't work off of optimism."

"I'm telling you the truth."

"You better be. Because of the holiday, the time of the year, this is all going to have to wait a few days anyway. Hold tight a bit longer and we'll get this sorted."

"I took a big risk for you." Lane locates his John Baggs Jr. His Doc Maynard. There has to be an angle to stall her. Tables will be turned. "Don't let me down, Nina. I know you're a legit businesswoman who stands by her word. Not another Inez."

THIRTY

OLD PATCHEYE CONTINUES TO YELL from his wheelchair about towelheads and the impending apocalypse. Fox News graphics and their parade of blow-dried muppets dance across the TV screen at the Rimrock.

"I need your help now. I need you to talk to Nina," Lane begs Lonnie across the corner of the bar. "Tell her Inez has been buying oxy like every day. That it's a guaranteed fact that she's off the wagon."

"I don't sell pills."

"How'd Nina get 'em then?"

"That was a special favor."

"Do me a special favor too."

"It'd still be weird if I call her out of the blue to say that."

"So, say Inez owes you money, and you're looking for her." Lane stands up on the rungs of his barstool thinking of how he was unable to find Inez that day in the store. "Yeah, that's perfect, 'cause she's gonna leave town for a few days, long enough that it can't be proven whether she stayed clean or not."

"You know, for a fact, she's leaving?"

"I'm gonna make sure of it."

Lonnie runs his finger around and around the rim of his pint glass, considering.

Lane has no idea how he'll get Inez out of town for multiple days, but he'll figure it out. He always figures it out. "What about her dirtbag ex-boyfriend?" he asks Lonnie, fishing.

"Yeah, Kevin. Kevin from the islands?" Lonnie rests his pale, hairless arms on the corner of the bar. "I thought we were talking about a different dude before. I know Kevin."

Lane finishes his Rainier. "Piece of crap, right? He's like violent, huh?"

"He's a good enough guy. Used to have an ill vinyl collection before he got more into drugs. But even before, he was the kinda dude who's never got gas money or can't find his wallet when it's time to pay."

Connie, the bartender, asks Lane and Lonnie if they want more drinks.

"I'm still waiting for my paycheck. Any day now." Lane puts his palms up to Lonnie. "I mean, I've got my wallet, but . . ."

Lonnie nods to Connie while finishing his pint and then puts two fingers in the air to signal the order. "Did I tell you about me and Brenda?"

Lane shakes his head and pretends to be distracted by the TV for a moment.

"Brenda, the girl I'm seeing. Since Christmas."

"No. Or, yeah, you did. Cool. So, Kevin . . . what? Oxy-Contin too?"

"Yeah. But so what? This whole country. This whole war

in Afghanistan." Lonnie points up at the TV screen. "People say it's about freedom or oil, but it's about smack. Dude, the Taliban shut down the world's largest poppy fields. New World Order can't be having that."

Lane rolls his eyes.

"I'm telling you, dude. The Tripartite—or Trilateral? Trilateral Commission. Kissinger. The Rothschilds. They've all been in the drug game for years."

"Why do all conspiracy theories lead back to the Jews?"

"OK, how about Astor, you know Astor? Like Astoria, Oregon? Like Astor Place in New York. He was a Freemason."

"Or Freemasons." Lane reminds himself that this is the price of doing business, or arranging favors as in this case, with Lonnie. "And he was like a fur trader or some frontier shit like that."

"Fur and opium. Astor realized that people don't pull out their fillings or turn tricks to keep buying more and more beaver pelts. Dude was selling shiploads of opium to the Chinese ... by the ton, son. And how was he punished? What was the moral of his story? He made so much loot that he bought half of Manhattan. No punishment at all—he was straight-up rewarded. Later, the German company that manufactures aspirin sold heroin as a cough suppressant in pharmacies across the US. And now the shit's peddled as non–habit forming time-release pills by Connecticut pharmaceutical companies with sales reps in suits taking doctors on all-expenses-paid golf trips and handing out branded pedometers and fishing hats. So, Kevin ... he's the bad guy, right?

"I'm not judging, I'm— I need to know how bad of a guy he is, is all. Is he like dangerous?"

"Dangerous to who?"

"To me? To Inez?"

"Nah, not really."

"Not really?"

"Not at all. I mean, he's your run-of-the-mill burnout weed dealer. Probably never weighed a bag on a real scale or kept a P-and-L in his whole career."

"Wait, I thought he was dealing oxy?"

"I didn't say shit about dealing. He ain't cutthroat enough for that business. I heard he went to Club Fed for selling eighths of schwag weed to hustle up cash to buy Similac and Pampers. Not the sharpest tool in the shed. Kind of an emotional cat." Lonnie belches. "I even heard he borrowed from Frank Jr. and started crying when he couldn't pay the vig."

"Colacurcio? When?" Lane pushes close in on Lonnie's face but retreats as he smells what he guesses to be Wendy's in the burp.

"Like now. Around New Year's."

"Shit, man. Why didn't you tell me that before?" Lane sits back down on his stool to think.

The band starts playing the same cover of Van Halen's "Panama" as the last time they were at the Rimrock. "This fucking rocks," Lonnie notes, and then continues, "I thought you wanted to know if he was dangerous, not pathetic."

THIRTY-ONE

"CHRISTMAS *AND* NEW YEAR'S," INEZ says through the trailer's screen door. She's wearing a bra with no shirt and holds a wadded bath towel over her chest to impede Lane's view. "Can I invite you to my birthday so you can crap all over that too?"

"When's your birthday?"

"Jordan and I'll be long gone at that point." She pulls a sliding bra strap back over her shoulder and tosses back her wet hair with a whip of her neck. "Asshole." The cigarette she's hiding behind her back starts to burn her finger. She chucks it into the sink and waves the smoke away.

Three to four days. He knows that's how long oxycodone is detectable with a urine test. That's what the computer at the library told him, anyhow. Nina only has a few more days unless she has some DEFCON 1 scheme up her sleeve like a hair follicle test. Lane knows Nina won't miss her window of opportunity. Unless she can't find Inez, that is.

"Look, I'm here to talk to you about something important.

I mean it. About Kevin. I think you need to take off for a few days. Get out of town. Until the end of the week."

"Sure, I'll jump on a flight down to LA. No, Palm Springs. Chill out a few days."

He starts to raise his voice. "I'm serious."

"You have to be realistic to be serious."

"You know the Colacurcios?"

"Uh. I used to be a bikini barista. In Lake City. What do you think?"

"I've got bad news." Lane pauses long enough to let her imagination visit a few worst-case scenarios. "Kevin's got debt with them. And he can't pay."

"And?" she laughs. "That's his problem."

"It's to Frank Jr." He wants to make sure she understands the implications.

"Those fat fucks ain't Mafia. They're old sleazeballs who own some strip clubs, happen to be Italian and watch too many movies."

"You don't want Kevin showing up here or at Fred Meyer all desperate, causing a scene. Taking your money. Or worse."

"I can handle myself."

"Can you? Can you handle yourself? And Jordan? And all of the legal stuff? Why don't you go to Yakima for a few days? Take the Greyhound. Stay with your grandma. Until he sorts out his situation."

"Sounds nice and all, but I can't leave my job. Or my mom. Or my son. Or nothing." She looks around the room for the time and finds it on the microwave. "I gotta get to work now."

Inez leans forward to grab a shirt and pulls it over her head. She catches him looking.

"You like that?"

"Like what?"

"You think you're all cool and know shit. But I can tell."

"Tell what?"

"*Right* . . ." She lights another cigarette. "And stop judging. Smoking ain't illegal, especially not in your own house."

Schmidt cans litter the trailer. Lane asks if she's drunk.

"A beer. Maybe seven. What? You never had a drink either?"

"What if you get tested?" He thinks of Wanda's descent from deadhead to diabetic drunkard.

"Like drug-tested?"

"Yeah, for booze. Or other stuff."

"Ain't gonna happen." She rises to her tiptoes and turns as if she's about to dance but thinks better of it. "I'm sorted."

"This Kevin thing can change all of that. Believe me. Call into work. Tell them you have the flu, and I'll drive you to the Greyhound station. My paycheck should be ready. Let's go get it, and I'll pay for your bus ticket." He taps into the late-night self-empowerment infomercials that he feasted on during his first weeks at home. "This is your chance to change your life, to make things better for you. Not just you, but you and Jordan. Don't let your past or those around you define you. Um, like search out the power within you." He almost starts to buy his own bullshit and is no longer sure if he's talking to her or himself.

She opens the screen door and hangs her towel on a mildewed nylon line under the awning.

Lane grabs the back of her hand. "Come with me. Right now. I've got a car. Let's go get my check."

She is quiet. Perhaps weighing the merit of his warning. There is some concern behind her bluster. He can feel it in the slackness of her arm. The desire to give in. To stop fighting. But she'll require more convincing.

She tries to pull free of his hand.

He tightens his grip, then thinks better of it and lets her go. "OK, then. Stay here, and I'll be right back to get you."

"But I have my shift."

"Call in sick. And, for God's sake, don't go anywhere until I get back."

AS THE RED LIGHT ON Ninety-Fifth is taking its time, time that Lane doesn't have, he cuts a right turn across the linoleum store's parking lot and bails to the side streets. He can make up some time this way, so long as he doesn't stop at the intersections.

He punches the dashboard as he thinks of how Mia controls all access points and continues to write the rules as they go. How is it fair that he can do nothing but struggle to adapt? Lane already tried to get back in touch with her a half dozen different ways. He *69ed her number from the deli landline, but it wouldn't go through. He told Fred Meyer customer service that he misplaced the number for a new customer who wants "like eight Wings n' Things party platters." They got him the incoming call list, but her number showed as blocked.

He—Lane Bueche—is used to being able to accomplish

whatever he puts his mind to. With the suspended sentence and loss of financial aid, Lane focused on what needed to be done and, even if it took a few extra years, he graduated. He's already pulled himself up from nowhere. From nothing.

Lane has tried to take that same approach to the breakup. If he wants to fix it, he can fix it through sheer will and resilience. But his ongoing inability to contact Mia proves to him how little power he has. He is unsettled to the core of his being by the realization that no matter what he does, no matter how hard he tries—even with this hiatus in Seattle—it all depends on her whim.

A Plymouth backs out of a wooded driveway. He swerves, missing the rain ditch by a couple of feet and accelerates through the gravel shoulder, or tries to accelerate but the station wagon picks up speed like a lawn mower. He rights the ship and blazes through the next four-way stop without pausing.

Nothing has changed. Lane feels the same frustration, the same sense of isolation and impotence as when he collect-called his mom from a pay phone near Gramercy Park and set the whole Seattle trip in motion. He pleaded with her to buy him a flight home for the holidays. To not ask any questions. That he'd pay her back. Lane didn't cry until after he hung up.

He then dialed the toll-free numbers of every airline that flew to Seattle and begged for a bereavement fare for the supposed funeral of his father. He wasn't able to produce a death certificate, an obituary, the name of the funeral home or the name of a funeral director, but he was able to convey enough of a genuine sense of bereavement that one sales agent took pity on him and offered a discounted one-way fare. One that was discounted just enough for his mother to cover the cost. He'd been hoping for a round-trip, but one-way was OK because he had to believe that if he stuck with the plan to lay low in Seattle, to be conciliatory and remove the pressure from his wife, that things would return to normal, achieve equilibrium, in time for the start of the new semester.

Perhaps the problem is that he didn't work hard enough. Left too much up to her and now she controls it all. If only he could be back in New York and with enough money in his pocket that he could meet Mia on even ground as a peer.

The car glides into the Fred Meyer parking lot, and Lane dumps it in a disabled spot by the loading dock.

LANE WAITS AT THE CUSTOMER Service desk to pick up his first paycheck. He tears off the perforated edges and cracks open the envelope. He knows it will be unimpressive. He missed some days because of his injury. And had to pay his lapsed union dues. But there has to be some sort of mistake. The check is showing him back down at minimum wage: $6.72 per hour, an amount he surpassed a few years back. He got time and a half for New Year's Day, a full $10.08 per hour. After all is said and done, he's still looking at less than two hundred dollars.

It has to be a clerical error, he repeats to himself. When he finds Tom in the detergents and toiletries aisle, Lane demands he accompany him to the Customer Service desk to help straighten things out. If not, Lane will go to the union. He paid a pretty penny for that right, after all.

"You're my assistant." Tom picks something out of his molars and wipes his hands on the front of his pants. "That's what assistants make. The real value is more long-term. In the mentoring. The knowledge."

"You've gotta be— I never agreed to— Dude, I worked the hot case. The fryers. Isn't that worth like—"

"You're lucky you're still getting hours, Lame-o. You haven't been applying yourself."

He wants to drive his mom's car full-speed through the glass front doors, down the aisle and right into Tom and his ratfuck mustache. Knock the smirk right off his face. Back the Chevy Celebrity over him again and watch his brain squeeze out the top of his skull like a Push Pop. But Lane has enough drama and has to get back before Inez goes and does something dumb like leaves her trailer.

He takes a deep breath and looks down the length of the aisle and sees someone who looks like Inez. No, wait, it's her. He's sure of it. She's affixing her name tag to her green cloth apron. She's walking past the end of the row, heading toward the Home Essentials section.

"THE HELL'RE YOU DOING HERE?" Lane pulls her into the walk-in and shuts the door behind her. The vapor from his breath cleaves around her face, wrapping behind her ears and still-damp ponytail.

"Starting my shift. What's it look like?" she asks. "And you can't drag me in here like that."

"But I got the car. The check. You ... you can't be here."

"I changed my mind. Anyway, I never promised you nothing," she says, and tries to step around him toward the door. "Excuse me, Lane . . . *Excuse me*."

"You need to do this. For you." Lane returns to his doomed internal realm of melting glaciers, receding beachheads, burning forests, that familiar place where he watches all potential falling away in slow, unstoppable motion.

"I gotta do things for Jordan. Jordan and me, not just for me."

"This is for him too. You gotta trust me."

She exhales the word *trust*.

Lane knows when he needs to give a little. "Look, I'm sorry. I had a panic attack before. On New Year's. I didn't tell you, but I'm married. We're going through a hard time. And I'm dealing with a lot of—"

"I'm supposed to feel sorry for you?"

"It's that— You won't understand. I'm misunderstood. By a lot of people."

"You're misunderstood?"

"Yes. Unfortunately."

She tries to step around the other side of him. He blocks her again. "Get out of my way. Don't make me fuck you up."

"I can't be misunderstood? 'Cause I've fought to make a better life for myself? I mean, I'm from up the street here too. I've had to do what I've had to do. To make the right choices. Hard choices."

"You want to talk about misunderstood?" Inez says, "When Jordan was a baby he kept getting pink eye. Like all the time. I took him in. But I don't have a car, you know. Did you ever

try to take a screaming baby on the bus? You have any idea how
other people look at you? Judge you? Think that they know better? Could do better? Anyway, the clinic gave me antibiotic eye
drops. But after I used them, all that nasty eye shit came right
back. No matter how many times I gave it to him, he couldn't kick
it. When a college girl caseworker came by she started accusing
me of all this BS. She didn't even have any kids herself. But, point
is, we find out later that Jordan has allergies. Hay fever. Antibiot-
ics don't do nothing for that. But they already thought I was doing a bad job. I'm a negligent parent. Don't care about my child's
well-being. Nobody's gonna admit they were wrong."

"So, they're wrong then." He shrugs. "Don't play the victim. Take control of your own life."

"Yeah, they're wrong. But their opinions hold a lot more
weight than mine. I'm just a bikini barista with a drug
problem."

"What about your New Year's resolution?"

"That's why I'm here right now, huh?"

"I know you don't believe me but I—I feel like I've gotten
to know you a bit better and I do care about you. You and little
Jordan."

"Well, that's worth about, let me think: nothing." She gets
around him and unlatches the metal bolt. She is chewing gum
and smells faintly of alcohol. "Thanks for the pill, at least."

"The what?"

"The one on my sink. The one that helped me to not cry my
eyes out for being dumb enough to hope for something with
you again. Numb enough to feel OK with starting off another
year on the wrong foot. That was worth something."

THIRTY-TWO

LANE SITS IN ON THE bench in the trailer. He takes the check out of the cabinet, reads it over a few times and looks out the window at the trees. There are three Douglas firs on and around his mom's property. Each looks to be about twelve to fifteen stories tall and hundreds of years old.

Lane thinks about how the trees—the trees and the water—gave rise to this whole place. They cut down and sent the trees to build San Francisco's Victorians, kickstarting Seattle's industry. Bill Boeing founded his empire in Seattle because the trees provided the right wood for airplane wings. The surrounding waters saved him from having to build runways. The engineering culture for Boeing laid the groundwork for Microsoft, and Microsoft made the other tech companies possible here, in what was otherwise the middle of nowhere.

The tech boom delivered Seattle to the precipice of becoming the world-class city it had always wanted to be. But not here. All Lake City has going for it are still a few good trees.

He reads the check again. Inez didn't seem to think the

OxyContin was a big deal. She argued that it's a prescription. It's not a drug; it comes from doctors.

"If you got tested, you'd come up positive for opioids. Oxycodone," Lane told her.

"Not gonna happen. I told you," she said before slipping out of the walk-in and returning to work.

He understands that his problems are solved. It is soon to be a done deal. He can sit back from here. In seventy-two hours, he will be on a flight to JFK. A brick of cash in his pocket. Maybe he'll have to put it in his carry-on. He's never seen that much money and has no idea what it requires to carry it.

Three days or less and this whole nightmare will start to come to a close. Sure, he will still have to work through some stuff with Mia, but he will be back in New York, back in school and—if need be—in his own place until things get sorted.

Lane is ecstatic. Absolutely ecstatic. That's what he tells himself. The sensation is in the front of his brain. Behind the eyes. But it's not in his chest. Not in his body. He knows that he's excited. Or should be excited, at least.

He starts to explore the rest of his feelings but knows that he must not let insecurity get to him. Lane is disoriented and needs to cut himself some slack. It's been so long that he's developed a kind of Stockholm syndrome with his captives. He's in a deep pit, and he shouldn't expect to return to being his old self right away. These things take time. That's all. It's been a tough few months.

"Lane." He hears a female voice calling from his front yard. "Lane."

He pulls aside the lace curtain above the kitchen sink. Inez stands on his front lawn with a can of Schmidt in one hand and pulling Jordan by the elbow with the other.

Before he can get to her and tell her to quiet down, to put the beer away, to step around the side to speak with him in a civil voice, she shouts, "You want to make up Christmas to me? Christmas and New Year's?" She takes a pull from the can, making no attempt to hide it.

He leaves the trailer and gets close enough to see the whorl of hair on the side of her neck. *In a different life*, he starts to think but chases it from his mind.

"How'd you find me here?"

"People at work. They talk." She finishes the beer. "I gotta get my mom at the hospital. You want to make it up to me?"

LANE HELPS JORDAN UP ONTO the upholstered seat in the Northwest Hospital waiting room. The cushions have a sort of a worn-out, early '90s digital Navajo pattern. The creases around the edge and the lacquered wood frames are filled with flesh-colored crumbs. Psoriasis? Kids eating Saltines, Lane hopes.

He grabs the hand-sanitizer pump from the counter and juices out a liberal dose into his cupped palm. Racing against the rapid evaporation, he slathers it all over Jordan's hands and works it up the kid's arms to the elbow. Jordan shivers from the chill of the alcohol. His skin puckers with tiny white bumps.

Lane is not sure why Inez would keep the poor kid in his short-sleeved SANTA'S FAVORITE LITTLE HELPER shirt. Doesn't seem like a thoughtful choice for the first week of January. But a little cold never killed nobody. That's what Perry used to say to Dottie when she made Lane add on an extra Goodwill sweater under his coat. One that he would take off and hide in his backpack before school. His mom still suggests it now when he steps out of the house.

When Inez returns from Wanda's hospital room, Jordan is half asleep. Lane holds his head in his hands but sits on the first three inches of the chair, worried that he'll be consumed by bacteria and mites.

"Still waiting on the lazy doctor to sign us out. Might take a while," Inez says while rubbing Jordan's shoulders. He wakes up and goes straight into tears.

"I gotta go back there," she says.

"Wait, what am I supposed to do?" Lane puts Jordan on his lap and tries to pet him back to sleep with no success. "It's already been like forever."

"Take him out to eat. Come back in a few hours and my mom'll be ready to go home," she says, and walks through the swinging doors into the back hall.

THEIR EXPERIENCE IN THE HOSPITAL cafeteria is less than ideal. Lane should have known better. The place reminds him of the state liquor store. The library. But with food. His collar feels tight.

He buys the bread bowl with clam chowder for Jordan. The kid can't even hold the full-sized metal spoon. His mouth reaches right to the edge of the table, where an older woman with skin tags and a walker with tennis balls stuck on its back feet has just finished a paper cup of chicken noodle soup. No matter how many times he tells Jordan not to put his mouth on the table, the kid doesn't listen. They need a change of scenery.

Lane tries to belt Jordan into the car seat. Inez hadn't known how to do it either. She said that the caseworker gave the seat to her but she'd never installed it in a car before. Something about looping the lap belt through it. Lane stretches to try to pull the belt across Jordan in the seat. It is not long enough, and Jordan starts to cry again as Lane pulls it to try to buckle. Perhaps it's the wrong belt. Is he using the middle one? He digs into the seat, looking for the correct one, and something small and metallic jams between his thumbnail and cuticle. He pulls his hand out and it's bleeding, covered with crumbs or sand reminiscent of what's to be found in the upholstered waiting room chairs. He sweats, imagining the particles entering his bloodstream. Jordan cries. He gives up and puts Jordan in the car seat but free-floating from the actual bench seat of the car.

It takes three attempts and then letting the car roll across the parking lot in neutral to gain some momentum before the engine turns over. Too cold. Gas getting low. He's not sure.

Jordan screams. This is no longer tears but a protest. Lane is trying to drive as carefully as possible. Doesn't Jordan appreciate what all Lane is doing for him? He is driving like this because he has someone else's child in the back without an attached car seat. Even if he got in an accident and no one is hurt, it could detonate his suspended sentence, his plans, his life.

But the kid keeps screaming. Lane might need to stop for gas. It's unclear if the gauge is moving or not. But he doesn't know if the car will restart and he'll be stuck at some gas station looking like a child molester with some random kid having a temper tantrum.

He points the car toward the one place he knows he can go.

LANE'S MOM QUITS PACKING, ORGANIZING closets and cleaning with Toby to tend to Jordan. She gets a new diaper from the neighbor at the corner with the five kids. Inez hadn't thought to pack one. Or water. Or a snack. Or anything, for that matter.

"All he needed was a fresh diaper." Dottie peels and feeds Jordan a piece of American cheese. He plays with the plastic wrapper and repeats, *"Ma, ma, mas."*

Lane exhales. "I think he wants his mom. I can't believe she left me with—"

"I think that's Spanish for 'more,'" Toby says.

"The fridge is pretty thin right now," Dottie says, "but I could go up to Fred Meyer to pick up—"

"Jesus, let Lane do it himself." Toby storms out of the room and starts packing again.

"I was on my way, dude. I got it," Lane announces loud enough that it can be heard in the other room. He doesn't need anyone's help. Except to install the car seat. After messing with that for another ten minutes while Jordan wails, Chaz and Toby have to step in and figure out how to thread the belt through the frame.

JORDAN AND LANE WAIT TO order food at the Lake City Dick's. The place is packed. The lines from each of the Plexiglas ordering windows run back eight people or more.

Turning off the car makes Lane anxious. It's not like Jordan can help him push or drive. Nor can he leave the kid by himself in a running vehicle while he orders. The line is too long, and there are some scrubs about. Sullen redneck laborers in pickups. High school boys in letterman jackets chewing tobacco and shoving each other for fun.

Lane orders a chocolate shake, Deluxe and cheeseburger, plus the little plastic cup of diced onions. He decides to get a cheeseburger and fries for the kid. He tells Jordan to stay by his side as he counts out the cash. They don't need to hold hands or anything, but the kid needs to keep close in the crowd.

He considers putting the change into the charity box; it's nothing more than a few nickels and some pennies. But he holds on to it. As he looks down to put it in his pocket, Jordan is gone. Like not there at all: gone.

As Lane's adrenaline spikes and he spills his onions and change across the cement patio, he sees the kid standing to the other side of him. *Easy now.* Lane talks himself down off the ledge. There's no big trick to this. All sorts of total fuckups and burnouts have raised children. That neighbor at his mom's corner who gave them a diaper, is the same lady who accidentally ran over her own dog. Lane can manage one kid for a couple of hours. This whole society of overprotectiveness is to blame for his anxiety. When he was a kid, things were much more free-range. He's gotta relax and be normal, and things will go fine.

They open the trunk of the Celebrity wagon and sit on the back edge, Jordan's legs dangling over the bumper. Lane is starving. He takes a moment to pull the paper off of the cheeseburger and pass it to Jordan. The kid looks a bit awkward holding the burger with two hands in front of his face, but Lane is too hungry to dwell on it and tears into his Deluxe. And once he starts one, he doesn't like to risk putting it down and having the whole stack misalign.

Jordan is quiet. Lane notices the kid's dark eyes. Their long, black lashes. His soft baby cheeks and double chin. He must admit that Jordan is a damn charming little guy. And he seems to be enjoying the food. Good. That's what Lane needs, a moment of peace and quiet to get down some calories and get his head back on straight. He smiles to Jordan. "Is it good?" Lane feels the urge to hug him.

Jordan doesn't answer.

"When I was little like you," Lane says, "I used to come here with my folks. I mean, I don't remember being two. But when I was like eight or nine. And I'd always have that same burger as you."

Jordan is still silent. Timid, Lane thinks.

He leans in closer. The kid isn't even chewing, just staring off into the distance. Perhaps he doesn't like it? Lane remembers from Christmas that Jordan's not always a fan of red meat. But it does look as if he's eaten a few solid bites.

"You OK? Little man?"

The kid's eyes flutter. Is he breathing? No, Lane's imagining things, letting his paranoia get the best of him. He's inexperienced at the parenting game. OK, no, wait, this is happening. For real. Jordan's not choking so much as quietly not able to inhale. Accepting his fate.

What is Lane going to tell Inez? Anxiety ripples out to his

hands and feet, driving his heartbeat up his throat and into his jugular.

He tackles Jordan, folding him over the edge of the trunk and knocking the rest of the burger to the ground. Lane pounds the child's back with an open hand. Nothing comes out.

Lane starts screaming Jordan's name. A deeper loss of control peels open before him. *Why didn't I wait to eat my own food?* he repeats in his head as he slaps Jordan between the shoulders. *Why am I so selfish? What is wrong with me?*

"What is wrong with you?" a woman in a sweat suit and Seahawks jacket yells at Lane. "What are you doing to that child?"

Jordan coughs and then throws up part American cheese and ground beef, part whatever else was in his stomach on the pavement and the tips of the lady's off-brand performance footwear. The kid starts to take in air in frantic gulps that steadies into regular breathing, save for a quick second round of vomiting.

Lane delivers a burst of contrition to the woman until she backs away from the vehicle to scrape the toes of her shoes on the curb. He and Jordan sit in the car without speaking for a number of minutes until Lane's hands stop trembling. Until the people in line stop staring. Until he knows he's not going to have a heart attack. They watch the seagulls at dusk.

He picks up the remainder of the uneaten cheeseburger and lets the kid throw pieces to the birds.

Lane hand-feeds tiny pieces of subdivided french fries to the kid, leaving nothing to chance. Jordan is like a desiccated plant receiving water. His posture straightens, and he does something that could be construed as a smile. Lane offers him a sip of his shake, not sure if Jordan knows how to use a straw. Once he starts, he won't let go of it and sucks the rest of it down with no sensitivity to the cold on his palate. Lane feels a sense of accomplishment, if not fulfillment, that the kid has eaten. He did something right. The kid is still alive and now even kind of nourished.

Jordan climbs up onto Lane's lap and asks, "Mommy?"

"Mommy? Mommy Inez?" Lane wraps his arms around the child.

"*Sí.* Yes," Jordan shakes his head. Only when Jordan finishes relieving himself, when the smell comes to Lane's attention, does he realize that he needs to loosen his embrace.

"Mommy?" Jordan repeats.

He considers how long it would take him to hightail it back to his mom's place to grab another diaper from the neighbor but recognizes the immediacy of the situation. He holds Jordan's hand tight as they stand in line to get a cup of tap water, a grip of napkins and an extra paper bag from the order window.

THAT NIGHT WHEN LANE LIES in the bunk, watching the beads of condensation run down the bubble windows, he digs for that elusive excitement over his impending return to New York. He is excited, he tells himself again. That's why he can't sleep. It's a lot for his mind to compute. Putting Lake Shitty in the rearview mirror. Restarting school. Things with Mia. It's too much for one person to wrap his head around. That's why he lies on the thin plasticized mattress in the bunk rehashing the evening over and over again.

Earlier, when they returned to the hospital, he drove right up to the door. Inez wheeled Wanda out in a chair, and Lane bundled her into the passenger seat.

On the drive back to University Trailer Park, Lane watched Inez and Jordan through the rearview mirror. Inez lay across the seats with her head in Jordan's lap. He smoothed her hair and neck with a gentle adoration that made Lane wish to be a child again. To not understand the shortcomings of the adults around you. The backwardness of your neighbors. The hurdles and booby traps that life is about to throw in your direction. You and your mother. When that is the extent of the universe.

He couldn't see Inez's face, but he assumed she was smiling. When he did get a better view as they passed under a set of streetlights, he thought that he saw the tracks of tears curling down her cheeks.

He goes over it again and again while watching the condensation streak off the window and into the night. "I don't care," he repeats to himself until it sounds so forced he must admit that it's not true. He changes it to "I can't care," which becomes "It's not my problem," but he knows that, directly or not, he was the catalyst. And that he will benefit from her downfall.

LANE EXCELS AT A FEW different things. But his main forte, the thing that made him who he is, is his tenacity. He is more aware of his Darwinian realities than his more entitled cohorts at Columbia. Than Mia. He has to be. He's been made aware of his realities with greater frequency—his slender buffer between daily life and catastrophe.

During high school, he took a parks department Intro to Lifeguarding class at the Meadowbrook public pool up the street from his mom's house. He thought it'd be glamorous to become a lifeguard once he got into the UW. He'd meet girls. Be on campus. Work shirtless. Not smell like deep fat fryers. But he didn't have the funding to go to the UW straight out of high school and had to grind through years of poolless community college. He also wasn't a good enough swimmer to complete lifeguard training. But he did remember the rule not to swim too close to people who are drowning or they will drown you too. Take you down with them. You have to be defensive at all times. If you get close to someone who is drowning, you might have to punch them or even put them into a sort of half nelson before you can attempt a rescue. If they climb atop you, you should swim down underwater and not provide them a platform. What good is it if you both drown?

Then again, what good is it if you are the one who kicks them into the pool and walks away?

He is no monster. He tells himself that he wants to do the right thing. In this case, he's still not sure what the right thing is. He can't leave her to drown herself. Nor will he go down with her. But there is a middle path. Avoid the damage he has done. Get her off on her own and let the powers that be, the universe, whatever determine the outcome.

If he follows up with his earlier plan and gets her out of town, he can get the cash and get back to New York, and Nina will have to sort it all out with the judge. The justice system will make the right decision in the end. Whether that is Nina and Tracey. Or whether Jordan goes back to Inez. It's not

Lane's decision to make. He never should have been involved in the first place. And Nina can take the financial hit; he's sure she writes off that much on client lunches on random Thursday afternoons.

THIRTY-THREE

WHEN LANE AND NINA MEET up, it's on her turf: a new café in Green Lake. Sandwiched between a running shoe store and a women's fitness apparel boutique, it has poured concrete floors, semiprofessional local artwork for sale on the walls and ample space between tables so they can talk without intrusion.

Lane orders a double Americano. He doesn't want to be cliché and order a latté or be basic and order a plain coffee, although he considers dressing it up and asking for "drip" or a handcrafted "pour over." It's an iced coffee for Nina, but the barista says they don't have iced coffee at this time of year.

"I'm sure you can figure out how to make one," she responds and then turns to Lane. "It's an LA thing." Lane's never been there. Like all Seattleites, he grew up despising and being secretly intrigued by Southern California. It's like the gaudy and somewhat dilapidated mansion at the end of your block and all you can do is crave their imported sports cars while shit-talking how dysfunctional they really are, how much they ignore their children and how much they've sacrificed authenticity for crass materialism.

The barista serves up Lane's coffee and improvises for Nina by pouring hot coffee over ice cubes.

Lane knew high school friends with a dirtbag hippie dad from Eureka or with folks who got priced out of Hayward. But he's impressed that she is from LA and lived there as a real adult. He notes the highlights in her hair, the painstaking eye makeup, and asks if she grew up near the beach or was more of a Hollywood girl.

They collect their drinks and make their way to a table in the corner. Once they're out of earshot of anyone else in the café, she says, "Between us: I'm straight-up Inland Empire. Ontario, California. Colony High. Don't go back there much. Never, actually."

"Your secret is safe with me." He smiles as they sit. "What about your folks?"

"Pentacostalists. God, guns and NFL people. They couldn't even handle my two-month vegetarian phase in high school. The whole lesbian thing makes their heads explode." She takes one sip of her coffee through the straw, holds it in her mouth for a moment, then removes the lid from her cup and spits it back in. "Hold on."

Nina walks to the barista and tells him that he was supposed to figure something out, not fill up a plastic cup with undrinkable watered-down piss. Iced coffee, not coffee with melted ice water, for God's sake. When his hands start to flutter, she softens and reconsiders. "Just give me a normal latté."

She returns to the table. "I'm supposed to be working on

forgiveness. Mindfulness. Gratitude. All that shit. Step by step, right?"

Lane nods and takes a sip of his coffee.

"I know you're not there yet," she continues, "but being a parent changes you. It's not all about you anymore. You can't control everything. You have to build a lot of like empathy or it crushes you."

"Jordan is a pretty cute kid." Lane tries to not get into it with her.

"I've accepted that Inez, no matter how piss-poor of a mother she is . . . she has some level of brute maternal instinct that is trumping her rationality. She feels like she loves Jordan even if many of her actions show the contrary. But loving someone and being able to take care of them are very different things."

He capitalizes on her moment of reflection to reinforce his point that she should do the testing once he's out of town. He needs to be long gone. He can't be implicated in any way; there's too much riding on it with his legal scenario and all.

"You have no idea how hard this has been on Tracey and some good news is going to be so important. To her. To us," she says, learning forward in her chair. "You see, we also found out that Jordan's got a few, I don't even like the say the word, but handicaps. What they call 'indicators of learning disabilities.' Probably from all the drugs he got in utero. We have a line on the best specialized preschool in the city. Sold a house to a lady on the board. But we can't move ahead with the application as foster parents."

"Well, as soon as—"

"It's gonna cost, and Tracey is gonna have to chauffeur him halfway across town and back every day. But it's the one place that can support all his needs. This is what you're making possible for him."

"Next stop, Stanford." Lane finishes his coffee. "Like mother, like son, huh?"

"Yeah, but that'd be his other momma: Tracey. I went to San Joaquin Community College. Over by Rancho Cucamonga. Worked events at the DoubleTree straight through."

Lane starts to perspire. Not from the coffee. A cold, anxious sweat that stings as it bleeds out from his pores. He wants to reiterate his negotiating points and get out the door before she further clouds his decision.

The barista arrives at the table with Nina's coffee and a handful of coins that he sets down in a stack in front of her.

"What's that?" she asks the barista.

"Your change. Difference in price."

"Seriously?" She hands it back to him, throws in an extra couple of bucks and waves him off. "Keep it. C'mon."

Lane tries again as the barista walks away. "I'm outta here in a couple of days, and I wanted to say that I'm—I'm glad this all worked out. A few bumps in the road but, you know, assuming we don't see each other again, I wish you and your family the best."

He gets a head rush as he stands up. She too rises, then leans across to give him a hug. He hugs her back with one arm, trying hard to conceal the sweat eating its way through his shirt. Trying hard to think of what to say next. He doesn't want to tell any more lies but can't think of any acceptable truths.

"I had a feeling about you, Lane," she says. "I'm good at seeing potential in people. Picking talent . . ."

He digs in his jacket pocket, pulls out her pager and slides it across the table. "It's alphanumeric."

"C'mon. I didn't say it all dorky like that." She puts it in her purse and passes him the iPod, headphones and all.

LANE WALKS TO FRED MEYER up the network of alleys with the iPod in his ears, even though the battery is dead. The cut on his leg has healed to the point that it itches when he walks too fast and blood rushes to his feet and calves. He keeps a solid pace for a block or three and then stops to scratch, but not so hard as to disturb the scab.

Inez will have to leave soon, and it is going to be hard to force that hand all over again. It's a few days, is all. He kneels in the alley, scratching his calf through his Dickies. Inez is nothing if not obstinate.

He comes to terms with the fact that he's going to have to tell her the truth. Not the real truth. He's not crazy. But something close enough to the truth that she will understand the need to disappear. He is going to have to tell her that she's going to get tested. That she needs to get out of town now. He won't say how he knows, or he'll say he heard it around the neighborhood. No, he heard it from Lonnie. Lonnie, his friend from high school who somehow knows Jordan's Aunties. It's a risk. It's flying close to the mountainside, but it will accomplish what it needs to do to exit this swirling disaster with his money and not directly harm either Nina or Inez more than he can stomach.

"They're gonna come and test you," he practices. Who are "they"? He can't say. He doesn't know. The Aunties? The state? No, not that specific. Not that close to the true truth. But, yes, this can work.

He'll be straight-up. Or straight-up enough. Lane could live with that on his tombstone or his entry when he gets a page on that new online *Wikipedia* thing:

Lane Bueche
The Bill Clinton of Lake City Way

Born into sub-ideal circumstances in North Seattle, 1974. Famed autodidact. Academic savant. BA University of Washington. PhD Columbia University. Expert on various important subjects. World-renowned humanitarian. Lived in Manhattan, New York City. Married to patron of the arts Mia Featherstone. He helped people, got stuff done and was always straight-up (enough to help people and get stuff done).

He is getting closer to Fred Meyer. Once he talks to her. Convinces her. Then he'll drive her to the bus station downtown. Help her pay for the ticket and then he's in a quick countdown to cashing out his check and getting on a plane. Whether he hears back from Mia or not. He'll have independence now. He'll be in control and have time and space to make things right.

Lane avoids Tom. Avoids the deli. Looks in the employee break room. The Home Essentials section. By the lottery machine. No Inez.

When he finds her in the hidden smoking section, she's in tears.

She won't answer him. Won't look up. Won't even hint at what's wrong. She is crying and smoking with a jacket draped over her shoulders and her head on her knees.

He puts his hand on her back and passes it up and down her spine, trying to soothe her. "Let me help you. You have got to get out of town for a few days, Inez."

She continues to cry. Her mascara melting down her face. Snorting to clear the tears and mucus pouring from her nose. She takes a drag and doesn't respond.

"What about Yakima? Say your grandma is sick and you can't be reached for a few days."

She shakes her head and wipes at her nose and mouth with her sleeve. "We already talked about this."

"Think about Jordan."

"My money. My and Jordan's money. It's gone."

"Kevin? Shit, I told you."

"He showed up at my place," she says between sobs.

"Did he threaten you?"

"He enlisted. Came to say goodbye to me and Jordie. He's off to basic training. Then Afghanistan."

"With your cash. What a piece of—"

"No, he left money. His signing bonus. Sold all his shit too. His decks. Mixer. Left the cash for us."

She clears her nose, spits on the floor in front of her and continues, "My mom. She took it. All of it."

Lane runs out of his boilerplate condolences after a minute and listens to her coughing and clearing her nose.

"I shoulda never got my hopes up. Maybe this is all wrong and I'm not right. I'm not cut out for this," she cries.

"If you believe that, then it'll become true. But you can change. Anybody can if they work at it. You can be a good mom. You're already halfway there because you want to be. Stick with it. That's all. It's no big mystery."

"And you know this from your own personal success as a parent?" Inez asks. "I think it might be too late for me. When you're broke and you had your dreams crushed enough times to understand that you're always gonna be poor, you're supposed to know better than to get your hopes up."

"My life coulda gone a million directions, and I never decided that's as good as it was gonna get for me."

"You're a white dude. With a mom who supports you, not vice versa. You can learn to talk better and change your clothes and hair and then look like any other successful person."

"That's a rather parochial approach. Totally disregarding the depth and impact of the class dynamic." Lane checks for new graffiti on the wall. There is a crude version of Tom. The mustache and hair are accurate. Erect penises spurt on his visage from three angles. "But your mom ... Can't you get it back? I mean, how'd you get robbed by somebody with no legs?"

"Who said she robbed me? She's my mom, dude. She needed it for an insulin monitor. The one covered by Medicaid doesn't do crap and is half the reason she ended up in the hospital again."

"Why would you— I thought you were trying to—" Lane flounders. "Look, regardless, you still need to get out of town for a few days. I heard—through people who know stuff—that they're gonna get you tested. For drugs. For sure."

"I told you, I don't—"

He kneels down so they are at eye level and puts his hands on her shoulders. He can feel the heat of her face, smell the salt in her tears. "Trust me: it is going to happen." A tear beads on her bottom lip. He leans in to kiss her, to taste it right off her mouth. To protect her. Make it all stop. But, instead, he stops himself.

She uses her shoulder to wipe the tear from her lips. "I got my first overnight with Jordan tonight, but come by tomorrow morning and—"

"What the fuck, you two?" Tom bursts into the smoking area like he's won a game of hide-and-seek. "How many times've I— I'm writing both of you up. Get back to work. Right now."

Lane stands up. "She's on her break. And I'm off today... *Tom*."

"The hell're you doing here, then? You know you can't be doing none of this romancing stuff at work. Inez, down to my office right now."

Neither moves. Lane looks to the drawing on the wall and checks it against Tom's face.

"Did you draw that?" Tom squares up to Lane. "Let's go. Right now. Both of you."

THIRTY-FOUR

"THINGS'VE BEEN COMPLICATED SINCE WE spoke the other day." That's all she gives him.

Lane grips the receiver. Things have been complicated for him too. He figures that goes without saying. He presses Mia for more details.

"I went to my framer with this really delicate painting on a banana leaf that I got on my Ecuador trip."

"When were you in Ecuador?"

"You know . . . recently. But you remember my framer, right? The one on Thirty-Second. The parking was full. The lot around the corner too," she says with increasing agitation. "There was no way I was going to waste my time trying to street-park. Anyway, it was a disaster. I ended up having to drive halfway downtown to this other ghetto framer, and then I missed my Reiki. Or not totally missed it but the first half hour of it. Which may as well be the whole thing. You know how long it takes to get an appointment with Sage? Anyway, I was so pissed—"

She becomes aware of Lane's silence. That he's stopped af-
firming her grievances. She trails off.

He remembers the argument they had when he told her
about his conviction for selling the weed to the student with
the Jeep and she said, "You should have known better: Wran-
glers are total high school cars."

"I thought you didn't have money," he says, regretting it
before he finishes the sentence. He needs to punch a pillow.
Get outside. Walk this off.

"My dad, he—" She tries again: "Sorry, that's not what I
want to talk about anyway. That's me being nervous. And
I think, no, I know . . . Well, I've thought about it and I want
to try to talk things through, Lane. In person. Things with us.
See what we can figure out—together."

"I'm gonna be there. I'm gonna come see you. Give me a
few more days." As the words barrel out of his mouth, he gets
more and more disoriented.

"I thought that things would be different. But I haven't felt
what I felt with you again," she says.

"What do you mean 'again?' Felt with whom?"

"I don't— You know."

"No, I don't know. With fucking Bray?"

"I told you: he and I weren't, we weren't— Nothing like
that. I've been feeling things out. Getting to know myself. Figuring what was right for me."

He has a million and one questions but doesn't want to
scare her off. This conversation is the little spark from the
flint, smoldering in the dry straw. He must care for it. Nurture it. Give it the right amount of oxygen. Too much, too

fast, and it will fade back into nothing. Yes, best to handle it in person.

"I'm looking into a flight on Saturday. JFK. Can I come to the apartment?" he asks, his voice breaking apart toward the end.

"Let me see. I have to deal with my—you know, stuff. But, yes. I'll call you. I—I miss you, Lane," she says.

"Me too," he says. "But you know that."

LANE'S MOM AND TOBY ARE both inside the trailer. Packing. Cleaning. Organizing. Reorganizing. They better not have found his check in there. Or worse, misplaced it. Thrown it out.

Lane sticks his head in through the door. "I'll have my things out of there tomorrow. I'm heading home. To New York."

He and his mom smile at each other. She sets down a bag with kitchen goods including reused Ziplocs, aluminum foil and her electric can opener. She hunches out the door and gives Lane a hug. "I knew it'd work out, Lane. You always make it work."

"Congrats, Lane," Toby says, his ponytail whirling around to catch up with the rest of his head. "Sounds like you might end up leaving before us."

"Yeah, I thought you'd be outta here by now," Lane replies.

"We did too." Toby picks at a rusted hinge on a cabinet.

"Gotta get new tires for the RV," Lane's mom says. "Guy at Les Schwab says there's no way we'll make it over the Siskiyou Pass."

"Under normal circumstances, I'd go for it and hope for the best." Toby puts his arm around Lane's mom and pulls her close inside the cramped space. "But I got the world's most important cargo onboard now."

Lane's smile betrays nausea.

"We wrote up a budget," she says, showing him a pencil-marked page torn from a notebook. "Need to work a few more days to be sure we got enough to make it down. Gas ain't cheap neither. Gonna be tight."

"I'm looking to pick up some quick work. Let me know if you hear of something," Toby says. "Gotta make it happen fast 'cause my buddy in Laughlin can't hold on to my gig down there forever."

The phone starts ringing in the kitchen. It rings the third, fourth time. Lane starts to get nervous.

"Isn't Chaz gonna get that?" he asks.

"He's at work," his mom says.

"The teenagers?"

Through the window, Lane can hear the answering machine pick up. It's Nina's voice.

"Lane. It's important. Give me a call."

IT'S AS IF THE DIAL on gravity has been turned up. It is hard to keep his head upright. His organs feel heavy. Lane must focus to maintain his breath.

Lane steadies his hands and calls Nina's number back. *Power pose*, he repeats to himself while he tries to break out of the crushing force all around him. He shouldn't be so unnerved by the noise of the teenagers playing video games in the other room. Or his mom and Toby debating whether they should go on I-5 through Fresno, 95 through Reno or go for it and head to Twin Falls and drop straight south on 84 and 93.

Nina answers after the first ring. Lane goes immediately on the offense with a firm, bloodless "I thought you were gonna deal with things from here, Nina." Daring her to throw a monkey wrench into his plans less than a day before he can cash the check. He looks at the clock on the kitchen wall and counts the hours until the bank opens tomorrow morning.

"Easy now, Lane. Why the bad attitude?"

"We had a deal, right? I did my part and now you do your part. It's done."

"You haven't heard yet. Have you?"

"Heard what?"

"It's done."

"What do you mean? What'd you do?"

"Me? Nothing. Her boss said she was—"

"Tom?"

"Whatever his name is . . . he surprise piss-tested her the other day at work. Caseworker's been notified. Which is huge because they were giving me a lot more grief about testing than I'd anticipated."

"What's gonna happen to her?"

"Hard to say. She hasn't even gotten the news yet," Nina says, more matter-of-fact than gloating. "She'll lose her job, which will put an end to the charade of 'progress' she's been selling. She could go back to jail for violating probation. Not sure. It's the judge's hands that are tied now. Jordan'll be ours. Before the day's over tomorrow—at the latest."

"What if she freaks out and, like, tries to hurt herself?"

"If the tables were turned, would you have shown the same concern for me? For Tracey?"

"Yeah, of course I would. It makes me sad that she—"

"Congrats, Lane. Be happy. You're gonna get what you want, and Jordan is guaranteed a stable, healthy home. A good life."

"A different life."

"Yeah, different in a good way. But he'll still get his Spanish. And maybe we'll even let him meet up with her when he's older."

"They're not Mexican, you know."

"Whatever, Lane. Who gives a fuck? You worry about you . . . That's what you're good at, right?" Nina says.

He imagines Inez's face when she gets the news.

"Go ahead and cash your check tomorrow," Nina says.

"Oh yeah, the check. Is that dated for tomorrow?"

"*Right*. Look, I knew you had it in you," she says. "Remember Lane: sometimes you gotta make that wolf soup."

He thinks about it, and agrees with the wider point, but isn't sure she's correct about the role assignments. Maybe they're all wolves and Jordan is the piggy. Maybe they're all piggies and the wolf is life.

He gets off the phone and stumbles to the bathroom where he dry-heaves until Toby starts knocking on the door to ask if he's OK.

THIRTY-FIVE

"DOTTIE OR LANE? I'M NOT seeing it."

"Take a wild guess." Lane twirls the heavy black pen tethered to the faux marble countertop by an aluminum ball chain. He's ready to sign whatever he needs to sign, get his money and get out the door. He walked into the bank already brimming with impatience and is now well past his limit.

The teller with the blond helmet of hair, shoulder pads and a ruffled, striped blouse informs Lane that she has located a record of his account but it has been closed due to lack of funds. For more than a year. That he needs an active account in order to cash a check of that size.

When he protests, she responds, "This is a bank. Moneytree is down the street."

Who is this lady to peg him as someone who would go to Moneytree? She appears to have copied her style from thumbing issues of *Golf* magazine and watching movies about Wall Street while, in reality, working as a teller at the two-bit stale-carpeted Lake City branch of Bank of Whatever that still has sand-filled ashtrays in the waiting area.

Doesn't she see the white headphone coming out of his pockets? Does she recognize his leather shoes? The only thing this bank has going for it is that it was the last spot robbed by Scott "Hollywood" Scurlock, arguably the most successful bank robber in US history. He only knows this because Scurlock was killed in a shootout with dozens of cops (or killed himself; it's also debatable) a few blocks up Lake City Way as Lane was sitting down to a frozen and canned Thanksgiving dinner with his mom in 1996.

Lane asks the teller to open a new account for him. He's in a rush, so please be quick with the paperwork. Time is of the essence. He called Inez multiple times last night and this morning, and no one answered the phone. He's gotta get there in person. He can't stop checking the wall clock as the lady taps the keys on the 1980s PC with a spinach-colored screen and yellowed plastic casing. When she calls his name, it's to tell him that the account is active but he'll still have to wait up to six business days for the full check to clear.

He pulls the pen so hard that the chain rips out of the plastic base affixed to the counter. After some use of "an elevated voice," as the woman described it, he reconsiders going to the checks-cashed place. It's within walking distance, so she won't even have to see him get into the beat-down Chevy Celebrity. But, after some reconsideration of his reconsideration, he can't bring himself to participate in that sort of usury and gives himself thirty minutes to pull off Plan C.

LANE HOLDS THE BANK'S GLASS doors for Dottie, who marches in wearing her reading glasses with their bedazzled strap and her anorak over her terry cloth bathrobe. She holds the signed check in her left hand, the paper flapping like a windsock as the heated bank air rushes out the open door.

For a fleeting moment, Lane wonders if it should pain or embarrass him to have his mother do the transaction for him. Not to mention in front of this same bank cashier. But there's too much at stake. Too little time.

The teller brings the cash to Lane's mom and counts it out across the counter. As the hundreds and fifties flop down into stacks, he thinks about that earlier flight from New York back to Seattle. The one he said he'd repay his mom for. He could do it right now, but he needs the money more than she does. They're going to nowhere Nevada. He needs it for New York. Manhattan. At a critical point in his life. Critical in the development of his career. He'll pay her back down the line when the time is right.

His mom slides the stacks of bills down the counter to Lane. It's more money than he's ever seen in cash before. He can smell the cotton fiber, sweat and sharp ink. He hunches over the bills and tries to fit it all into his pockets. He folds the stacks in half when possible. The paper pushes into his skin. His pants bulge. He knows everyone is looking at him.

Out at the car, Lane goes to the trunk and pulls out a plastic Fred Meyer bag. The thick kind they use to keep the rotisserie chickens warm. He empties his pockets. Stuffing the cash into the bag like Hollywood Scurlock with sirens bearing down on him. Bills fall out of the bag, and he rams them back in with a fist. Right in front of his mom. He decides to keep about five hundred in his pockets, although he does not go out of his way to be precise with his counting.

"What time is it, Ma?" Sweat streaks down his sides, even in the cold weather.

She doesn't have a watch. "'Bout ten, I think. Give or take."

He tries to hide the bag in the trunk's tire well, but it is rusted shut. Lane slams the trunk closed and bundles his mom into the car in one extended motion.

The engine chokes and dies. "It's predictably unpredictable under a quarter tank," she says.

"It says full."

"Gauge ain't worked since Ronnie. Remember Ronnie?"

"Ronnie who ran the vinyl-siding pyramid scheme out of our living room? Or the one who ripped the tank off the toilet?"

"The toilet tank was Don. Donny. He was climbing— trying to change a light bulb."

"At 4 a.m.?"

The teller watches them through the glass doors as Lane pushes the Celebrity across the lot with his mom behind the wheel. With enough momentum, the station wagon turns over, and Lane sprints around to the passenger side as the vehicle rolls out into light Lake City Way traffic.

"Cool if I drop you at the bus stop?" he asks his mom. "I don't have enough time to take you all the way home."

INEZ ISN'T HOME AT UNIVERSITY Trailer Park and neither is Wanda. Or at least they're not answering the door. Daisy is barking her ass off and appears to be the only one on the grounds.

Lane curses himself. That he's too late. That they've already taken Inez and Jordan away. He walks around the trailer and climbs atop the plastic cistern to peer in through the sliver between the foil and the edge of the window. It looks empty inside. He feels an acid pit of shame in his abdomen. Jordan will have the chance to flourish with Nina and Tracey, but he feels the vast space inside of the trailer. A hole he has helped rip open.

Daisy's teeth hit the window, ripping foil away from the glass and streaking it with saliva just inches from Lane's face. He jumps backward, falls from the cistern and lands on his ass.

As he sits on the ground, rubbing his sore thighs and lower back to the ongoing soundtrack of pit bull barking, he wonders if she's been arrested. Or, if not, how far she could go with no money. He surveys the downtrodden trailers. Garbage piled on the lawns.

He is confused by his impulse to cry, thinking that he might never see her again. He is a charlatan, and he knows it. A real piece of shit.

No, she can't be far.

ON HIS WAY BACK OUT of the trailer park, he sees the old-timer sitting in a lawn chair and drinking a tallboy.

"Hey there, Santie Claus," the old-timer says. "I thought that was you."

Lane asks if the man has seen any police or any cars, in general, coming and going from the Annex this morning.

The man doesn't move but wants to know what it's worth to him.

Lane grumbles and then digs in his pocket, gets out of the car and walks over to the man in the chair. He passes him the smallest bill he has. A fifty.

"No," say the old-timer.

"No? No, what?"

"No, I didn't see nothing."

"I gave you fifty bucks, dude. You gotta tell me something more."

"You want me to make something up?"

"No."

"Well, there you have it then."

LANE DRIVES THE LENGTH OF Lake City Way looking for Inez and Jordan at bus stops. He keeps the driver's-side window rolled down. The January cold helps him stay awake. Alert. And it hurts a bit. Like he knows he deserves.

What would he do if he were her? Where would he go? But he's not even sure how much she knows at this point. When he gets to Fred Meyer, he decides to look for her inside. It's a reasonable guess that she is picking up her last check.

He's uneasy about turning the car off, so he leaves it running next to the double doors in the upstairs parking lot. He plans to do a sweep through the store in five minutes or less. But he risks losing a lot more than the beater car. He takes the key out of the ignition and heads in, still with the plan to keep it as fast as possible. That way he should be able to avoid Tom too.

She's not at Customer Service. Not getting her check. Not in the break room or the smoking section. He heads back up the escalator and can see his car through the glass doors when he runs into Tom, leaning up against a counter, telling stories to a new female cashier with braces and a high-strung laugh.

"Hey, Lame-o, you meet Charity?" Tom good-ol'-boys him. "Started today. Yesterday?"

"Hi." He nods to her. "Can I speak to you for a second, Tom?"

"Guy's a bit queer." Tom smiles at Charity. "Watch that he don't try to, you know . . ."

They take a few steps toward the door. "Before you say anything," Tom says in a monotone, "know that I can—"

Lane shoves Tom in his shoulder with his right palm. "Why'd you have to do that to her, man?"

"Easy now, kid, don't make me slap the shit outta you." Tom straightens his tie and looks over his shoulder to be sure Charity or another employee didn't see. "Inez got the employee handbook in training. Same as everybody else. No double piercings. No shoulder-length hair on men. No drugs. And, of course: no fucking people at work."

"I didn't— She's my friend, dude."

"Friend?" Tom laughs.

"Yeah, *my friend*. Nothing like that happened."

"Shit. I fucked her. Didn't you?"

Lane shoves Tom again. Hard. With both hands. Square in the shoulders. He falls against a spinner rack of garden seeds. Charity gets a full view of it and lets out a scream that is as much surprise as alarm. Tom's face burns red, and he swings back with a lopsided haymaker, missing widely. Before Tom can punch again, Lane is out the door and running. He doesn't want to risk a dead car in front of his crazed and mortified assistant store manager, so he continues up and out of the lot and hides in the hedge across the street until he's sure Tom is gone.

When, in fact, the car won't start, Lane sneaks down to the loading dock and knocks as hard as he can until Cheese and Rice answers. The clerk says he can't leave the deli unattended. That would be breaking the rules. Lane promises to go to Mars Hill with him. To heed his advice about college. He'll find God. Whatever to make the kid feel magnanimous so he'll come upstairs and help Lane push his car across the lot. "C'mon, Biz," Lane coaxes.

As Cheese and Rice pushes the back bumper, Lane sees Tom come out through the double doors. The engine coughs and then turns over. Lane bids farewell to the deli clerk before adding, "We still have nothing in common, dude."

Tom runs as fast as he can, which isn't particularly fast, and pants, "Don't come back. Ever. You goddamn prick." Lane floors it out of the parking lot, past the row of hedges and onto the back street. He looks into the rearview mirror to see Tom chewing out Cheese and Rice as they stand in the middle of the lot.

THIRTY-SIX

OUT OF IDEAS. OUT OF options. Lane pulls into his mom's gravel driveway.

He can envision the sideshow. It is coming. As soon as the social workers and Nina realize that Inez has taken a runner.

He'll deal with his money and buy his ticket. Then he'll return to her place again, check the bus stops. Where else could she be?

As he gets out of the car and heads around toward the trunk to get his money, Lane spots her smoking a cigarette over by the garbage cans. Casual. Like she's taking one of her fifteens at work. Except she has a tattered blue suitcase and her young son at her feet. Jordan is shivering. Underdressed.

Lane hugs her out of instinct but is still surprised that she receives it and returns the embrace with an unexpected level of affection, if not need.

"How'd you know?" she asks as she releases her grasp.

"I, uh, saw Tom." Lane pets Jordan atop his head. His hair

feels unwashed. The kid smiles, reaches up and holds on to Lane's index and middle fingers.

Inez looks off toward the Douglas firs in the distance.

Lane continues, "Tom told me that you and he, that you two—"

She doesn't give him a chance to finish the question. "You jealous?"

Lane shakes his head.

She studies his face and returns to looking at the trees, "You *are*. You're jealous."

"No. No way. Not at all. But, Tom?"

"Did you know he was the home run king of the union softball league? In '97. And again in '99." She puts her hands over Jordan's ears. "I don't know what it was. It was like something savage took over in me. Something animal. I had no choice."

Lane is crestfallen. His shoulders roll forward. He no longer cares if it's obvious. He going to make a point to act dejected.

"See? I knew you liked me." She puts out her cigarette. "And give me some credit, dude. I wouldn't touch Tom with your pussy."

"I don't have a— I don't even know what that means." He then mounts a vigorous defense to prove that he knew she was messing with him the whole time. He was playing along. She wants to know why he was jealous then, why he cares. He denies it, but now it is his turn to avert his eyes and study the gravel and weeds in the driveway.

"I still think you like me," she teases.

Lane hits back. "The fact that you came here now tells me that you're the one who likes me . . ." He watches as she pulls her hair back and smiles.

"Yeah, 'cause at least you got a car now."

A SIREN IN THE DISTANCE catches his attention. Lane hurries them out of the exposed driveway, and they get Jordan into the back seat of the station wagon. The suitcase weighs a lot more than it looks when Lane heaves it into the trunk. He tries to think of ways to get the bag of cash to a safe place in the trailer without her noticing. He holds it in his hand and starts to stuff it into his pants, but she comes around the back of the car.

"What's that?" She points to the bag, as he rushes to tuck it back under a blanket and slam the trunk shut.

He waves her off with his outstretched palm. "Nothing," he says, and spirits her back into the vehicle.

"The look on your face . . ." She laughs.

"I told you: that bag's got nothing." He fumbles to start the station wagon and notices his mother watching them through the kitchen window.

"No, the look . . . about Tom."

"Oh, that. Yeah. Right." The engine turns over. Lane nods to his mom and wipes at his brow with an exaggerated pass of his hand to signal relief.

"Well, you wouldn't be so jealous if you were with me and Jordie last night, man." She details for Lane the fiasco of the overnight. Jordan didn't sleep well in the bed she made for them on the couch. He was up on and off for most of the night. He cried for two hours straight at one point, and Inez lost her cool, grabbed him by the shoulders and screamed at him to stop. Not out of real anger but out of frustration coupled with the limited impulse control brought on by sleep deprivation. "I never felt so tired in my life. This mom thing is fucking crazy." She turns to Jordan in the back seat. "Sorry. Don't repeat that word."

"WHY CAN'T WE STAY AT your place for a day or two?" she asks at they reach the top of the hill past Lane's mom's house and pull out onto Lake City Way. "After things settle down, I'll talk to the judge. This is all a big misunderstanding, you know."

He insists that it's not a misunderstanding. That it's very real and she either needs to accept this or hit the road. She says that she can't and won't go back to how it was before. Back to jail. Having Jordan in limbo.

"Then you gotta get out of town. Outta state. Like right now," Lane says. They stop at a red light, and Lane looks over both of his shoulders and scans the oncoming lanes for police cars. "What about the reservation? Can you apply to keep him under tribal law?"

"I was like twelve last time I was there. I don't even know if I'm Indian enough. I gotta talk to my mom."

"Call her from Yakima. C'mon, let's go. Over the mountains. I'm taking you to the bus station."

"I dunno about Greyhound right now. About taking Jordie on that long of a bus ride. The whole thing sounds sketchy."

He thinks for a minute. "I'll drive you there. To Yakima. Then you can figure all this out."

She searches for a response. Her hand locates his, resting on the front bench seat. She slides her palm atop the back of his hand.

"Where's his car seat?" He flees from the moment. Takes it back to the practical. Logistics.

"I came on the goddamn Metro. You ever try to carry a car seat, a kid and a suitcase on a city bus?"

He looks at Jordan in the rearview mirror. His poreless skin, black hair and handful of crooked teeth. The kid peers out the window and shouts something indecipherable at a passing garbage truck. Lane feels a sense of quasi-fatherhood, that he is responsible for the child's well-being. "If we get pulled over without a car seat, you see, I've got a suspended sentence—"

"Well, they're going to call this a kidnapping or close to it. So I don't think the car seat is your biggest worry, Lane."

"Kid? Nap?" Jordan repeats.

"Don't sweat it, little man." Lane turns and tries to soothe Jordan. He swivels back to Inez and whispers, "You're his mother, right? The court hasn't contacted you yet, right? And I don't really know the first thing about the situation, right? So, let's say you're taking an unapproved in-state trip for Jordan to meet his extended family. His grandma. Not totally kosher. But not the end of the world. And you can see what they try to throw at you from there. Make your decision on better footing when you have some more leverage over your situation."

She leans across the bench seat and kisses him on the cheek. She holds up a hand to block Jordan's view and stretches farther to kiss him on the mouth as he drives.

"Will you stay with us then?" she asks. "For a day or two. For a little bit."

"I dunno. But I'll make sure you're OK."

They kiss again as he gets lucky and hits a green light at the main intersection of Lake City Way and 125th.

THEY DRIVE PAST THE FLOORING store with its changeable-letter billboard that reads HAL LAWSON IS A CROOK.

The neighborhood used to have a movie theater. A creek. A bowling alley. The theater is now a Mennonite church. The creek is buried in cement drain pipes, only surfacing in a few ravines full of ferns, nettles and discarded furniture. The bowling alley is a parking lot for Laidlaw cheese buses, with razor wire all around it.

If only the people who lived here showed some personal pride and gave a damn about their community, about the future of this place, Lane thinks.

Maybe it's because he's hungry, but he does notice a new crop of restaurants up the length of Lake City Way. There's a pho place. A Thai bar, a halal market and a Mexican storefront jammed with canned hominy, mangoes and posters for five-dollar and ten-dollar international calling cards.

He steps on the accelerator. Food can wait. They're not going to stop before they get out of town, out of King County or further.

But he has to fight the growing sense that there could be the seeds of potential in the neighborhood. Not potential by normal standards, but a local, mutant strain. A few green-cross signs for medical marijuana dispensaries catch his eye. He drives by an old dry cleaner that has been fitted with reflective windows and a perimeter gate. Young men load cardboard boxes into dropped BMWs and Lexuses. At a playground between low-rent apartments, women in hijabs watch over their children spinning on a merry-go-round. Inez even tells him that there are plans underway to resurface the creek. Could it be that the gentrifying, homogenizing city's last northern frontier will become the most original and authentic part of town? Was Lake City was finally going to—

Nah, fuck this place, Lane thinks.

"IT'LL BE GREAT TO SEE Grannie. For Jordan to meet her. I used to write her as a kid," Inez muses. "You know, maybe things all happen for a reason."

Lane smiles through the fact that he can't tell how much gas is in the tank and feels what may be a sputter in the engine. He dismisses it as his imagination.

"Thank you, Lane." She turns to him. "Maybe I was wrong about you."

They make it as far as the trailer park before the engine starts to choke and seize. Lane can no longer deny it. He looks over his shoulder to see if there are any cops, swears under his breath so Jordan won't hear, and they coast into the Shell station.

"Don't thank me yet." He isn't sure if he's joking or not.

He must leave it running. There's no other choice. They can't risk a dead vehicle this close to Inez's place. The rain has started, and the wind picks up. He gets the pump going and jumps back into the car with her and Jordan.

Inez rubs her palm on this thigh. "You're right: Once things settle, I'll talk to the judge. It'll be fine. These, uh, Aunties, they can foster another kid, no problem."

"Yeah, but be prepared. Nina and Tracey'll put up a fight. I bet they want him as much as you do."

They see two cop cars driving down Lake City Way, and they duck below the windows of the vehicle. Lane peeks back over the edge of the glass in time to see them turn into University Trailer Park.

"Nina?" she asks.

"She won't give up. I'm guessing. From the situation. I said, 'I *bet* that—'"

"No, how do you know her name?"

He feels like she pulled the emergency brake in a moving vehicle. "You told me?"

She shakes her head.

"You must be forgetting." He takes the iPod out of his pocket and starts pushing buttons. Not rattled at all. Totally chill.

"I couldn't have. I only know Tracey's name. Just Tracey. She's the one adopting. They're not married."

"Maybe Jordan told me? Right, Jordie?"

No answer.

Lane and Inez stare at each other across the front seat.

THERE'S NO WAY TO EXPLAIN it. Not well. To make it sound good. He tries. As best as he can. About Nina. The luau. Her plan. How he thought he was helping out Jordan. How it was never supposed to get so complicated.

"I could've just let it play out, but I realized— You see, I'm here now, and that's what really matters." He's not sure if Jordan is listening along and if the kid understands or not. He hopes not. It's a bad sign for your argument when you're evading the judgment of a toddler.

"You wanted to help Jordan. Like you said: to do the right thing." Her face is hard. Trying to convince herself that the situation is still somehow salvageable. She takes the iPod out of his hand and clicks through the song list on the screen. "This thing's cool. But your music is way shittier than I guessed."

"OK, look, I mean, if I'm totally honest, I wanted to help . . . me. But I wanted to do the right thing too, if I only knew what that was. And I didn't know you yet. And now that I know Jordan, know you, that I even feel like we're maybe— Listen, I'm still trying to do the right thing. For you and Jordan."

Her expression starts to crack. She rubs her eyes with her hand and keeps rubbing them so he can't see her cry. He reaches for her knee. She slaps his hand away without even looking. Jordan starts crying too.

"You're . . ." She cries. "You're filthy, Lane."

He strains for some levity. "*Filthy* filthy? Like Seattle filthy? Or just regular 'filthy?'"

She cries harder. "Just . . . lame."

Lane sees the cashier walking across the lot but doesn't hear what he's saying and doesn't even notice that he shouting. There is too much going on inside of the car. A loud rap on the glass gets his attention.

"Are you crazy, man? Turn off your car when you fill it," the man shouts, a Sonics hat pulled down low over his eyes.

"Hold on." Lane dismisses the guy through the window and tries to soothe Jordan.

"Shut off your goddamn car, man. Before you blow up my station."

"I said, hold on." He turns back to Inez. "You understand, don't you? The truth is: it's that, I guess I don't have anything more figured out than anyone else." His vision blurs with tears.

"Do I suck as a mom?" she asks with her hands still over her face. "Be honest."

The gas station attendant starts around the other side of the car.

"What does my opinion even matter? What do I know?"

"Answer me."

"You're new to this, but I have confidence in you. Yes."

"That sounds nice. But I don't trust a word out of your mouth."

He watches her lips as she talks and then cuts in. "Please, Inez, I think maybe I, no, I know, I lov—"

"Especially not that." She clears the final tears from her eyes. "Not that."

The attendant pounds on the window and holds on the driver's-side door handle, "Did you hear me? Shut your fucking car *off*."

Lane opens the door, "Dude, there's a kid in the car. Watch your language."

"I called the police," the man shouts. "Turn off your car off and pay me right now."

Lane steps out of the vehicle. "Take it easy, man. We need just another second—" The wail of sirens closes in from beyond the bend in Lake City Way.

Inez jumps across the bench seat to take the wheel and throws the shifter on the steering column into DRIVE. She blows Lane what he thinks is a kiss, although she could be flipping him off. He can't be sure.

He could stop her. Sprint to open the door, grab the shifter, grab the key. But he doesn't. His body goes slack. He feels a sense of calm, a release of the tension in his neck and temples. He breathes in and feels the cool air go all the way to the bottom of his lungs. His chest expands. And then it all goes out. The sirens get closer.

The car rolls forward, straining against the pump in the gas tank, stretching the fuel hose as far as it can go. It's Lane's last chance to stop her. Instead, he leans forward and yanks the pump handle out of the tank, freeing it just in time for the car to peel out of the station. The clerk runs behind the vehicle, screaming for Inez to stop.

Lane picks the gas cap up off the pavement and holds it in one hand with the pump in the other, and watches the top of Inez's head as she swings the sixteen-foot-long station wagon into traffic. Jordan stands up in the back seat and waves to Lane. It looks like a wave. He can't be sure of that either.

They disappear, along with his rotisserie chicken bag full of money, up and around the top of Lake City Way toward the freeway, mountains, reservation and beyond.

He feels a leaden sadness roll down behind his eyes. A premature and permanent departure from a world he had only started to explore. Loneliness, again. But something else. A small sense that he touched some sort of unadulterated greater good. Then he thinks of Nina and Tracey, and the feeling evaporates.

The incoming police car blazes by without stopping and turns down into the trailer park. Lane gives the attendant one of the fifties from his pocket to get the guy to stop yelling.

He starts walking.

THIRTY-SEVEN

LANE STANDS IN THE DOORWAY of the garage and watches Chaz and one of the teenagers load his belongings around the cardboard boxes on the upper shelves.

"I know it's not the best, but it's for a couple of days, right?" his mom says. "I gotta pick Toby up. We're gonna try to replace one or two of the worst tires and hit the road."

Lane leans into the doorframe to relieve the blisters on his feet. He didn't come straight home. He walked as if each stride would burn off another layer of grime added on by his life, by his choices, and get him closer to the core of who he is or who he could be.

"Heard you're going back to New York," Chaz says. "Made it work, huh?"

"Something like that."

The teenager nods in near admiration as he finishes putting Lane's books on the shelf. Next to his Cub Scout gear, *Star Wars* toys and a stack of old *Mad* magazines.

Lane surveys his belongings. It's not much. Nothing really.

Some dirty clothes. Books that he hasn't read. He asks Chaz and the teenager if he can be alone to talk with his mom.

As soon as they're alone, she says, "Chaz is gonna front us some cash so we can at least replace the flat and get down there before they give Toby's job to somebody else."

Lane looks out the window to see Chaz packing a dip and roughhousing with his inbred offspring. "Aren't you supposed to be getting rent from him, not borrowing cash?"

"It's OK. He's like a son to Toby," she says.

"Like a son," he says to her, to nobody in particular. He pulls his remaining cash out of his jacket and hands it to his mom.

"No, Lane, you need that."

"Think of it as payback for the flight. The one you bought."

"That's too much."

"I kinda lost your car too."

"My car? How'd you—" She holds the money. "But, Lane, you need—"

"So do you. Make sure to tell Toby that the ten bucks he loaned me is in there. And to buy some more Rainiers too."

He gives her a long hug and helps her up in to the driver seat.

"You sure you know how to drive this thing, Ma?"

She sits on the purple TV-watching pillow to boost her up enough to see out the windshield. She taps the pillow and says, "I always loved these things."

"I know," he says, and closes the door for her.

LANE LIES ON THE CAR seat in the garage listening to the radio. He searches for local broadcasts with any bulletins about

Inez but doesn't find any. The rest of the news is grim enough on its own. The first American soldier died in Afghanistan. A plane crashed into a mountain in Pakistan and more soldiers died. This whole national vengeance quest may not be as straightforward or gratifying as we've been led to believe. He's not motivated to get up and turn off the radio, but he'd like to dissociate himself from his reality for a bit longer. Lane works on trying to fall asleep even though it's light-out and he's not tired.

As he starts to fade off, a series of loud car horn blasts pierces the quiet. Lane bolts up off the bench and looks out the window to see Nina's Mercedes parked partway on the lawn. He had been waiting for something like this to happen. Nina or the cops.

He's almost to the door of her car when it swings open and Nina steps out drinking a pint bottle of vodka. "What'd you tell her?"

Lane sees Chaz and the teenagers all standing in the living room window staring at them. Chaz starts toward the door, but Lane waves him back. The teenagers' eyes are wide with excitement.

"I don't know what you're talking about," Lane says. "Take it easy.

"You take it easy, you white trash liar." She lunges at him but staggers to the side, missing him by more than a foot.

He considers playing dumb. Saying he hasn't seen Inez. That was his plan before she showed up. And Nina can't prove otherwise. But he is tired of evasion. Tired of positioning.

All he can think to say is "I'm sorry."

"I never should've trusted you."

He is a paragraph into telling her what happened before he realizes the lack of a stutter. In fact, her insults pass right through him. He understands that she is hurt, and he takes a moment to reflect on why.

"You're not listening to me, Lane," she spits. "Nobody took Jordan. Jordan is at home with Tracey right now."

Lane stops talking.

"Inez dropped him off with Tracey and kept on going God knows where," Nina says.

"OK, wait a minute . . ."

"She left me. Tracey left me. Kicked me out of my own house. Inez told her the whole story. About you and me. The luau. My plan." Nina bursts into tears. "How did she know?"

He shrugs.

"You told her, didn't you?"

He can't muster any reaction.

She drops the bottle and leans against her car.

Lane puts his arm on her back. She shakes free.

"I was trying." She starts to sob.

"Me too," Lane says.

Nina keeps crying.

"Go back to Tracey," he says. "She'll come around. C'mon. Nina Radcliffe always gets her way, right?"

"Fuck you, Lane. You think you can hug me like it's all OK?" She slaps him across the face, grabs her pint bottle and stands up. "Enjoy New York. You're still a loser."

Nina gets in her car and backs up off the lawn, leaving deeps ruts of mud behind her. Lane keeps his feet planted in the overgrown grass while rubbing the red palm print on his left cheek.

THIRTY-EIGHT

"HE'S NOT WHO I THOUGHT he was," Mia says.

"Your dad?"

"No, my dad's as big of an asshole as ever." Her mouth is getting dry, her tongue clicking against her palate. "That guy. The consultant. It's not like he can watch *Charlie Rose* with me like you used to. He doesn't want to talk about globalization. He doesn't even have an opinion on the Tobin tax, at least not one he'll share with me." She trails off and then resets. "When do you get here?"

He picks up the manila envelope with the annulment papers he hasn't looked at since Christmas Day and thumbs through the stack. "I don't know. I don't know anything. Who I am. Where I'm going."

"I know who you are, Lane ... I know that I want you here. Need you here. We can figure it out."

He pauses. "I'm not sure."

"What do you mean?"

"I mean: I'm not your bunny rabbit." He swallows. "You know, to pet to— never mind."

"To death?" She goes quiet. Processing. "What does that make me then? Some sort of semiretarded migrant farmhand?"

"Migrant? No, you know, 'I will hug him and pet him and squeeze him . . .' like in *Looney Tunes*."

"Yeah, that's from—um—don't they offer tenth-grade English in Seattle?"

Lane had always feared that she'd realize he was little more than a few well-placed archipelagos of memorization in an endless ocean of ignorance. "Sorry, I had a job in tenth grade and didn't have time to read all of the assigned books."

Mia lectures him about how her life isn't all easy just because her family has high expectations, values education and is prudent with money. She had to work hard too. Endure social politics. Navigate her own mental and emotional instability. Accept that money often supplanted love in family relationships.

His thoughts wander and fade into adrenalized white noise as if he were working up the nerve to grab the most expensive bottle of wine off the liquor store shelf and book out the door. Then it all erupts back out of his mouth.

"You can't hope to understand me, my life, my path—even riding shotgun on it—if you can opt out whenever you feel like it. And I can only visit your world as some sort of budget tourist who got a lucky upgrade. An exchange student, at best. With you as, like, my host mom or Rotary Club sponsor in it or some shit."

"I'm not sure that I . . ." She changes course and mumbles

something about him being confused. He can hear her breathing, her mouth drier than before.

"Thank you, Mia."

They both try to figure out what to say next.

"Thank you for what?" she asks.

He holds a few moments as if he is considering.

"Lane? Thank you for what?"

"I don't know . . . For all of it." He hangs up and lets the papers spill from his hand into the trash.

LANE STANDS IN FRONT OF the Washington State Liquor Store up on Lake City Way. He looks through the window at the rows of wine. The vodka section. The wall of bourbons. Tequilas.

He counts out the change in his pocket. It's around two dollars. He counts it again to be sure. He wonders where Inez is. If she is happy. If she has thought of him. If she is becoming the person she could be. He may never know, and he needs to be OK with that.

He heads inside. The same clerk is behind the register in her orange vest.

"Long day, Shirley?" He extracts a single tallboy from the cooler case.

She counts his change, rings him up and slides the can into a brown paper bag.

When he steps outside, it starts to pour again. Not a hard rain but Seattle's thin needles of water through the saturated air. He stays under the awning, admiring the wet pavement leading out to muddy grass and blackberries.

He cuffs down the top of the brown paper, but it still soaks with beer and gets in his mouth. It doesn't bother him. He stares out over the horizon. The sun setting to the west. It is low enough, between the earth and the clouds, that its pink light reflects back down off the bottom of the cloud cover and silhouettes the pine trees atop the distant hill line.

Cars speed up and down Lake City Way. This is his land. His domain. If not his, then whose is it?

A red Chevy Cavalier Z24 pulls up in front of him and the passenger-side door swings all the way open. The interior is white-walled with smoke.

"Holy shit," J.C. says to Robbie. "I told you it was Lane. The one and only Lane Bueche."

Lane considers the pronunciation and lets it go.

"What up, man?" Robbie pulls J.C.'s seat handle and starts pushing it forward so Lane can climb into the back. "Where you going?"

"Remember Lonnie?" Lane says. "I was gonna walk up and meet him and his girl for their GED class. They need a new instructor or something."

"Lonnie has a girl?" Robbie ponders out loud.

Lane finishes his Rainier. "Crazy shit happens like every day."

"Get in, dude," J.C. says. "We'll give you a ride."

"You sure?"

"Weed's free. And you don't gotta pay no gas money."

Lane tosses his can into the garbage, feeling a quick pang of guilt that it's not the recycling, and climbs into the back seat.

ACKNOWLEDGMENTS

I'd like to thank everyone who supported and encouraged me directly or indirectly through this winding, multiyear process.

Thanks to my earliest readers Duffy Boudreau, David Lipson, and Maria Dahvana Headley; to Jonathan Evison (whom I met at the Rimrock) for telling me years ago that he would get behind this book and help me make it happen, and then did exactly that; to my lawyer extraordinaire, Caitlin DiMotta; to Jim Thomsen, who got the manuscript cleaned up and ready to sell; to my unflappable and always thoughtful editor, Harry Kirchner, who took this from manuscript to a real book; to everyone at Counterpoint (and Catapult) for supporting my vision for this story, bringing it to fruition, and being everything that publishing can and should be. Thanks to all of my friends who blurbed this book, joined me at book events, or supported in any other way to get the word out.

I would also like to thank my parents; my brother and his family; my children; and especially my wife, Tábata, who makes everything possible.

THOMAS KOHNSTAMM is the author of the memoir *Do Travel Writers Go to Hell?* and owns a digital multimedia studio where he produces a variety of video and animation series. *Lake City* is his first novel. He lives in Seattle with his wife and two children—and wrote this book, his first novel, in Lake City.